THE ADVOCATE'S KILLER

TERESA BURRELL

SILENT THUNDER PUBLISHING

COPYRIGHT

Cover Art by Madeline Settle
Edited by LJ Sellers

Library of Congress Number: 2020907745
ISBN: 978-1-938680-33-5
Silent Thunder Publishing
San Diego

DEDICATION

To all the doctors, nurses, law enforcement officers, firefighters, grocery clerks, delivery workers, truck drivers, other first responders, and any other essential people who are literally risking their lives to fight the Covid-19 pandemic. I, along with so many others, feel very isolated at times, and then I remember I get to stay home, while *you* do not. You are true heroes and I, for one, appreciate you.

To the real Suzie White and all the Suzie Qs who have suffered the anguish of sexual molestation. Especially those who are stuck inside with the violators, due to this isolation, and have no one to report to or anyone to save them. My heart aches for you.

ACKNOWLEDGMENTS

A special thanks to those who made this book possible.

Apollo Madrigal
Bob Pullman
Addison Thomas
Robin Thomas
& JP

Thanks to **James Williams, Sr**. for choosing the title for my book. I also appreciate the suggestion you made for a plot line, even though I didn't use it, it led me to something that worked for me. You are always an inspiration, not only to me, but to all those around you.

And My Loyal Beta Readers:

Beth Agejew
Linda Athridge-Langille
Vickie Barrier
Melanie Cardullo
Alisha Henri
Judy Jacobs
Gena Fortner Jeselnik
Crystal Johnson
Sheila Krueger
Janie Livingston
Joy Lorton
Rodger Peabody
MaryAnn Schaefer

Colleen Scott
Uma Swati
Nikki Tomlin
Brad Williams
Denise Zendel

OTHER MYSTERIES BY TERESA

THE ADVOCATE SERIES

THE ADVOCATE (Book 1)

THE ADVOCATE'S BETRAYAL (Book 2)

THE ADVOCATE'S CONVICTION (Book 3)

THE ADVOCATE'S DILEMMA (Book 4)

THE ADVOCATE'S EX PARTE (Book5)

THE ADVOCATE'S FELONY (Book 6)

THE ADVOCATE'S GEOCACHE (Book 7)

THE ADVOCATE'S HOMICIDES (Book 8)

THE ADVOCATE'S ILLUSION (Book 9)

THE ADVOCATE'S JUSTICE (Book 10)

THE ADVOCATE'S KILLER (Book 11)

THE TUPER MYSTERY SERIES

THE ADVOCATE'S FELONY

(Book 6 of The Advocate Series)

MASON'S MISSING (Book 1)

FINDING FRANKIE (Book 2)

CHAPTER 1

Monday, a.m.

Attorney Sabre Brown stopped outside Courtroom One and opened the text she'd just received. An image of a bloody body made her gasp. A man lay on the sidewalk, battered and broken.

"Oh my God!"

"What is it?" asked Bob Clark, her best friend and colleague.

Sabre handed him her phone.

Bob studied the photo. "We know this guy."

"What?" Sabre leaned in to see the photo again.

Bob took a closer look. "He sure looks like that social worker…what's his name?"

"I don't know. All I saw was a lot of blood and a contorted body."

Bob held the phone out for Sabre. "Look, isn't he a social

worker? You know—your friend from that trial you just had. Dickolson?"

Sabre glanced at the image again. "You're right. That looks like Jim. And it's Nicholson, not Dickolson."

"Dickolson suits him better." Bob moved his thick glasses down and looked again. "I can't tell for certain, but I think that's him. I never liked that guy."

"Me either, but I didn't want him dead." Sabre shuddered.

"But he *is* the social worker on that nasty case you just had, right?"

"Yeah, the Baxter case. We did the trial last week. He wanted to send Hannah, my six-year-old client, home with her mother who was still living with her boyfriend, the guy who molested her. The mother told Nicholson the boyfriend was gone, but he never checked to see if she was telling the truth."

"How did *you* know he was still living there?"

"I went to the house, knocked on the door, and he answered."

"So, it didn't take rocket science to learn that." Bob shook his head. "That guy was the laziest person I've ever met."

"I know the social workers are overwhelmed and their caseloads are too high, but no one else in the department would've made that kind of mistake."

"Who sent you this?" Bob asked, handing back her phone.

Sabre walked over to the bench in the hallway and sat down. Her petite body hadn't changed, but she suddenly felt older than her thirty years. As she leaned over to examine the text, her shoulder-length brown hair hung down in her face. "I don't know. I don't recognize the number."

Bob followed but stayed on his feet.

"Why would someone send me this photo?" Sabre asked, shaken by the idea. "And what if it really is Nicholson?"

"Is there any message?"

"No, just the photo."

"Call the number and see what happens." Bob started to pace.

Sabre hit the info button, then pressed the phone icon to call back. She shook her head. "I'm getting a busy signal."

"Could be a burner phone. Maybe it was Richard Wagner or Mike Powers. Those guys have a strange sense of humor."

Sabre looked up. "Maybe. Mike was on my trial. Perhaps he thought I should know. But I have Mike in my contacts. If he sent it, his name would show up. Besides, I doubt if he has a burner phone."

"He could've used a burner-phone app. He's pretty good with tech stuff."

"Why would he do that?"

"To yank your chain. Especially if it's not really Nicholson. What if he saw the photo, thought it looked like the social worker, and decided to prank you?"

Sabre thought for a few seconds. "No, that's a little much even for Mike." She stood up. "I have another hearing in Department Four. Are you done?"

"Yes, but I'll wait for you. In the meantime, I'll see if Powers is here and ask him. Maybe see what I can find out about Nicholson's living status."

CHAPTER 2

Monday, a.m.

Bob walked with Sabre to Department Four. They passed a heavy-set, bleached-blonde woman standing near the information desk. She looked up from her iPad and glared as they walked by.

Startled, Sabre said, "Did you see the way that woman looked at us?"

"She's my client. Lovely lady. I can't wait for you to get to know her." Bob chuckled.

"Yeah, I can tell from the report how lovely she is." Sabre glanced back to get another look at her. "She seems familiar. Was she here last Thursday?"

"Yes. Why?"

"She did the same thing that day. She scowled at me when I passed her in the hallway."

"She's a peach. Her case has been here a few times. The last one was about two years ago. I'll tell you about it later, pretty funny stuff. The case closed, but now it's baaaack." Bob stretched out the word in a creepy, songlike way.

They stopped at Department Four, and Sabre went inside.

Bob went to search for Mike Powers. He couldn't shake the uneasy feeling about the text Sabre received. She was his best friend and had been for many years. They'd met in juvenile court when they were on a dicey case together—one they managed to win—and they had remained friends ever since. They lunched together nearly every workday at Pho Pasteur, a Vietnamese restaurant a few miles from court, where Bob always ordered the same thing.

"Hey, Mike," Bob called to a man walking out the front door. "Wait up."

Mike Powers stopped until Bob caught up to him, and they continued outside. Mike was ten years older, but Bob knew his prematurely gray hair made him look forty-something too.

"What's up?" Powers asked.

"Did you hear anything about Jim Nicholson getting killed?"

"What?" Powers looked astonished.

"I guess you didn't."

"What happened?"

"I have no idea." Bob told him about the photo.

"Why would someone do that?"

"I don't know. I was hoping it was you. I thought you might be goofing around."

"Me? I'm not that sick."

"Yeah, I didn't think so."

"Are you sure he's dead? Maybe it was someone's idea of a bad joke."

"The guy sure looked dead, but I'm not even certain it was Nicholson. I'll make a few calls and see what I can find out."

"Good luck," Powers said. "I need to run. I have to pick up my son from school. He got sick and threw up in the classroom."

"Later."

Bob walked back inside the courthouse and looked around. He spotted a social worker he knew and walked toward her. "Hi, Sally."

"Hi, Bob. Nice to see you."

"You too. Why are you in court today?"

"I have a new detention that's a little sticky, an eleven-year-old who keeps running away. Are you on detentions this morning?"

"No, but I wish I was. I always enjoy having cases with you." He paused. "Do you know a social worker named Jim Nicholson?"

"Sure. He's in my unit. Why?"

Bob didn't want to start a rumor, just in case the photo was fake. "You haven't seen him this morning, have you?"

"No, in fact, our supervisor was upset because Jim missed a meeting this morning and didn't call in."

"Has he done that before?"

"Not that I'm aware of." Sally scowled. "What do you know about Jim?"

"Nothing for sure yet," Bob said and hurried off. He sat in front of Department Four until Sabre came out. He updated her on what Powers and Sally had said.

Sabre opened the text again and stared at the photo. "It sure seems real, and it looks an awful lot like Nicholson." She handed the phone to Bob again.

"It does to me too, but you can do anything these days with Photoshop," Bob said. "Are you okay?"

"I'm fine. It's a little strange, but we're used to dealing with kooks, right? I can't let it bother me."

"Good. Want to go to Pho's for lunch?"

"Sure."

They walked out the front door together. Just as they stepped outside, Sabre's phone beeped. She scanned the text. "Now this is just getting too weird."

"What did it say?"

Sabre read the message out loud. "I'm sure that pic made you happy. LHO."

CHAPTER 3

Monday, noon

Sabre called JP Torn, her boyfriend who worked as a private investigator, and asked him to join them at Pho's for lunch. She didn't tell him about the texts, only that she needed to show him something.

His truck was parked in front of the restaurant when they arrived. He stepped out and approached as Sabre exited Bob's car. She watched JP—a tall, handsome man—walk toward her and realized how lucky she was to have him. They had taken a long time getting to this place in their relationship, but it had been worth the struggle. His whole face smiled when he saw her. She loved the way he always made her feel—like she was the only one in the room.

"You sounded mysterious on the phone," JP said, walking up in his usual cowboy boots and black Stetson. He touched her lightly on the shoulder. "Is anything wrong?"

"Yes. No. I'm not sure." She showed him the text messages.

JP's face turned red with anger. "What the heck is this? Do you know this guy?"

"He looks like a social worker I blasted in court last week, Jim Nicholson."

"Is he dead?"

"He sure looks like it, but I don't know. Bob talked to a social worker in his unit this morning, and she said Jim had missed a meeting without calling. But that's all we know."

"The message is signed LHO," JP said. "Do you know anyone with those initials?"

"Bob and I have been wracking our brains to come up with someone, but nothing."

"What do you want me to do?"

"I want to have some lunch. I'm starving. And then you can try to determine if Nicholson is dead or alive."

They walked up to the front of the restaurant and saw a handwritten sign posted on the door.

WE ARE CLOSED
FOR BUSINESS.
SORRY FOR THE
INCONVENIENCE.

"What?" Sabre's stomach growled in complaint. "They were open on Friday and didn't say anything about closing up."

Bob studied the sign. "It doesn't say they moved," he noted. "There's no forwarding address. They can't close on us. What are we going to do for lunch?"

"This day just keeps getting better and better," Sabre said.

"Yeah," Bob replied. "It's enough to make my hair turn white."

Sabre and JP laughed. Bob was only in his thirties, but at his rate, it wouldn't be long before he was completely white.

"Now what?" JP asked.

"We need to find another Vietnamese restaurant," Bob answered. "One where I can get my usual number one-twenty-four."

"Good luck with that," Sabre said. "You know it won't be the same. You're pretty spoiled with Pho's food."

"I know." Bob took a step forward. "Want to try In-N-Out?"

"I've had enough for one day," Sabre said. "I don't have court this afternoon, so if you don't mind, JP can take me back to my car and maybe we can figure out if Nicholson is still alive."

"Good idea," JP said.

Sabre and JP met at her office where they both commenced making phone calls. Sabre called Maxine Quinn, a supervisor at the Department of Social Services, and asked about Nicholson. All Maxine knew was that Jim Nicholson had not come in to work that morning. Sabre didn't share the messages she'd received.

JP was still on his phone when Sabre hung up. He nodded and turned his speaker on.

"Curt, I have you on speaker. I'm here with Sabre. She's the one I was just telling you about."

"Hi Sabre," Detective Curt Marlow said. "I hear you received a couple of rather disturbing texts this morning."

"Yeah, they're a little creepy."

"You don't know anyone with the initials LHO?"

"No, I can't think of a soul."

"We found his body this morning at an apartment complex in Point Loma. He was lying on the pavement at the edge of the parking lot, just below his third-story window. There was already a crowd when we arrived, so anyone passing by could've taken the photo. With cameras on every phone, anyone can take a picture these days."

"But whoever it was sent it to me."

"Or posted the image online and someone else sent it to you. You'd think our jobs would be easier now with all the photos and videos that are captured when something happens. But in some ways, it's harder. First, we have to find all the digital footage, then authenticate it. The worst problem is keeping it from going viral before we can investigate." He paused. "Anyway, that's my problem, not yours."

"Is it Nicholson?" Sabre asked.

"Yes. We haven't disclosed anything to the public yet, but a local TV reporter was at the scene, so I expect you'll see it on the news this evening."

"How did he die?" JP asked.

"It looks like Nicholson fell from his third-story apartment window. We were leaning toward a suicide, but this information might change things."

"What do you need from me?" Sabre asked.

"Come by the department with your phone please. In the meantime, forward the image and the follow-up message to me, then text me the phone number it came from. And if you get anything more, please send that too. JP has my number."

"Okay, I'll do that right away."

"I'd like to see you as soon as possible. When can you bring in the phone?"

"You're not going to keep it, are you? I can't function without it."

"I have a tech guy here now. So, we should be able to download the data, get your statement, and get you out of here within an hour."

Sabre looked at JP and mouthed, "Can you go with me?"

He nodded.

"We'll be there in about twenty minutes," she said.

CHAPTER 4

Monday, p.m.

Sabre had imagined Detective Marlow as a short, white man with a Columbo look. Whenever she spoke with a stranger on the phone, she conjured up an image based on their voice. When she met them later, she usually discovered the image didn't fit. This was no different. When she walked into Marlow's office, she was pleasantly surprised to see an attractive African-American with a mustache. Sabre seldom found facial hair sexy on a man, but Marlow pulled it off, even with a toothpick in the corner of his mouth. He stood about five-eleven and weighed a lean one-seventy. Marlow smiled pleasantly when JP introduced them.

Sabre handed the detective her phone. He stood and started toward the door. "I'll be right back."

Sabre thought she noticed a slight limp in his step. When he was gone, she asked JP about it.

"He was a marine. Served in the Iraq war and was hurt when a tank exploded. He considers himself very lucky."

"And the toothpick?"

"He's chewed on those almost as long as I've known him. He was a smoker when we met. He quit that habit cold turkey and traded it for another, albeit a much healthier one."

"Good for him."

Marlow returned and sat down at his desk. "That shouldn't take too long."

"So, how does this work?" Sabre asked. "Will you be able to trace it?"

"Maybe," Marlow said. "We ran the number you sent, and it appears that phone may have been destroyed already. We tracked it to the scene where the photo was taken, but we already knew the person had been there." He flipped his toothpick to the other side without skipping a beat. "How long after you received the photo did you get the text message?"

Sabre thought for a second. "I talked to Bob for a bit and then did a quick juvenile court hearing. I think it was about fifteen or twenty minutes later."

"We tracked the second message to the crime scene too, and it seems odd that the person would hang around."

"Maybe they live in the same apartment complex."

"We've considered that, and we're checking it out. But there are over three hundred residents in that complex, so it won't be easy. We'll start by checking anyone with the initials LHO, or LO, or with a last name that starts with O." Marlow looked at Sabre. "The question is why someone would involve you. What can you tell me about your relationship with Nicholson?"

"It's strictly professional. We've had five or six cases together over the years. Most recently, he was the social worker on a case that went to trial last week. His recommendation to the court was to send a six-year-old child home to a mother who had let her boyfriend molest the girl. I discovered the offender was still living there. That jerk should have been in jail, but the D.A. was afraid they couldn't make the case with Hannah's testimony, so he's probably going to skate. Anyway, Nicholson's supervisor overrode his recommendation, and he changed it at the last minute. The case still went to trial because the mother contested it."

"Was Nicholson upset because he had to change his recommendation?" Marlow asked.

"I don't think he cared that much about it, but he was embarrassed that his sloppy work was detected, and he looked pretty bad on the stand."

"I'll need a list of everyone who was involved in that trial."

"I can tell you who the attorneys were and the social workers, but as for my client and the witnesses, I'm not sure I can do that without a warrant. And if you get a warrant, you might as well get the records from DSS because theirs will be more comprehensive than mine. They'd also be quicker because I'd need time to delete my work product from my files." Sabre didn't mind cooperating, but it was always a hassle when she had to give a file to the cops.

"Well played." He smiled. "You said you had other cases with Nicholson. How long ago was the last one?"

"Six months or so," Sabre said.

"Anything unusual happen with that case in regards to Nicholson?"

Sabre shook her head. "Not that I can think of. A baby was born on drugs because the mother was using when she was pregnant. Even Nicholson couldn't mess that up."

"I take it you didn't like him much."

"He was a nice enough guy, very friendly …."

"But?"

"He was a lousy social worker. He was inefficient and lazy and seemed to spend more time avoiding work than doing it."

"What other cases did you have with him?"

"I had one just a month or so before the tox-baby. The father on the earlier case was an attorney whose new wife, the stepmother, was accused of hurting his child. We never took jurisdiction because the father kicked his wife out, filed for divorce, and took care of the child."

"Any others?"

"I know I had a few in years past, but I can't remember what they were or anything unusual about them. That's another reason to get the information from DSS. They'll be able to pull any cases Nicholson was on and see the attorneys assigned."

"Have you had any contact with Nicholson outside of the courthouse?" Marlow's toothpick stayed lodged in the corner of his mouth.

"I met with him at the Department of Social Services a month ago to discuss that case." Sabre smiled. "I also ran into him once at Starbucks a few weeks ago, but other than that, I've never seen the guy outside of court."

"Why do you think someone might send you that photo?" Marlow asked.

"I have no idea. Anyone who works at court around me would know I didn't respect him. The attorneys all share their social-worker nightmares, and everyone seemed to have the same opinion of Nicholson. Since I recently had a trial with him, lots of people knew what I thought."

"Was there anyone on the case who might have had more anger toward him? One of the parents maybe?"

"The father wasn't thrilled with Nicholson's recommendation to send his daughter home to her mother. But I think that was more grandstanding than anything else, because he wasn't that involved with the child. The mother was upset that Nicholson changed his rec at the last minute, but she knew it was the supervisor's doing, so she wasn't that mad at Nicholson himself." Sabre shook her head. "I think you need to look at other cases if that's where you're going with this. I'm sure he's done more serious damage along the way."

Marlow continued with questions until a young man brought in her cell phone and handed it to the detective.

"We're all done, sir," he said. "The report was emailed to you."

"Thank you, Grant." The young man left, and Marlow said, "Let me read the report real quick and see if it brings up any questions." He turned to his computer, opened a file, and read through it. A look of concern crossed his face.

When the detective turned back, JP asked, "Anything you can tell us?"

"It appears that whoever sent the text to Sabre also called CBS news. The 9-1-1 report came from someone else, but the calls must have been pretty close together because the news vans rolled in right behind us."

"So, the messenger wants some attention."

"We're hoping he or she wants it enough to have stuck around for the cameras." Marlow turned his attention to Sabre. "We may have you look at the footage to see if you recognize anyone."

"Whatever you need."

"Keep in mind that we still haven't ruled out suicide. Of course, that doesn't change the fact that someone wanted to harass you with a photo of a dead body."

CHAPTER 5

Monday, p.m.

JP and Sabre pulled out of the parking lot. "Where to?" JP asked.

"Just take me back to my office so I can get my car. I have some work to do there anyway." Sabre glanced at the time on her phone. "Aren't you picking Conner up from school?"

"Yeah, since it was his first day at the new school, he wanted to see what it was like before he started riding his bike." JP smiled to himself. "He also reminded me that he'd be sixteen soon and wondered when he could get his driver's license."

"What did you tell him?"

"I said I'd think about it, but that we needed to talk to his dad too." JP turned to Sabre. "Want to ride with me? There's not really enough time to take you back to the office first."

"I'd like that. I'm anxious to see how his day went. I can't believe how early the academic year starts now. This is only

August. Didn't we start in September when we were in school?"

"Yep. The day after Labor Day."

As they drove to Conner's high school, Sabre thought about how much things had changed in such a short time. A couple of months earlier, she and JP had been discussing their future, and she'd commented about not being sure she wanted children. Now, JP was the foster parent for his ten-year-old niece, Morgan, and her fifteen-year-old brother, Conner—whose parents were both in prison. When they'd had that conversation, JP didn't even know where his brother Gene was or that he had a niece and nephew. Sabre stayed with them most nights and fell right into a parenting role along with JP. She loved the children, and most of the time she liked the whole arrangement. There were times, however, when she felt unsure of herself and wondered if she'd taken on too much. If JP felt the same, he had never voiced it, and he always seemed comfortable in his new position.

"All the paperwork is filled out and approved for visits with Gene, if you still think it's a good idea," Sabre said.

"Conner and Morgan are both anxious to see him, and neither seem scared about going to the prison."

"How about if I make an appointment for next Sunday?"

"Will you go with us?" JP asked.

It wasn't high on her list of things to do, but she knew it would be easier on the children if she went. "Sure."

As they pulled up to the front of the school, Sabre saw a tall, lanky boy with wavy, sandy blond hair walk out of the building. Conner was always easy to spot. He was just as handsome as his uncle and his father. There was something about those Torn boys. Conner was talking with another student who was shorter and stockier. Sabre hoped that was a sign that he'd already made a friend. The two boys split when they reached the sidewalk, and Conner got in the backseat of the truck.

"So? How did it go?" Sabre asked.

"It was fine. No one at this school knows me, so I figured my recent run in with the law wouldn't make it on the school radar, but it did. This girl in my class, Faith, knew my old girl-friend, so word got around real quick."

Worried, Sabre turned to face Conner. "How did they treat you?"

"Most everyone was cool. I didn't get any name-calling or anything. Mostly, it made me feel like a celebrity or some-thing, which I didn't really like that much, but it could've been worse. They asked a lot of questions. It was all kind of weird, but I don't think it'll last long."

"That's good," Sabre said. Conner had spent several months in juvenile hall on a false murder charge, but that was over now. They needed to move on. "Do you like your classes and your teachers?"

"Most of them. Algebra was great. English may be a little tough. She seems pretty strict, and it's not my best subject."

"If you need help in English, I'm not your guy," JP said, "but I bet Sabre excelled in it. She excels in everything."

"I'll be glad to help you with English if you need it." Sabre locked eyes with Conner. "Just don't get behind in any subject, and you'll do all right. So, ask me right off when you need help. Don't wait until you're so far behind you can't catch up. Okay?"

"Okay."

No one spoke much on the drive back to her office except for JP's comment that Morgan would have been chattering if she were there. They pulled into the parking lot behind Sabre's office, and she stepped out.

"I'll be home in time to meet Morgan after school," Sabre said. "I know she's only across the street, but I thought the first time she might feel better if someone was there for her."

"I'll do it," Conner offered.

Sabre loved the closeness Conner and Morgan had. It reminded her of the relationship she had with her own brother, Ron.

"That would be nice," Sabre said. "I'll see you all this afternoon."

JP got out of the truck and walked with her into the office. "Why don't you get your stuff and come with us?"

Sabre touched his cheek. "I'm fine. I'm not alone here. Jack and Elaine are both still around, and I won't be long."

"Promise me you won't be here alone."

Sabre kissed him lightly on the lips.

"Promise," JP repeated.

"I promise."

As soon as JP left, Sabre pulled all her case files with Nicholson as the social worker. She knew she had others, but she could only remember the names on the last three. She had no way to cross-reference by who DSS had assigned as social worker. She had just started to peruse the files when Elaine, her long-time receptionist, walked in with a handful of call slips. Elaine had been working in the office with two other attorneys, when Sabre rented the space. The tall, spunky woman was in her fifties, and *today* her hair was red.

Sabre reached for the pink slips. "Hi, Elaine. Anything important in here?"

"The court clerk from Department Four called and said the Sellers case continued until Thursday. The other calls I'm not sure about, but you did have one that was pretty strange."

A quiver ran up her spine. "How strange?"

21

"He just said to watch the six o'clock news tonight."

Sabre shuffled through the call slips. The message had no name, just the time. "This came in right after I left here."

"Yes, you hadn't been gone more than a couple of minutes."

"He didn't leave a name?"

"No."

"Tell me exactly what was said."

"I answered and he said, 'Please give Sabre Brown a message for me.' I asked his name, and he said, 'Just tell her to watch the six o'clock news tonight, CBS local channel.' And then he hung up."

"He didn't ask to speak to me?"

"No, just wanted me to pass the message on."

"Did the voice sound familiar?"

"No, but I get so many calls all day long, there are only a few clients or social workers I recognize."

"You're sure it was a male voice?"

"Yes, I'm sure of that."

The call had come in right after she left. *Was he watching her?* Sabre remembered the stalker she'd had a few years back. Feeling uneasy, she packed up her files and left the office.

CHAPTER 6

Monday, p.m.

Sabre arrived at JP's house just as Morgan was getting home from school. Before anyone could ask, Morgan announced, "I love my new school. They have these pods with two class-rooms together, but they're not really together. There's a wall between them, but it's removable. It opens up like a big accor-dion. That's the way the teacher explained it, but I thought it looked more like a great big book. We had the wall open for part of the day, and you know what?"

"What?" Sabre asked, thinking how attached she felt to this cute, little girl with soft brown curls and tiny red glasses. Sabre had recently discovered that Morgan had worn glasses since she was eighteen months old. She had a condition called nystagmus, which made her eyes move repetitively, like a 'tick-tock,' as she called it. To focus, the girl would often tip her head to the left and a little forward.

"It was astonishingly quiet," Morgan said.

"Is *astonishingly* your word for the day?" JP asked.

"Yes, and there were a lot of astonishing things about my new school."

Morgan's father had taught her to build her vocabulary by learning a new word almost every day. Sometimes it took her longer than a day to get comfortable with a word, so usually three or four days went by before she moved on. The agreement with her father was that she had to look up the word and use it as often as she could. When they first started it, she was only five, and he would look up the words for her. When Gene went to prison, Conner helped Morgan until she was old enough to do it herself. She said the word game made her feel closer to her dad.

"So, what other astonishing things did you see at your new school?" Sabre asked.

"Lots of things, like the science lab. We're going to study the stars. Isn't that cool?" Morgan didn't stop long enough for an answer. She went on about everything new she had discovered.

Conner shook his head. "She hasn't stopped talking since we left the school, and now she's repeating what I already heard. I'm going to my room." He smiled at his little sister. "Later, Morgonster."

"Tell him not to call me that."

"Don't call her that," JP said, but with little conviction as usual. It was easy to see that Morgan didn't really mind, so he let her brother tease her.

It wasn't until after homework, dinner, and Morgan's bedtime that Sabre got a chance to tell JP about the creepy message she'd received. She'd taken a few seconds to record the six o'clock news so they could watch it together without interruption. She turned the television on and brought up the news.

"You're just telling me about this now?" JP looked upset.

"There was nothing you could do earlier. I didn't want the kids to see the news or our reaction to it."

"There *is* something we, or you, could've done. You could've called Marlow and told him."

"I did that."

"I could've come to the office."

"I left right after I got the message."

Sabre started the recording and fast-forwarded until she saw the relevant footage. The announcer made a disclaimer that the content was sensitive. That was followed by film showing a body lying in a heap on the ground with one leg twisted back, blood all around, just like the photo she'd received. The caption at the bottom of the screen read: *Suicide? Accident? Or Murder?*

"Those reporters have no idea what happened, but they have to sensationalize it," JP said.

"If they knew the cause of death, they could report it. I suspect they're not getting much from the cops."

"The cops don't know." His tone sounded a little irritated.

"Don't get defensive. I'm not blaming anyone. I'm agreeing with you. No one knows anything yet."

Just then, Nicholson's photo flashed on the screen, and the announcer said, "The body has been identified as James G. Nicholson, a San Diego County employee. He was fifty-two years old and was a child case worker for the Department of Social Services for twelve years. We've talked to several people here in the apartment complex, and most say they didn't really know him well. He'd lived there for several years, but apparently kept to himself."

JP put his arm around Sabre and pulled her close. "I'm sorry I was testy. I just worry. I still don't like you being at that office."

"JP, it's not like this guy has threatened me or wants to kill me."

"You don't know that."

CHAPTER 7

Tuesday, a.m.

Sabre stood in the tiny attorney lounge—previously a broom closet—looking through detention reports, when Bob walked in.

"I don't know why they call this a lounge. There's no place to *lounge*. We only have one chair, and it's a straight back. The rest of this tiny room is for mailboxes and reports."

"Hi, Snookums," Bob said, smiling. "You're wound up this morning."

"You'd think they could find a room where we could actually relax if we need to."

"That's gonna happen," Bob said, sarcastically. "I see you're on detentions this morning. I was hoping you would be. The public defender was representing the minor on one of my cases, but she had to conflict off because of her involvement in the domestic violence charges that were previously filed on the case. It was set over from yesterday. Hendrickson is the name."

Sabre shuffled through the box of documents. "I don't see a petition for it."

Bob looked after she did. "You're right. It's not there. I'll make you a copy of mine. It's an old case that keeps coming back."

"What are the allegations?"

"Dirty house, alcohol abuse, domestic violence, internet addiction, a little insanity. My client, the mother, is a wacko. Wagner represented the mother at first, but she fired him. That was a long time ago. She's actually a pretty cool, interesting woman." He said the description in a slow, deliberate way. "Actually, she's cool some of the time, but interesting all the time. I like to call her the 'praying mantis.' Her husbands or boyfriends, we're not sure which they are, keep dying."

"What do you mean by that?" He had Sabre's full attention now.

"Well, only two so far—that we know of. One just disappeared." Bob let out a small laugh. "Maybe she ate him, like the female praying mantis does after sex. Since he's not around, we can't be sure."

"Is she killing them?"

"We don't really know."

"Bob, you're talking crazy. Has she been charged with murder for either?"

"Nope, but I like to think she's guilty of it. Makes the case more fun." He smiled and shifted into too-much-information mode. "I'd hate to be a praying mantis. You get one shot at sex and you're done. I guess that's better than some black widow species that practice cannibalism sex. Not all of them do, you know. But the ones that happen to survive can't have sex anymore."

"How do you know this stuff?"

"Late night insomnia internet reading."

"You're sick."

Bob made copies of his paperwork and smirked when he gave the file to her.

"What was that about?"

"What?"

"That Cheshire Cat look you just gave me. What are you up to?"

Bob waited while she glanced through the reports he'd just given her. When she looked up, he started for the door.

"Bob," she called out. "Is this the crazy lady who's been glaring at me?"

"Oh, gee, I guess it is." He smiled. "You'll love her. Let me know when you're ready or if you have any questions. I'll be glad to fill in the blanks."

"Like you just did? I think I'll read everything for myself. I'll get a better understanding of the case."

Bob was almost out of the room when Sabre spotted a petition with his name on it. "Hold on. I think you're on this case. The child's name is Suzie White."

He came back in and she handed him a copy. "I remember this case," Bob said. "The child was removed from the parents because Grandpa was molesting her. The parents moved out, went through some programs, and the child was returned to them."

"Well, the case is back, and so is Grandpa." Sabre glanced at the allegations. "Dang! Don't these people ever learn?"

"Apparently not," Bob said. "I'll let Powers know. He represented the father. But you'll need to take the child because her attorney was Edlene McKenzie, and she's on the bench now."

Sabre read through the old reports about Suzie White.

The case initially came to the attention of the dependency court when police responded to a report of child molestation at the grandfather's house. Suzie, her thirteen-year old brother, Darrin, and their parents were living with the paternal grandparents because they had been evicted from their home for not paying rent. Two months ago, the father lost his job at the Shell station. Mother was working part-time at Jack in the Box. When the father was questioned about any inappropriate behavior by the grandfather, he said he had seen his father-in-law on two occasions touch Suzie's groin area, but he couldn't be certain it wasn't just her leg, or that it was intentional. The father admitted that there had been reports of the grandfather having "sex-play" with his other granddaughters. He also said it wasn't unusual for the grandchildren to sleep with grandpa because grandma worked nights as a security guard.

"What's wrong with these people?" Sabre asked.

"Which part?"

"They knew Grandpa was messing with these kids. How could they not stop it?"

"They needed a place to live, I guess. I don't know. I have a theory that people are basically selfish—and stupid."

Sabre continued to read.

The grandfather, who worked as a part-time preacher, was investigated, but no arrest was made. The case was filed in Juvenile Court; the parents moved out of the grandparents' home; no contact was to take place between the grandfather and the child; and six months later the case was dismissed. A new case was filed today based on a welfare check by the police who found the parents and the children living at grandpa's house.

"Is your client that numb?" Sabre asked Bob.

"She means well, but she's not the brightest star in the sky.

She's very dependent on her husband, so they continue to walk together through the hallway of life with their heads in the clouds and no electricity or running water in their home."

"That was both poetic and sickening."

"I don't pick 'em. I just represent them. By the way, dear old Grandpa is here."

"He's here at court?"

"Yup. He claims he's innocent and wants his day in court."

"Well, he's not getting it here. He can have it in criminal court."

Bob smiled and left the room. Sabre read through the three other petitions on calendar that morning. One was a tox-baby, the mother's second child born on drugs. Debbie Collicott represented the mother, but the newborn needed counsel.

The second petition was a little more complicated, even though it also involved a tox-baby. Several days earlier, both mother and baby had tested positive for opiates in the hospital immediately after the delivery. However, the mom was only fifteen and, as a minor, she would need a child advocate too.

In the third instance, a four-year-old child had been picked up in a drug raid, and no one seemed to know who he belonged to. Sabre had no idea where that case might take her, and she felt sorry for the little boy no one was claiming.

Sabre read through the reports for the new petitions, finished two review hearings in Department One, then walked down the hall to Department Four to do the detentions. Bob and Mike Powers were there when she arrived.

"We're ready on the White case," Bob said.

Sabre laid her files on the table. "Let's do it."

Judge Hekman, a gray-haired woman in her late sixties, called the case, and the attorneys introduced themselves and their clients, along with County Counsel, Linda Farris.

"Your Honor," Sabre said, turning to the grandfather who was sitting in the back of the courtroom.

"I got this." Judge Hekman cut in before Sabre could finish. The judge stared at the offender, a skinny old guy with sparse gray hair. "And who are you, sir?"

"I'm Suzie's grandfather, Thomas White."

"Suzie's *paternal* grandfather?"

"That's right."

"The same Thomas White who is named in the petition, the alleged perpetrator?"

"That's correct, ma'am, but those are false allegations."

"That may be, Mr. White, but these are confidential proceedings, and you will have to leave."

"I don't care if he's here," Suzie's father said before his attorney could stop him.

"I do." Sabre and County Counsel countered in unison.

"And so do I," the judge added. "You can wait outside until the hearing is over, and your son can fill you in if he chooses."

The grandfather didn't move.

"Sir, leave my courtroom now."

The bailiff, Mike McCormick, walked toward him. By the time he reached the gate, Mr. White had stood. The bailiff kept going and, without touching him, escorted him out of the room. The rest of the case went off without a hitch. The parents denied the allegations in the petitions. They asked to have their child returned as soon as they acquired housing. The court ordered foster care with supervised visitation for the parents and no contact with the grandfather. As a wrap-up, the judge set another hearing date to address the issues.

Everyone left the courtroom except Sabre, who remained at the counsel table, while Bob and Powers took seats in the back of the room. Next up was the Spencer case. Wendy, an emaciated fifteen-year-old, had greasy, light-brown hair streaked by the sun, and amber-colored eyes. Sabre thought she had a real beauty that would be unmatched if she got cleaned up and added a few pounds. The teenage mother nervously hugged an older woman bedecked in jewels and wearing a bright purple dress covered in beads, then took her seat at the counsel table. A teenage boy, the alleged father, took a seat next to her.

After Judge Hekman appointed Sabre to represent the baby, the court clerk said, "We need attorneys for the minor-parents."

"Mr. Clark, are you available for an appointment?" Judge Hekman asked.

"Of course, Your Honor."

"Good. Meet your new client, Wendy Spencer."

"And you, Mr. Powers? Do you want a new case?"

"Yes, Your Honor."

"You'll be representing the father, Carlos Vega. Please meet with your clients and be back here in fifteen minutes."

CHAPTER 8

Tuesday, a.m.

The Spencer Case

Child: Baby Spencer, newborn (F)
Parents: Father—Carlos Vega & Mother—Wendy Spencer
Issues: Physical Abuse, Drugs
Facts: Baby born positive for methamphetamines.

To make sure she hadn't missed anything, Sabre stood in the hall and read through the report again while she waited for the other attorneys to meet with their clients. The young couple had been living in Arizona, where they scammed several emergency rooms to get Vicodin and whatever other meds they could get. Looking for new drug sources, they moved to California just a few days before the baby was born.

"You ready?" Bob asked as he approached.

"I'm ready." Sabre tucked away the paperwork.

The participants filed into the courtroom and took their

seats, with the young parents next to their respective attorneys. The older woman in purple took a seat in the back as Bob instructed her to.

"In re: Baby Girl Spencer," the clerk said, calling the case.

The attorneys introduced themselves and their clients for the record.

"The grandmother is seated in the courtroom, Your Honor," Bob said.

Judge Hekman made official appointments for the attorneys, and both parents entered denials to the allegations.

"Can this petition be amended to include the child's name?" The judge looked at County Counsel Linda Farris.

"The parents haven't named the baby yet, Your Honor," she responded.

"Is that correct?" Judge Hekman asked the parents.

"That's right," Wendy said.

"Why not?"

"Because we haven't found the perfect name yet."

"You need to do it soon, young lady." The judge didn't look happy.

The woman in purple raised her hand.

Hekman glanced back at her. "You're the baby's grandmother?"

"I'm Wendy's grandma from Louisiana. My name is Tallulah, which is the Choctaw word for *leaping waters*."

The judge looked at County Counsel. "Is this child of Native American descent?"

"Not that we've been able to ascertain, Your Honor, but this is new information. I haven't actually met Miss Tallulah yet," Farris said.

"Follow up on the Choctaw information and make sure the proper notices are given to the tribe if needed."

The grandmother raised her hand again, and the judge acknowledged her.

"I was named after the waterfalls in Georgia." Tallulah rubbed her necklace as she spoke. "I'm not of Indian heritage. I came here to help this girl. Is it possible this baby can be put up for adoption?"

"It's way too early to have that discussion, ma'am. What is your last name?"

"Waters."

"Thank you, Tallulah Waters." The judge turned to Wendy. "Have you been attending school?"

"No, I've never gone. I moved around a lot. I can read a little though. I watched a lot of Sesame Street."

"Where are your parents?"

"I don't know. I haven't seen them in a couple of years."

Judge Hekman looked at the father, Carlos. "What about you? Are you in school?"

"I was until about six months ago."

"What happened?"

"I quit going."

"Where are your parents?"

"Tucson, Arizona."

"Do they know where you are?"

"Yes, I called them a couple of days ago to tell them about the baby."

County Counsel Farris spoke up. "Your Honor, we've been trying to locate the baby's maternal grandparents, but we haven't found a trace of either. We've also made attempts to reach the paternal grandparents, but so far have been unsuccessful. We have an address and phone number, but our calls haven't been answered. We're trying other means to reach them or any other family members we can find."

"I don't care if you have to use carrier pigeons, find the relatives," the judge spouted. She stared at the woman in purple. "Do you know where Wendy's parents are?"

"No, ma'am."

"When did you last see one or both of them?"

"Actually, I never have."

"What? How is that possible?" Judge Hekman was scowling now.

"I'm not exactly Wendy's grandmother, but I'm part of her extended family."

"And who made the extension, you?" When the woman didn't answer, Hekman pressed her. "What do you mean 'not exactly?' Are you related to Wendy Spencer or not?"

"I'm not, but I'd like to hire an attorney for her. Can I do that?"

The judge paused before responding. "Technically, since the petition is not filed on her as a minor, you can hire another attorney to represent her as the accused mother. However, Wendy has a very capable attorney right now who is an expert in dependency law. As I said, you're still free to hire someone else, but since the mother is a minor, I will keep Mr. Clark on the case as her guardian ad litem."

"What's a guardian ad litem?" Wendy asked.

"It's someone to represent, not just the legal issues, but your best interest as well. They sometimes conflict on these cases." The judge turned to the woman in purple. "I'm afraid I'll have to ask you to leave the courtroom until we're done. These hearings are confidential, and since you're not *exactly* related, you cannot be in here. Do you have anything else you'd like to add or ask before you leave?"

"No, ma'am."

The bailiff stood and escorted her out of the room.

"There is no address listed for either of you," the judge said to the young couple. "Where are you living?"

"Nowhere right now," Wendy said.

"You have to be somewhere. Where did you sleep last night?"

"With some friends."

"What is the address of these friends?"

"I don't know." Wendy shrugged. "They just took us there."

Hekman looked directly at the teenage father. "Do you know the address?"

"No, I don't."

"Do they live in San Diego?"

When Wendy didn't answer, Bob whispered something to his client. She whispered back, and Bob spoke up. "Your Honor, my client does not know the exact address, but she thinks it was El Cajon. She's only been in this area a few days and does not know her way around. She's also not certain where they'll be staying tonight."

Hekman ordered the baby to remain in foster care with supervised visits, then she set a jurisdiction hearing. She locked eyes on the young parents. "Our goal is to reunify you with your baby, if that's what you want. We don't know how long that will take. It depends primarily on you. The first thing you need to do is find a place to live. The social worker should be able to help with that. If you don't cooperate with CPS and you don't do the programs I've ordered, your parental rights could potentially be terminated. Do you understand that?"

Both teenagers nodded, and Wendy said, "Yes."

"You both have very good attorneys, so be certain to make your wishes and concerns clear to them. And give any information you can to the social worker so she can find any appropriate relatives. Understand?"

Again, they both nodded.

"You need to speak up," the judge said.

With a little prodding from their attorneys to use words, they both replied, "Yes."

After the teenagers and their attorneys left the courtroom, the judge turned to County Counsel. "You might want to consider filing petitions on those parents as well. They should both be under the jurisdiction of the county, especially her. She's only fifteen. He's seventeen, so if you can get ahold of his parents, that may take care of him."

"The social worker is already on it, Your Honor."

Hekman pivoted to Sabre. "Counselor, see if you can find out who that woman in purple really is. I don't like what I see."

CHAPTER 9

Tuesday, a.m.

Still in court, Sabre had two more detentions: the little boy with no parents, known only as Miguel, and the Hendrickson case with Bob. Very little information was given about Miguel, except that he had been dropped off at the drug house about six months previously by a *coyote*—a human trafficker who brought him across the border for a fee. One of the women in the home said they kept him because they didn't know what else to do. Sabre decided to have JP investigate, but not until after she saw the little boy.

The judge went through the usual steps, appointing Sabre to represent, detaining the child in foster care, and setting a jurisdictional hearing. As Sabre left Department Four, she saw Bob sitting on a bench talking to the woman in purple, so she walked over.

"Tallulah," Bob said, "this is Sabre Brown, the baby's attorney. I don't think you've formally met."

"Hello, ma'am," Tallulah said.

"Nice to meet you." Sabre looked at Bob with raised eyebrows, as if to say, *Do you mind?*

Bob waved his hand. "By all means, join us." Sabre sat and Bob continued. "Tallulah has been telling me about her life in Louisiana. She taught at a charm school for teenage girls."

"I didn't know they still had those."

"They do in the South," Tallulah said.

"How long have you known Wendy?" Sabre asked.

"A long time. She's a dear, dear girl." The woman stood. "I must be going now. I need to take the kids home."

"And where is home?" Sabre asked.

"Wherever they want to go."

"We'll walk out with you," Sabre said. They started down the hall, and Sabre repeated her question. "How long did you say you've known Wendy?"

Tallulah ignored her. "There they are now." She picked up her pace and caught up with Wendy and Carlos. "Nice meeting you," she said over her shoulder as they hurried off.

Sabre walked outside, with Bob following.

"Where are you going?" Bob asked. "We still have the Hendrickson case."

"I want to see what she's driving."

They watched as Tallulah and the teenagers hurried to the parking lot and got into a fairly new, silver Lincoln Town Car. Sabre keyed the license plate number into the note app on her phone.

"I guess being a charm schoolmarm pays pretty well for Leaping Waters Waters," Bob commented, his tone skeptical.

They walked back into the courthouse and headed to Department One. Sabre went inside and sat on the far right side of the counsel table. Bob entered shortly after with his client, Vicki Hendrickson, the mother on the case. She stared at Sabre and headed straight toward her. When they got closer, Bob took the seat next to Sabre, blocking his client's view of her.

"Thanks," Sabre whispered.

Bob winked.

After being appointed to represent the child, eleven-year-old Unity Hendrickson, Sabre asked for a continuance so she could interview her client.

The judge gave her orders, then turned to the mother. "Do you understand?" Hekman asked.

"Yes, Your Honor," Vicki said in a deep southern accent.

"That concludes the morning calendar." Judge Hekman gathered up her files and walked out.

Vicki Hendrickson left the courtroom too, but not before staring daggers at Sabre one more time.

The bailiff stepped toward Sabre. "Welcome to the praying mantis case."

"I don't think she likes me very much."

"Because you're too pretty."

Sabre blushed. "Thank you, Mike. You're very kind."

"Do you have time to eat?" Bob asked, as they walked out of the courtroom.

"I'd like to, but where?"

"We need to try new Vietnamese restaurants until we find one we like."

"You mean that *you* like. I'll eat most anything."

"I don't know what else is around here, but we can google it."

"Let's hit In-N-Out today, then you can find new places to try later. I don't have a lot of time. I need to see my new clients."

"That'll work."

"I was surprised to hear your client had a southern accent," Sabre said, as they walked toward their cars.

"So was I." Bob furrowed his brow. "Last time she had an Irish brogue."

"Why is it called a *brogue*? Why don't they just say accent?"

"Some linguists believe the word derives from the Irish word *bróg*, which is a type of shoe traditionally worn by the Irish as well as those from the Scottish Highlands."

"I'm sorry I asked." Sabre cocked her head. "That was rhetorical. I didn't really expect you to answer the question."

"Then you shouldn't have asked."

"How do you know so much trivia?"

"I read a lot."

"Maybe you should go on *Jeopardy*."

"Maybe I will."

CHAPTER 10

Tuesday, p.m.

The White Case

Child: Suzie White, Age 7 (F)
Parents: Father—Thomas White, Jr. & Mother—Georgia
White
Issues: Neglect, Sexual Abuse
Facts: Suzie was allegedly molested by the paternal grandfa-
ther, a member of their household. Parents continued to live
with him.

After lunch, Sabre drove straight to Polinsky Receiving Home.
Before heading inside, she glanced at the file again. Comfortable that she knew the facts, she headed into the facility and
waited in the interview room until an attendant brought Suzie
to her. The thin little girl stood about four feet tall, and her
blonde hair fell in curls to her shoulders. She looked angelic,

except that her haunted blue eyes had dark circles around them, as if she hadn't slept in a while.

Sabre smiled. "Hi Suzie, I'm your attorney. I'm here to help you."

Suzie stared down at the floor and didn't respond. Sabre looked around the room to see what she could do to get the girl relaxed enough to talk. She spotted a large, pink Barbie house. "Do you like to play with dolls?"

Suzie shook her head.

Sabre walked toward the corner where they kept toys and books. "Come on, let's see if there is something you like over here."

Suzie followed and searched the shelves without saying anything. She picked up a coloring book and a box of crayons.

"Do you like to color?"

"Yes." Her voice was almost a whisper.

"I do too." Sabre reached for another coloring book.

They sat down at a table and got busy with the crayons. Sabre explained that she would represent her in court and told the girl about the rules of confidentiality. "Do you understand?"

Suzie nodded.

"Do you have any questions?"

"Can I see my brother?"

"I'll try to set that up for you. Tell me a little about him."

"His name is Darrin, and he's funny. He calls me Suzie Q."

"Do you two get along well?"

"Yeah, he's good to me, 'cept when his friends are around."

"What does he do then?"

"He mostly ignores me." For the first time, she gave a half

smile. "But it's okay, 'cause I ignore him too when I have friends over."

Suzie stopped talking and was silent for about ten seconds.

"What is it?" Sabre asked.

In a very soft voice, Suzie asked, "Will Grandpa go to jail?"

"I don't know for sure, but he might. Is that what you want?"

"No," she said quickly. Then she shrugged. "I don't know."

"Why did you ask?"

"Because Daddy said if I told on Grandpa, he'd go to jail, and that it would be all my fault." Suzie's shoulders were hunched to her ears and she looked very tense. "I just want him to stop touching me."

Sabre had an urge to find Suzie's father and punch his face, but instead she took the little girl's hand in hers and said, "Suzie, take a deep breath. None of this is your fault."

Suzie looked at her, breathed in deep, and dropped her shoulders. When she did, tears burst from her eyes and sobs came from deep within. "No one ever believes me."

CHAPTER 11

Tuesday, p.m.

The Miguel Case

Child: Miguel, age 4 (M)
Parents: Unknown
Issues: Neglect, Abandonment
Facts: Child was smuggled across border and left with strangers.

Sabre remained in the interview room at Polinsky. She took a deep breath and prepared herself for her next client. Her heart melted when she saw him. Miguel was a happy little boy with dark curly hair and big brown eyes who spoke very little English. "Hóla," he said with a smile as he walked in the room. He spotted the toys and ran directly to them. He handled several, then discovered the Legos and ignored the rest. He sat down cross-legged on the floor and began to build a tower.

"Hóla, Miguel," Sabre said, joining him on the floor. She

was proficient in Spanish, having studied it in college and spent time in a school in Guadalajara, where she sharpened her conversational skills. Yet she was feeling a little rusty and realized she needed to use it more often. But speaking to children was easier than to adults because their own vocabularies were limited. She continued their conversation in Spanish. When she told him her name was Sabre, he jumped up and swung his arm like he was slaying a dragon. Miguel found it quite humorous that her name was *sword*. She tried to explain that it wasn't the same, then gave up because he thought it was so funny.

"Who have you been living with?" Sabre asked while they played with the stack of Legos. Miguel seemed only to be interested in the height of his structure.

After he added a few more layers to his tower, he said, "Aunt Trina, Aunt Angelina, Uncle Jorge, Uncle Diego, and Uncle Alejandro." He paused. "And sometimes Uncle Lorenzo." He stopped again.

"Is that all?"

"No."

"Who else?"

"Manuelito, but he's just a baby, and Antonio, who's bigger than me."

"How much bigger?"

"A little, not much." He stood and raised his hand above his head six inches. "This much. He's not four. I'm four, but he's more than that."

"Does he go to school?"

"No." Miquel sat back down and stacked more Legos.

"Do you remember when you came to live with these people?"

"Yes."

"How long ago was that?"

"A while." He shrugged. "But my mamá is coming to get me."

"She is?"

"She said she would."

"When did she say that?"

"When she left me to go to America." He paused and his eyes widened. "What's taking her so long?"

"I don't know, but I'll certainly try to find out."

Suddenly his happy brown eyes turned sad. "I want my mamá. I hope she didn't forget me."

"I'm sure she didn't. I bet she's having trouble finding you, but I'll do everything I can to help with that. What's your mamá's name?"

"María."

Of course it is, Sabre thought. That wasn't going to be much help. "Does she have another name?"

"María Luciana."

Sabre tried to build out the base of the Lego stack as Miguel added more blocks to the top. Suddenly, it gave way and came crashing down. Miguel giggled at the sight.

"Yay!" He shouted. "Let's do it again."

As they started another structure, Sabre encouraged him to put a few more on the bottom to make it wider for stability.

"Miguel, do you know your last name?"

A little smile crossed his face, and he looked at her sheepishly, but didn't answer.

"You do know it, don't you? It could really help me find your mother, if I knew."

"My name is Miguel Luis Gonzales Bigotes." He rattled it off as though he'd said it many times. Then he rubbed his chin, as if he was stroking a beard.

49

Sabre laughed. "Your last name is *whiskers*?"

Miguel smiled proudly.

"Did you tell the social worker your name?"

He shook his head. "I was told not to tell anyone."

"Who told you that?"

"Uncle Alejandro. He said everyone at the house would get in big trouble and maybe go to jail." The boy shrugged. "But they did anyway, even though I didn't tell anyone my name. The cops came and took them away."

"Do you know why they were taken?"

"I heard the cops say 'drugs.' They asked a bunch of questions."

"What did you tell them?"

"Men come there and buy things, but I don't know what." Miguel added more Legos to the tower. It stood about eighteen inches and was starting to get shaky. "Are drugs bad?" he asked.

"Illegal drugs are bad."

"Are my tíos and tías in jail now?"

"I'm not sure, but you won't be going back there to live. You'll stay here for a while, and we'll try to find your mother. You may go live with another family for a while, but we'll see about that. Are you doing okay here?"

"It's nice. We have lots of bananas. I like bananas. Antonio and Manuelito are here too."

"Have you talked to Antonio?"

"We got to sit together today at lunch, and we played on the bars."

"Miguel, do you know your father's name?" Sabre kept her voice soft.

"Yes, señora."

"Can you please tell me what it is? It might help me find your mamá."

Miguel lowered his head, then raised only his sad eyes. "Papa's name is Manuel Gonzalez. He works hard, but now we don't see him."

Sabre handed him another block. "What do you mean by that?"

Miguel just shrugged, his happy little face no longer smiling.

"Was your papa coming to America with you?"

"No, mamá said we won't see him anymore because he worked too hard."

Sabre wasn't sure what to make of the information, but she knew whatever it was, it made Miguel sad.

"Thank you for telling me your name and your parents, too. I'll only use that information to help you, but I have to tell the social worker so she can help look for your mother as well."

The Lego tower wobbled as Miguel added the last block—then it tumbled. He smiled as it crashed, but he didn't giggle as he had earlier.

CHAPTER 12

Tuesday, p.m.

Sabre sat in her office putting together the files from the new cases. It was nearly five o'clock when JP called. "Will you be home soon?" he asked.

"I have to finish up a few things. I got four new cases today, and I have several hearings for tomorrow that need some work."

"Is anyone in the office with you?"

"Elaine and Jack are both still here."

"Please leave when they do. You know I don't like you there alone."

Sabre loved that JP cared so much, but it annoyed her when he suggested she might not be able to take care of herself. Still, she knew he was right about one thing; she needed to be careful. Whoever sent those texts could be as dangerous as the guy who'd stalked her previously. She knew sometimes she took chances that she shouldn't, giving JP good reason to be concerned. What bothered her most was that there were so many crazies out there making everyone vulnerable.

"I won't," she said. "I'll pack up my files and be home shortly. Do you need me to stop at the store for anything?" Sabre knew the answer would be no, but she offered anyway. JP had become quite the shopper since Morgan and Conner moved in. He even checked the coupons and got the best deals. He also did most of the cooking, with Morgan's help. The girl really seemed to enjoy it and was pretty good. She had done a lot of cooking with her grandma when she lived at home. Sabre prepared a meal now and then, but she wasn't much of a cook and had no desire to learn. Fortunately, JP never expected it of her.

"Just get your pretty, little self on home to me. That's all I need."

After dinner, Morgan asked for help with her math. JP looked at Sabre, raising one eyebrow.

"I'll be glad to help you," Sabre said.

"I have to write an argumentative paper comparing short stories we read in class to real life," Conner said as he sauntered into the room. "I don't really know where to start." Conner didn't ask for assistance that often, so when he did, they knew he needed it.

"That's right up your alley, Ms. Brown," JP said. "You can always put together a fine argument."

"Thanks." Sabre winked. "But you're just saying that because you can't do the grammar part of the paper."

"I never claimed to be a good student. Me helping with an English paper is like a blind man in a dark room looking for a black cat," JP said. "Why don't you help Conner and Morgan, and I'll clean the kitchen?"

"It's a deal."

Sabre sat down at the table with the two children, occasionally checking Morgan's math, which was seldom wrong. Sabre knew Morgan just wanted the positive feedback rather than needing instruction. Conner, on the other hand, took more time. She asked him questions about the stories they'd read and encouraged him to type his arguments. When they were done, she checked for grammatical errors.

After the kids were finished, they finally went to their rooms, and Sabre sat on the sofa with JP. He pulled her close.

"This is nice," he said.

"Yes, but I still have a lot of work to do. How busy are you right now?"

"You mean right this minute, or with case work?"

"With work. Do you have time to take on new assignments?"

"Of course, anything for you darlin'. What've you got?"

Sabre told him about the Suzie White case and asked him to find out how much the family knew about the molestation. She wanted to find a relative Suzie could be placed with who wasn't caught up in protecting Grandpa.

"I'll see what I can do. What else?"

"I'm representing a little boy named Miguel Luis Gonzales Bigotes who is from somewhere in Mexico. I'll visit him again tomorrow and see what else he can tell me, but we need to find his mother." She explained what had happened.

"Okay. I'll reach out to my friend at INS and see what he might know." JP's brow furrowed. "You said you had four new cases. What's happening that triggered so many new ones?"

"Full moon, maybe. I don't know. There've been a lot more filings lately."

"What are the others?"

"The Hendrickson case is a rerun, but the minor's attorney had to recuse herself because she had a conflict. Bob represents the crazy mother, who, by the way, has already decided she doesn't like me." Sabre told him what had happened at court.

"And the basis for the petition?"

"Neglect, dirty home, alcohol, and the mother's poor judgment. It seems she spends more time on her tablet than she does parenting."

"Is she a gamer?"

"Games, social media, I don't know for sure." Sabre shrugged. "The case was filed twice before, same issues each time. The first round was only in the system about six months, then the mom got her act together, and the case was closed. The last time, it took longer."

"Is there a father in the picture?" JP asked.

"Oh, about that. He's dead, and so is one of her previous partners. Another one is missing. Bob calls her the 'praying mantis.' He thinks she's killing them."

"Wonderful," JP said sarcastically. "What would you like me to do?"

"Get a full rundown on the dead/missing men. You can read what's in the social worker's report, but it's a little sketchy. No charges have been filed against the mother, but apparently there has been an investigation."

"And the last case?"

"A tox-baby without a name. And there's a strange woman who has inserted herself into the family, and I want to know who she is. She calls herself Tallulah Waters and claims she's from Louisiana. All I know for sure is that she drives a silver Lincoln Town Car. I'll text you the license plate number." She checked her notes and sent it to JP. "Oh, and she wears bright purple clothes with crazy jewelry."

"Yeah, that ought to go a long way in finding her," JP said facetiously.

"She tries to act like a Southerner, but I don't know how much of that is put on. She claims she was named after a waterfall in Georgia, but I'm not convinced Tallulah Waters is even her real name. Have fun." Sabre stood, "Now, I have some work to do."

"Will you do me a favor?" JP said in his usual soft tone.

"Of course. What?"

"Think about your caseload and see if you can come up with anyone who might have sent those texts."

"I've given it a lot of thought. I have a few crazies on my cases, plus a few who might want me dead, but I can't think of anyone who might have killed Nicholson."

"How about if you make a list of the *crazies* and the *Sabre haters* and pull the files for me. Might as well add the files where Nicholson was the social worker. Let me look through them and see what I can find. Please don't leave anyone out. I can eliminate them myself, if a connection seems farfetched."

"Maybe it was just a one-time thing. Someone who knew I had argued with Nicholson and thought the messages would be funny."

"But why the burner phone?"

"Part of the joke?"

"Just humor me. Give me the list and the files and let me satisfy my own curiosity."

"Okay, but there are cases I had with Nicholson that I can't remember. Elaine will search the files when she has time, but that could take forever. I'll call Maxine Quinn, the social worker who helped with Morgan and Conner, and see if she can check the records without violating any rules."

Sabre sat at the table with her laptop and files for the next day. She read through the reports and jotted down notes. She was already tired and wanted to go to bed, but she knew this was the new routine. Now with the kids in school, homework time had been added to the schedule.

Sabre opened a new Excel sheet, labeled it NICHOLSON, and created columns labeled Case Name, Attorneys, Social Workers, Parents, Witnesses, and Notes. She would humor JP, but she wanted to believe it was all a hoax. As she prepared her cases for the morning hearings, she occasionally added a name to the Excel sheet for JP.

After a while, Morgan came into the room. "Sabre, will you tuck me in?"

"Of course, sweetheart."

Morgan smiled, walked to the sofa, and gave JP a kiss. "Goodnight, Uncle Johnny."

"Goodnight, Munchkin."

After tucking Morgan into bed, Sabre finished JP's list, printed it, and handed it to him.

"Dang, girl, that list is as big as Dallas."

"You said to be thorough. And if I think of anyone else, I'll let you know. If you want to come by the office tomorrow, Elaine will pull the files and you can work on them there. I'll also have Elaine make copies of the new cases so you can start on those too." She kissed his forehead. "You're gonna be a busy boy."

"Busier than a one-legged man at a butt-kickin' contest."

CHAPTER 13

Wednesday, a.m.

The next morning, JP sat at Sabre's desk, working his way through the Excel sheet she'd given him. He jotted down questions as he went, starting with cases Nicholson had worked. JP planned to shift to Sabre's new cases when Elaine brought him the files. He was more concerned about protecting Sabre, but she'd made it clear that the new cases were her priority.

The most recent scenario with Nicholson seemed the most likely, so he read through the entire file, but nothing triggered a reason why someone would kill him or target Sabre. Until he discovered otherwise, JP planned to operate under the assumption that whoever killed the social worker had also sent the texts.

He called Marlow. "You got anything new on the Nicholson case?"

"It looks like a suicide, but we haven't found a note or anything that really supports it. The front door to his apartment was locked, and there were no signs of a struggle on the balcony."

"What about his neighbors?"

"We have no witnesses who actually saw it happen, and the one who claims to have seen him hit the ground isn't really credible. The main reason we're keeping it open is because of the messages Sabre received."

"If someone killed him, they're good at what they do."

"Tell Sabre to be careful. Right now, it doesn't seem like the perp is after *her*, but you never know. That text was strange."

"I'm trying, but Sabre can be a little hard-headed sometimes." JP hung up.

A moment later, Elaine came into the office. "Here are your copies of Sabre's cases."

"Thanks."

"Always a pleasure, Cowboy." She turned to leave. "Just let me know if you need anything else."

He glanced through the files, then picked up his phone and called Pedro Torres, his friend at INS. He told him about Miguel Luis Gonzales Bigotes, then asked, "How would I go about finding his mother if she is in Mexico?"

"Do you know the mother's name?"

"All we have is Maria Luciana, but I don't think that's her last name."

"If the child's last name is Bigotes, then her first surname should be Bigotes as well, but we don't know what her second surname is. In Latin America, the child is given two secondary names, the father's surname, followed by the mother's paternal surname."

"But if she got married, wouldn't she have her husband's last name?"

"No. Latin American women don't typically change their names. So, if I were you, I would start with the surname Bigotes. It's not real common, so it'll be easier than others. Do you know what area they're from? The town, maybe?"

"No, but Sabre hopes to learn more from Miguel."

"If she can get him to describe the place or area, I might be able to narrow it down."

"I'll see what I can find out and let you know."

"When you get me more information, I'll do what I can. I hate to see these children separated from their parents."

JP thanked him and hung up. Next, he called two relatives on the Suzie White case and made appointments to stop by their houses later. Then, he looked through the other files in which Nicholson was the social worker. He noted the name and a few other details of the attorney, Daryl Anderson, whose girlfriend had beaten his daughter. He called Anderson's office to make an appointment and was told he'd have to wait until Monday and that the attorney was in a meeting. JP took the new case files, all his notes, and left. It was only a few blocks to Anderson's office in a high rise on Broadway, and he planned to drop in.

Once inside the building, he took the elevator to the tenth floor and found the offices of Anderson, Brockton & Whales. He approached the receptionist and asked to see Anderson. JP wondered if it was a requirement for these law firms to only hire receptionists who were young and attractive. It seemed the same wherever he went. Perhaps the only thing requested for their applications was a current photo.

"I'm sorry, he's not available right now. Would you like to make an appointment?"

"I know he's here," JP said, bluffing. "Please tell him there's a private investigator here to see him and it's personal.

Tell him if he wants me to share with you just how personal it is, I will."

JP waited while she made the call. To her credit, she repeated his words almost verbatim. She hung up and said, "Right this way."

She led him down a hall into a private office with a view of the bay. A man in his late forties in an expensive navy blue suit sat behind a large oak desk. Anderson stood when JP extended his hand, but he didn't invite him to sit.

"Nice view," JP said, as he walked to the window and looked out at the water.

"Thanks. It makes my job a little more pleasant."

"Thanks for seeing me."

"You piqued my curiosity, but I only have a few minutes. What can I do for you?"

"I'll get right to it." JP stood in front of the lawyer's desk. "I know you had a juvenile court case a while back. And before you get concerned about the confidentiality issues, I'm the private investigator for the minor's attorney."

"That case is closed, and my child is fine." Anderson sounded a little defensive.

"I'm sure she is."

"I haven't seen my ex since the divorce. I've moved on, and frankly, I don't bring women home anymore. My daughter is the most important thing in the world to me."

"I'm not here to question your parenting."

"So, what do you need?" Anderson picked up a pen and clicked it open.

"Do you remember the social worker on that case, Jim Nicholson?"

"Yes, I saw on the news last night that he died. It looked like a suicide. Is it?"

"It probably was."

"But you're not sure?"

"I have some reasons to believe he may have been murdered, but I can't share those with you right now."

"And the police?" He clicked the pen again.

"As far as I know, they're looking at suicide."

"What does it have to do with me?"

"Do you know anyone on your case that might be angry enough to kill Nicholson?"

Anderson responded, "No. The case never got past a juris-diction hearing. When I found out what was going on, I got rid of the witch. Once the paperwork was done, they closed the case."

"Nicholson didn't give you any trouble?"

"No, in fact, he did very little." Anderson kept clicking the pen. "I took care of everything myself."

"What about your wife? Was she angry?"

"Not enough to kill anyone, if that's what you mean." The attorney glanced at the pen and laid it down. "Besides, she's already found another sugar daddy, and she got way more from me than she deserved. I just wanted it over quickly so I could get my daughter's life back on track."

"No other relatives were involved?" JP tried not to feel discouraged.

"No." Anderson glanced at the large clock built into the wall. It had no face, only numbers and hands, and those covered a ten-foot radius. "I have an important meeting in just a few minutes." He walked to the large glass door and opened it.

"Thank you for your time." JP nodded and left.

CHAPTER 14

Wednesday, a.m./p.m.

The Spencer Case

Child: Baby Spencer, newborn (F)
Parents: Father—Carlos Vega & Mother—Wendy Spencer
Issues: Physical Abuse, Drugs
Facts: Baby born positive for methamphetamines.

JP skimmed the first set of case notes, then headed for El Cajon to have lunch with his old friend, Deputy Sheriff Greg Nelson. They had been rookies together many years ago and had remained friends. Their paths had crossed on several cases in the last ten years, and occasionally they socialized, mostly over a beer. They met inside Burger King.

"What prompted this lunch date?" Nelson asked.

"I'm here because I'm so hungry I could eat the north end of a south-bound goat."

"You know what I mean. Why are you here with me?"

"Maybe I just wanted to see my old friend."

"If that was the case, we'd be meeting for a drink, not eating at a fast food joint. So, I'll let you buy me lunch, and you tell me what you need." Greg handed over a folder. "Here's the police report you wanted on Vicki Hendrickson, which I could have emailed. So, what's up?"

"Let's get some food first." JP stepped to the counter and ordered hamburgers, then asked Greg about his family while they waited. When the food came, they took it outside to sit where it was quieter. JP told him about the teenage parents and the woman in purple. "She claims her name is Tallulah Waters and that she's visiting from Louisiana. But I think she might be an El Cajon resident. Does her name ring any bells?"

"I can't say that it does. And Tallulah would be a hard name to forget."

"I suspect it's not her real name." Sabre had shared her distrust of the woman.

"Why would anyone pick a name like Tallulah?" Greg made a face.

"She said it means *leaping waters* and that she was named after a waterfall in Georgia."

Greg stopped eating, looked up, and grinned. "You're kidding."

"No, I'm serious."

Greg shook his head. "Is she a big woman, wears bright colors, and so much jewelry it's a wonder she can walk around?"

"You know her."

"I sure do. She's used the names Niagara, Palouse, Feather, Rainbow—all waterfalls. She's obsessed with them. In fact, on the street, her place is known as *The Falls*. She's an old hooker who has since turned madam. She moves around a lot, but she never leaves El Cajon or Lakeside. Her clientele seems to find her wherever she goes. Her *girls* all use names of waterfalls too. We left Ms. Falls alone for a long time, until recently."

"What's your interest now?"

"She's starting to take in underage girls, and their drug use has become more prevalent. She used to be adamant about not allowing drugs or minors at The Falls, but she must be hurting for the business."

"Do you know where her establishment is now?"

"She recently moved, but we're close to nailing her. I'll let you know if we do."

The White Case

Child: Suzie White, Age 7 (F)
Parents: Father—Thomas White, Jr. & Mother—Georgia White
Issues: Neglect, Sexual Abuse
Facts: Suzie was allegedly molested by the paternal grandfather, a member of their household. Parents continued to live with him.

After a quick glance at the second file, JP drove to the address for Daniel White, Suzie's paternal uncle. His wife, Brenda, invited JP inside the small, stucco tract home. The main room was a little messy, but livable, and he expected it would pass a social worker's inspection. He introduced himself as the PI for Suzie's attorney.

"So, you work for Suzie's lawyer, huh?" Brenda said, her pudgy face unsmiling.

"That's right."

"Pops sure doesn't think much of her. She really ticked him off by not letting him stay in the courtroom for the hearing."

"I don't know anything about that."

"I think it's kind of comical myself. Not too many people stand up to Pops." She smiled.

JP explained that they were looking for a possible placement for the girl.

"We'd love to have Suzie here with us," Brenda said. "Ain't that right, Daniel?"

"Sure." Daniel didn't stand, but he glanced up from the television long enough to say, "She's a good kid."

"It's a real shame what Pops did to her," Brenda volunteered. "I feel so sorry for that little girl. She didn't deserve that. Her parents knew too. I don't know why they stuck around."

"What makes you think they knew what was going on?"

"Suzie's mother told me. She wanted to leave, but they didn't have the money to get a place. And her husband, Thomas Junior, said it wasn't all that bad and convinced her things would be okay. I told Georgia to come live with us, but Daniel and Junior don't much get along, even though they're brothers. Holidays are about all they can handle. We seldom make it through those without an argument between the two of 'em."

"You think Suzie is telling the truth?"

"She wouldn't lie about a thing like that. And she's not the only one in the family, you know. He was doing the same thing with little Becky, his other granddaughter."

"What does your husband think about it all? Does he believe Suzie?"

Brenda rolled her eyes. "I'm not sure what Daniel thinks. You can ask him, if you can get his head out of that television. He has to go back to work." She pointed at her husband on the couch. "That man sits around all day watching soap operas and game shows. I can't wait until he's out from under my feet."

JP walked over to the couch and took a seat across from Daniel. "Do you mind answering a few questions?"

Daniel paused his program, "What do you need to know?"

"Do you believe what Suzie says about her grandfather is true?"

"I don't know. Kids these days see a lot of stuff on television, and sometimes they make stuff up. I'd hate to see the old man go to jail over a misunderstanding." Daniel's eyes flashed in anger. "I think it's pretty chicken that Junior blew the whistle on him after all Pops has done for him and his family. Pops takes him in all the time, gives him a place to live when he's down. It doesn't seem to me like Junior's very grateful."

JP started to really dislike the guy. "I don't think Junior was the one to turn him in, but that's not the point. Have you talked to your father about what happened?"

"Yeah, he says he didn't do anything. He might have accidently touched her once, but he didn't do anything else."

"Do you believe him?"

"I give him the benefit of the doubt."

JP thanked them both for their time and left. *Suzie wouldn't be staying with them.*

His next stop was to see Frank White, the other paternal uncle. Again, the woman of the house invited him in, but he didn't sit anywhere. The place was filthy! Empty fast-food cartons were everywhere, some still containing leftovers. The kitchen floor hadn't been swept or mopped in months. Frank wasn't home, but his wife seemed sure Frank would believe his father over Suzie. She also said she would be willing to have the child in her home. JP didn't stay long and didn't feel the need to speak to Frank. This home would never be approved, based on the condition of the house itself, without even considering Frank's attitude.

From there he drove to see Suzie's paternal aunt, Anita Gage. She arrived at the same time he did, and they introduced themselves on the porch.

"I don't have long because I have to pick Becky up from school, but you're welcome to come in for a few minutes." Anita stepped inside and JP followed. She lived in an old, but clean neighborhood, and her house was the same. She offered JP a beverage, which he declined.

"I'll get right to the point. We're trying to find a placement for Suzie while we figure things out. Would you be interested if your home was approved?"

"I would love to, but I can't. I'm a single mother, and I work full-time. There's just no way I can take on another child."

"Is there anyone else in the family who could take care of her and protect her?"

"No," she answered curtly. She crossed her arms. "I'm mad as hell at this whole family, especially Georgia."

"Why is that?"

"She knew what Dad was doing to her own daughter, and she didn't do anything about it. What's worse is she took my daughter, Becky, to see him when I specifically asked her not to. I told her many times I did not want my child around him when I wasn't there. Now Becky is scarred for life." Her voice grew louder and angrier as she spoke. "Not one of them will stand up to Dad. He helps them out when they need it, and they're afraid their cash cow will cut them off if they don't do what he says."

"Does he help *you*?"

"No. He's offered, but I won't take anything from him. I seldom see him, and my daughter will never see him again if I can help it."

CHAPTER 15

Wednesday, p.m.

The Bigotes Case

Child: Miguel Bigotes, age 4 (M)
Parents: Father—Manuel Gonzales & Mother—Maria
Luciana Bigotes
Issues: Neglect, Abandonment
Facts: Child was smuggled across border and left with
strangers.

As Sabre drove to the Receiving Home to see Miguel, his social worker called to say the boy had been moved to a temporary foster home. Sabre asked Siri for directions and headed to National City, arriving fifteen minutes later.

The foster parents, Suzanne and Horst Barabasch, were of German descent and German was their first language. However, they both spoke Spanish and English as well. Sabre had other children in their home before and was pleased with how caring they were. She thought they would be a great fit for Miguel. They were older and retired, but full of energy and loved children.

Miguel was in his room watching cartoons when Sabre walked in.

"Do you want to play with Legos?" Miguel asked.

"Sure, but don't build it too high so it falls down," Sabre said.

"But that's the best part."

"Okay, build it as high as you'd like."

They started to stack blocks, but this time Sabre didn't bother to give the structure a stronger base. After a couple of towers crashed, Sabre prodded the boy. "Miguel, do you know the name of the village or town where you lived?"

"I can't remember."

"Was it big or small?"

"Small, I guess."

"Was it bigger than this town, or smaller?"

"Smaller."

"Have you ever been to Mexico City?"

He shrugged.

"What about Guadalajara?"

Miguel's eyes lit up. "I have cousins there. I've been to see them and my auntie."

"Is it far from where you live?"

"Yeah."

"Did it take you a whole day to get there?"

He laughed. "No."

"When you go there, do you spend the night?"

"No, we come back home again the same day."

That narrowed things down a bit. Sabre spotted a small pottery cup sitting on Miguel's dresser. She picked it up. The cup was beautiful, gray with a blue-and-brown cascade of flowers and leaves. It was very familiar to her. "Is this yours?"

"Yes, I brought it with me, from my village."

Sabre turned it over and saw the word *Mora* across the bottom. *Bingo!* She used her phone to take photographs, capturing the design as well as the signature on the bottom.

"Miguel, did you bring anything else with you?"

His gaze dropped to the floor, and his eyes filled with tears. "I had a picture of me and Mamá, but it's at the house where I was living. Can you get my picture for me?"

"I don't know, but I will try. How big was the picture?"

Miguel held up his little hands about six inches apart. "This big."

"Was it in a frame?"

"Yeah, but the glass got broke."

Sabre arrived at her office and parked on the street. A space happened to be open, and she didn't plan to stay long. As she walked to the door, she admired the old Victorian house, glad that someone had the foresight to convert it to office space rather than tear it down. It was her first law office and felt like home. She reminisced about when she'd found it. She had been fresh out of law school and determined to start her own practice, unlike most of her friends who'd gone to work for firms. In hindsight, it was probably not her best move. She'd struggled for the first two years and almost threw in the towel a couple of times, but her career had worked out in the end.

She stepped onto the porch. A padded manila envelope with her name on it sat by the door. She picked it up and went inside. She greeted Elaine, who handed her opened mail and half a dozen call slips. Sabre spotted Jack Snecker in his office, stopped at his door, and said hello. She admired his space and thought someday she'd have something similar. It was the largest of the three offices and had once been the living room in the old home. A beautiful bay window gave Jack a view of the street from his large mahogany desk. Sabre's favorite part was the fireplace and the settee that provided a cozy sitting area for guests.

As she walked down the hall, Sabre noticed there was no return address on the envelope. She passed David's office, but it was empty as usual. He seldom ever practiced law anymore. He spent most of his time with his ice cream trucks, a business he'd started several years earlier. Sabre entered her own office and laid all the envelopes on her desk. She shuffled through the call slips and decided everything could wait until tomorrow. She flipped through the mail and tossed half of it. Finally, she opened the manila package and pulled out a framed photo. Sabre gasped. Staring up at her was Jim Nicholson's bloody face. "Oh no!"

CHAPTER 16

Wednesday, p.m.

Sabre heard the frame clang on her desk before she realized she'd dropped it. She sat, staring at it, as Elaine and Jack ran into the room.

"What happened?" Jack asked.

Sabre pointed at the photo, and Jack started to reach for it. "Don't touch it," she said. She took a deep breath and told them about the messages and the death of the man in the photo.

"You need to call the police," Jack said.

"I'll call Detective Marlow. He's handling the case. Did either of you see who dropped off the package?"

"No." Elaine shook her head. "Nor did I hear anything. I had no idea it was out there."

"I didn't see anything either," Jack added. But someone could easily come up to the door without my noticing. If I'm at my desk, I have a very narrow view."

"I didn't see it when I came in after lunch," Elaine said.

"It was leaning against the door, so you couldn't have missed it," Sabre said.

"Then it must have been dropped off in the last hour."

Sabre picked up her cell phone and called Detective Marlow. He told her not to touch anything and that he would be there shortly. After Jack and Elaine left, she called JP and gave him a quick rundown.

"Call Detective Marlow," JP said, cutting in.

"I already have."

"I'll be right there."

"What about the kids?"

"I just picked up Conner, and he can get Morgan. They'll be fine. Are you okay?"

"Yeah, I was a little upset when I first saw the photo, but I'm fine now. The picture can't hurt me."

"Are you alone?"

"No, Elaine and Jack are still in the building."

"Please ask Jack to stay until I get there."

"I'll be fine."

"Please," JP begged. "Do it for me."

"Okay."

While Sabre waited for Marlow to arrive, she called her friend Maxine Quinn at DSS and explained the incident. "Could you do me a favor?"

"Sure, what is it?"

"I had several past cases in which Nicholson was the social worker, but I can't remember the older ones. I know you have privacy issues to deal with, but all I need are the names of the cases we worked together. Do you have a way of cross checking that?"

"Yes, indeed. The cases are listed in the database with the attorneys of record. The cops have all Nicholson's files now, and I gave the detective a list of those that you were on, so I have it at my fingertips."

Sabre forwarded the list to Elaine and asked her to pull the files. A few minutes later, JP walked in, followed by Marlow shortly after. The detective questioned everyone and bagged up the evidence, all the while chewing his toothpick.

When he was finished, JP walked out with him. "Are you any closer to finding out who killed this guy?"

"No, and I'm getting pressure from the brass to close the case. The physical evidence we have so far points to a suicide, although there is no strong indication he wanted to end his life. We checked Nicholson's health record at Kaiser. We thought maybe he had been diagnosed with cancer or something, but no. He seldom went to the doctor, and his most recent tests were all good. He visited a clinic once for a migraine, and another time, some tests were ordered, but he never followed through."

"Did you question his associates?"

"We talked to a few friends and co-workers, who saw no signs of depression. Although, he didn't have many friends, and none seemed that close. Everyone seemed to think of him as a loner."

"What about family?" JP asked.

"He has a brother who lives locally but is out of the country right now, plus a half-sister who lives in North Dakota. We contacted her, and she said Jim called the day he died. We were able to verify the time as shortly before his death. She didn't think much of it at the time, but when looking back, she thinks the call could have been a goodbye."

"Someone could have forced him to call her."

"I know, but there is no sign of struggle, no fingerprints that can't be explained. In fact, the guy couldn't have had much company because we lifted very few prints in his apartment that weren't his. Nothing was wiped clean. If it was a murder, it looks like a perfect crime."

"So, you're giving up?" JP wasn't ready to accept that.

"No, and this incident with Sabre will keep the case open for a while. But I'm stumped as to where to look for a perpetrator, other than within Jim Nicholson's cases. We're going over those with a fine-tooth comb, actually all of his cases, not just the ones Sabre was involved in."

JP shared the information he'd learned from Anderson, the attorney.

Marlow frowned. "Thanks, but be careful you don't step over the line. I don't want you interfering with my investigation."

"Right."

"Look, JP, you're a cop, albeit retired, so I understand that no matter what I say, you're not going to sit back and do nothing while your girlfriend is harassed. I wouldn't either. But you need to bring me anything you find that's out of the ordinary. You hear?"

"You bet."

JP went back inside and asked Sabre if she was ready to leave. She ignored his question and said, "Miguel has a cup made of pottery from his village."

"And?"

"It might help us find the village where he lived."

"How?"

"I recognized the art. I'm pretty certain it's from Tonalá. When I was studying Spanish in Guadalajara, I did some sight-seeing in the area. We went to Tonalá and Tlaquepaque and saw some pretty cool stuff."

"His cup could be a fake. What keeps artists in other areas from copying the designs?"

"They could, but different areas have different types of pottery." She shrugged and gathered up her files. "It's all we have right now. After talking to Miguel, I was able to ascertain that he doesn't live far from Guadalajara, which would be accurate if he's from Tonalá. It's our best shot. So, I'll have someone look at the pottery to confirm my suspicions."

"I guess it's worth a try. But finding pottery in Mexico seems like looking for a particular squirrel in the woods." JP winked. "So, are you ready to go home now? I'm not leaving until you do."

"I'm done here, but I'm not ready to go home yet."

"Sabre, where are you going?"

"To the house where Miguel was living when DSS picked him up.

"The place where the drug raid went down?" Sabre heard the stress in his voice.

"Yes. I need to get a photo for him."

"I can do that for you," JP said. "It seems risky."

"Then go with me. If anyone is still there, they probably don't speak English, and you won't be able to communicate with them."

"Okay, but please let me take the lead."

"Sure."

CHAPTER 17

Wednesday, p.m.

The Bigotes Case

Sabre climbed into JP's truck, and they drove toward the raided house, hoping someone had returned and would be cooperative. Several of the people who'd been apprehended were on INS holds. At least two others were in a local jail, awaiting trial. This was a long shot.

JP cut into her thoughts. "I'm sorry about that photo you got. If Marlow doesn't find who's sending these things, I will."

"I know." Sabre put her hand on JP's knee. "I'm really okay. I was surprised when I saw it. The red, bloody close-up got to me, but I'm fine now."

"By the way," JP said, "I haven't had a chance to tell you about my lunch with Greg Nelson today."

"How did that go?"

"He gave me the investigation reports on Vicki Hendrickson. Her first husband, Harvey, Unity's father, died in a car accident. Vicki and Unity were with him." JP pulled onto I-15 heading south. "It was late at night, and Harvey had been drinking; he had a blood-alcohol level of point-two-eight. He was out cold after the accident, so Vicki took the baby and went for help, but it was too late. He was dead when the ambulance arrived."

"Why didn't she call?"

"Apparently, she couldn't find her cell phone. Vicki wasn't considered a suspect because nothing suggested foul play. Although, the couple had a fight at their friends' house just before they left. It was a Fourth of July party, and everyone was drinking."

"According to the DSS report, the second husband left her," Sabre said. "No one knows where he is, which isn't unusual. Bob thinks she ate him." She snickered. "The third died of a heart attack. I don't know if they were married or not. Vicki claims they were, but there's no marriage certificate to prove it. Was there a report on that one?"

"He died at home, and Vicki called for help. They conducted a cursory investigation since he died at home, but apparently the heart attack was legit." JP exited the freeway.

"Talk about being unlucky in love."

"For the men, for sure." JP smiled. "I also inquired about Tallulah Waters and found out she lives in El Cajon and has several young girls who live with her. The cops are pretty sure she's a madam. They've been watching her for a while."

"So, that's her interest in Wendy." The news infuriated Sabre. She had seen far too many kids exploited by adults, often the same people who were supposed to be protecting them. "She's got a lot of nerve showing up in court and claiming to be the grandmother."

"Yeah, that took some guts."

"We're close." Sabre pointed ahead. "The house should be down there on the right."

JP parked a half block from the address, then asked Sabre to wait in the car until he assessed the situation. "No." She shook her head. "But I'll stand behind you and slightly to the right when you knock on the door."

JP scowled, but climbed out without arguing. They walked up to the house, and he rang the bell. A woman in her mid-forties opened the door.

JP asked, "Do you speak English?"

"No, señor. Only a little."

Sabre stepped forward and spoke in Spanish, "We're here about Miguel, the little boy who was living here when the cops came."

"Is he okay?" the woman asked in her native language.

"As good as can be, but he misses his mother."

"Pobrecito," the woman said.

"I'm Sabre Brown, Miguel's attorney."

"He's only four. He couldn't do anything wrong."

"No, he didn't do anything wrong."

"Then why does he need an attorney?"

"The Department of Social Services has filed a court case to determine where Miguel should live. I'm trying to help him. Miguel said he had a photograph of himself with his mother that was left here when they took him away. He asked me to get it for him. Do you know where it is?"

"Un momento." The woman closed the door. She returned a few minutes later and handed Sabre a photo, still in the frame but with no glass.

"Thank you so much." Sabre smiled. "This will make him very happy. He misses his mother very much. Do you know her?"

"No. A coyote brought Miguelito and dropped him off. He cried for days, asking for his mother, but we didn't know where or who she was."

The woman spoke rapidly in Spanish, and Sabre had to ask her to slow down so she could follow the conversation. "What else did Miguel say?"

"The man who brought him said they had to separate at the border and would meet up later, but his mother never came. We figured she was probably caught and sent back to Mexico. We kept the boy because we hoped she would come back and find him."

"Do you know the man who brought him?"

"No, but I think Lorenzo does."

"Do you know Lorenzo's last name?"

"No."

"Was Lorenzo here when the house was raided?"

"No."

"Do you know where we can find him? We won't tell the cops. We just want to find Miguel's mother."

"INS got him. I heard they sent him back to Mexico."

"What is your name?" Sabre asked.

"Trina Lopez."

"Trina, one more thing." Sabre took out her phone and scrolled until she reached the photos of Miguel's cup. "Do you know what area of Mexico this pottery is from?"

"Of course, everyone knows." Trina smiled. "It's from Tonalá. The Mora artists have made that pottery for centuries."

"Thank you. You've been a big help."

Sabre and JP started to walk away, but the woman called after them. "Please tell Miguel his Aunt Trina loves him and misses him very much."

Sabre smiled. "I will."

She translated the conversation to JP as they drove back to the office. Inside, they picked up all the files Elaine had stacked on her desk, printed out from Maxine Quinn's list. At home, they cooked and ate like a family with no mention of work, but they both knew they had a long night ahead.

CHAPTER 18

Wednesday, p.m.

When the kids were in bed, JP and Sabre sat down with the stack of files they'd brought home. The cases dated back four years, and all seven had Jim Nicholson as the social worker. Sabre opened the Excel sheet she'd set up with various column headings: Case Name, Attorneys, Social Workers, Parents, Witnesses, and Notes. The plan was for her to add to the list as JP worked his way through each file, giving it a fresh set of eyes, starting with the most recent case and working backward. But that seemed to create too many basic questions.

"Why don't I give you a quick synopsis of each petition, then we can go into more detail?" Sabre asked.

"Good idea, darlin'. Just give me the bacon without the sizzle."

Sabre smiled. JP asked questions as they went, and Sabre added information and anecdotes that weren't in the files. "The most recent with Jim Nicholson is the Hannah Baxter case. You know the basic facts already. Hannah, six years old, was molested by her mother's boyfriend. She was removed, and Nicholson recommended return to the mother, who claimed her boyfriend was gone. I discovered otherwise and set it for trial."

"That was just over a week ago, and you won, right?"

"It was a very heated trial. The father wanted the child placed with his own mother, and I agreed. The court ordered placement in the paternal grandmother's home, which Nicholson had initially approved. It seemed like it was the right move since Hannah's father was in prison and her mother was still living with the perpetrator. If you remember, you investigated the grandparents' homes. The maternal grand-mother was totally inappropriate."

"She was the one who lived with the convicted sex offender. Like mother, like daughter."

"Right. Once the information came out that the mother was still with the perp, the judge ordered her to participate in ther-apy, parenting classes, and a twelve-step co-dependent program."

"Okay, I'm familiar enough with this case, unless there's someone you think I should give extra attention to."

"Nope. The one most upset with me was Nicholson himself. But I doubt he killed himself because of what I thought or did."

"He couldn't very well send you messages after he was dead." JP smirked.

"More importantly, he couldn't take the photo." Sabre suppressed a grin and opened the next file. "We're getting silly now, and we have a long way to go."

"So, the next case. When was it?"

Sabre checked the date. "The case was opened four months ago. An eighteen-year-old mother used drugs while she was pregnant and gave birth to a girl who was born addicted. She went through pretty bad withdrawals. The baby was taken from the hospital to a foster home. Three weeks later, she was placed in the home of the maternal grandmother. I'll do some follow up on this, but I think we can let this one go."

Sabre stretched her arms above her head, then rolled her head around. "Sorry, my shoulders are tired."

JP stood up behind her and commenced rubbing her shoulders.

"That feels great." She sat there for a few moments without talking, just enjoying the massage. "Thank you."

"You're welcome." JP kissed her lightly on the cheek and sat back down.

Sabre continued her summary. "The mother diligently went to her drug programs and parenting classes. She tested clean every time and was allowed to live in the home with the child, as long as she continued her recovery. Nicholson made the recommendation to allow the mother to live in the home, and nothing was contested."

"What about the father?"

"Unknown. According to the mother, he was a one-night stand, the result of too much alcohol at a club."

"She was only eighteen. What was she doing at a club?"

"Drinking, with a fake ID."

"Would Nicholson still be on the case?" JP asked. "If he were alive, that is?"

"No. Once the case goes to disposition, they get a new social worker, so he was only involved for about six weeks."

"Is the mother still clean and living with the grandmother and baby?"

"Yes, as of last week, but I'll follow up to make sure. I really don't see anyone or anything in that scenario that would trigger someone to send me bloody photos."

"Next?"

"You're already familiar with Lily Anderson, or at least with her father Daryl. The case was filed about seven months ago and only lasted a few weeks."

"The attorney whose trophy wife abused his daughter?"

"That's the one. But he immediately kicked her out, filed for divorce, and the case was dismissed."

"What was the wife's name?"

"Kelsey Anderson." Sabre had to glance at the file. "Her maiden name was Newhart."

"According to Daryl, she has already moved on to another sugar daddy, but I'll follow up on her." JP paused. "What else you got?"

"This case was from three years ago. Five kids, mother, father, and paternal grandparents living in a two-bedroom house in La Mesa. The issue was mostly poverty, but the home was filthy, cockroach ridden, and full of black mold. A dirty-home petition was filed, and the health department shut down the house. Nicholson, to his credit, found them better housing, and a friend of the father's connected him to a better job. I remember Bob gave them a bunch of kids' clothes that CJ had outgrown. It was one of my more positive cases."

"And they're still doing okay?"

"As far as I know. I haven't done any follow up, but if the case came back to court, as the attorney of record for the children, I'd be notified. They could've moved to another city or state though. If a case was filed elsewhere, I wouldn't be aware of it."

"It sounds like spending time on this one would be a waste."

"I agree." Sabre laid down the file. "Want to take a little break? I could use a cup of tea."

CHAPTER 19

Wednesday, p.m.

Sabre sat in front of her computer, her teacup close at hand. She picked up the next file. "Oh yeah, the Fisher case. You may remember this one from four years ago. You worked on it when Judge Mitchell was killed. It was another drug-baby petition, and both parents were volatile. The father threatened Nicholson when the child was taken from the hospital and placed in foster care. Then, at the detention hearing, the mother lost it and screamed that everyone would pay for taking her child."

"I remember well." JP stiffened. "The father, Dale Fisher, was a big guy with a muscular body, who threatened you at court."

"He didn't actually threaten me. He just got in my face and called me names."

"And he yelled, 'You better give me my kid back.'"

"That's true."

"Did he ever get his kid back?"

"No, the parents never got off drugs, didn't do their programs, and before we got to the two-six hearing, the father was back in prison."

"What happened at the hearing?"

"The parents' rights were terminated, and the baby was placed for adoption."

"It seems that could be reason enough to want the social worker dead and you harassed."

"Maybe, but neither parent even visited the baby after a month into the case. The mother tested twice, and both were positive. After that, she didn't test at all and although she signed up for drug programs, she never attended. The father never even signed up or got tested."

"So, you're sayin' they chamber-of-commerced it."

Sabre smiled. "Yeah, that's exactly the way I'd put it."

"I think I'll keep this one on my radar and see what I can find out." He pulled his elbows forward to stretch his back. "Next?"

Sabre picked up a thick file. "You also worked on the King case around the same time. It involved physical abuse. Two boys, ages two and twelve. The younger child's biological father, Isaiah Banks, beat his stepson, Kordell King, with a belt, leaving some nasty bruises. Then he hit him with his fist."

"Wait, I remember. That was the one where you almost got killed when you went on a home visit to see Kordell."

"I didn't almost get killed," Sabre protested. She had been scared, although she wouldn't admit that to JP.

"Someone shot at the house three times while you were there. If the grandmother hadn't warned you to get down, you could've been killed. You ended up covered in glass from the broken window."

"But I didn't get hurt. I just had to replace the windows in my car where the bullet went through."

"And you could've been in your car." JP's face was red.

Sabre knew he was getting angry and tried to soothe him. "But I wasn't. Anyway, it seems weird that the stalker would be anyone on a case that was from so long ago."

"How old are the kids now?"

"Devon would be about six and Kordell sixteen. Why?"

"Is the case still open?"

"No. Kordell's grandmother was given a guardianship after two years, and the case closed at that point. So, I don't know what happened to either of the boys."

"I'll see what I can find out. Was that the last file?"

"No, there's one from six years ago, Emily Cadle. It was my first case with Nicholson, and I wasn't impressed with him back then either. I'd like to think he just burned out over time, but he never really did his job well. He was lazy, always trying to find the easy way out. I represented the mother, and Bob had the father. It was our first case together, and we bonded over it. Nicholson became our common enemy, and that's when the relationship between Bob and I took roots. I hadn't really thought about it, but I guess we have Nicholson to thank for that."

"What was the situation?"

"The parents were charged with burning their five-year-old daughter with cigarettes, evenly placed around one of her ankles. Emily denied it. The parents were adamant that they hadn't hurt her, but they never offered a good explanation for the little round, infected areas. Bob and I couldn't reconcile why the burns were so evenly placed. It didn't make sense that Emily could hold still for five burns. In spite of expert testimony by a medical professional who said she could have endured it, the judge wasn't convinced either."

"So, what happened?"

"After a lot of research and a little luck, Bob came across an article about flea bites and how they could get under elastic and leave a row of bites in a perfect line. With a little more investigation, we discovered that Emily had been playing in a sandbox, got the bites, and scratched them until they got infected. The judge found *that* explanation more plausible than a five-year-old holding still while someone burned her with a cigarette."

"Did the parents hold a grudge against Nicholson?"

"Not as far as I know. They weren't ideal parents, but I'm pretty sure they weren't abusive either. If Nicholson had filed a case for neglect, he might have won that. They weren't angry people either, and it was a long time ago. Why would they send me a creepy photo?"

"I don't know. Maybe one of them killed Nicholson and thought you might appreciate it."

"Why just me and not Bob? He was even more helpful to them. And why after all this time?"

"Maybe the perp is an avenging angel, and they somehow heard about your latest run-in with Nicholson, and it triggered something."

"That's a stretch."

"Anyone else on the case who might be a suspect?"

"Not that I can think of. The only other player was the paternal grandmother. She wanted the child with her, but mostly because she hated her daughter-in-law. Grandma kept trying to point the finger at the mother. I think she was an alcoholic."

"Who, the mother?"

"No, the grandmother. The parents drank too much too, but they were better than Grandma."

"Nice family."

"They were pretty dysfunctional, but neither of them was violent or would intentionally hurt their child as far as I could tell."

"Are we done?"

"Yup." She looked at the time on her computer. "It's nearly midnight, and I'm zonked. I hope this gives you something to start on."

JP nodded. "I'll read through the cases, but so far nothing jumps out at me. I just hope we're diggin' where there's taters."

CHAPTER 20

Thursday, a.m.

The next day, JP sat at his home desk with Louie, his three-year-old beagle, nearby. As much as JP enjoyed having his niece and nephew around, the peace and quiet was a big welcome. Louie was good company and just enough.

JP's goal for the day was to contact everyone in the stack of files. He started with the most recent case, six-year-old Hannah Baxter, a molestation victim. He figured that was the most likely since Sabre and Nicholson had quite a difference of opinion, and people didn't usually wait too long to get revenge. JP checked every name, looking for possible suspects. He personally knew all the attorneys and had no reason to suspect any. The mother, of course, had the most to lose, but since Nicholson was on her side, she had no motive to kill him. The boyfriend, Fritz Eastland, had no real grudge against the social worker either. If anything, they would have more reason to kill Sabre than Nicholson. But if it was one of them, maybe they thought taunting her was worse than killing her. No, that was too big of a stretch.

JP called the parents' attorneys and got the same reaction from both. Neither thought much of Nicholson as a social worker, but otherwise, "he seemed like a nice guy." Nor did the attorneys believe their respective clients would feel revengeful enough to kill Nicholson. They gave JP permission to speak to their clients and said they would notify them. JP jotted down the new address for Fritz Eastland and Jackie Baxter. Apparently, they were still living together in spite of court orders.

JP continued to call everyone associated with the case, but no one rose to a level of anger or hate that might warrant murder. Sabre had made an appointment to visit Hannah later that afternoon, and he planned to go along and talk to her grandmother. But so far, JP hadn't found anything in the file that was unusual or inflammatory.

Time to move on. First, was the baby born on drugs and living with her mother and grandmother. He set the file aside. Sabre agreed to follow up and make sure everything was okay at the home before he spent time on it.

After a bit of research, JP found the last known address for Kelsey Newhart Anderson, the abusive stepmother on the Lily Anderson case. He googled Kelsey and discovered she free-lanced as a model. When he pulled up her photo, he could see why Daryl had been attracted to her. She was beautiful—tall, blonde, blue-eyed, with voluptuous lips. She wasn't really his type—he preferred a more natural look—but it was easy to see why someone would fall for her.

JP opened Google Maps and checked the locations. He lined up his stops so he would be close to Hannah Baxter's home at three-thirty, when he was scheduled to meet Sabre.

~

The Anderson Case

Child: Lily Anderson, age 7 (F)
Parents: Father—Daryl Anderson & Stepmother—Kelsey
Newhart Anderson
Issues: Neglect, Physical Abuse
Facts: Stepmother tortured Lily.

Kelsey Anderson lived in a high-rise condo in downtown San Diego, one with a keypad for security. JP waited until a couple approached and punched in the code, then caught the open door and followed them inside. He walked past a waterfall that dropped to a pond filled with goldfish, surrounded by tropical plants. He wondered if Daryl had paid for his ex-wife's elegant home. JP took the elevator to the fifth floor, found the apartment, and rang the bell. He was surprised when she opened the door—since he hadn't called ahead or checked in.

Kelsey's eyes widened when she saw him. Apparently, she'd been expecting someone else.

"Kelsey?" JP asked.

"Yes. Who are you?" She stood in the doorway.

"JP Torn. I'm investigating the death of Jim Nicholson. It was on the news a couple of days ago."

"I saw that. Didn't he commit suicide?"

"It looks like that on the surface, but we have reason to believe otherwise."

"Should I be concerned? For myself, I mean?" She touched the hollow of her throat.

"I couldn't tell you for sure."

"Then what does his death have to do with me?"

"Probably nothing, but I know you had some interaction with him about six or seven months ago."

She scowled. "I sure didn't kill him, if that's what you're suggesting."

"No, nothing of the sort. But the killer has reached out to someone connected to your case, and I'm checking to see if they contacted anyone else." JP paused. "Have you heard from anyone? Received any texts, emails, or phone calls?"

Kelsey shook her head. "No."

"When was the last contact you had with Jim Nicholson?"

"I only saw him once when he said Lily accused me of *torturing* her." She made air quotes around the word. "Which I never did. But Daryl believed his precious daughter over me and gave me the boot. The truth is Lily was jealous of me because I took too much of her father's attention."

JP looked over her shoulder at her apartment and gave her a tight smile. "It looks like you landed okay."

She seemed puzzled.

"From the boot." Before she could respond, he asked, "Do you have any contact with Daryl now?"

"No. I haven't seen him since the divorce. He was a big mistake. I'm concentrating on my modeling now, and that's working well for me."

JP took out a business card and handed it to her. "Please call me if you receive any unusual contact from anyone."

"Okay."

"And be careful. We don't know what this killer is up to."

Kelsey nodded and closed the door. JP heard the deadbolt lock. He hadn't turned up any information that would help, but he'd gotten a feeling for what kind of person she was. Probably not a *killer*. She struck him as more interested in money and attention than revenge.

CHAPTER 21

Thursday, p.m.

The Baxter Case

Child: Hannah Baxter, age 6 (F)
Parents: Father—Nick Baxter & Mother—Jackie Baxter
Issues: Neglect
Facts: Mother's boyfriend, Fritz Eastland, molested Hannah.

His next stop was to see Hannah's mother. Jackie Baxter lived with her boyfriend, Fritz Eastland, in an apartment complex off University Street—quite different from the building he had just left. For a second, JP thought about the inequities of life, but he believed people made their own luck—most of it anyway. Some just got a better start in life than others, but what they did with it after that was all on them.

He located unit six and walked up the rickety steps, passing a window with a screen hanging off. He knocked on the door, and a woman opened it.

"Jackie Baxter?"

"Yes."

"I'm JP Torn. I work for Sabre Brown, Hannah's attorney."

A flash of concern on her used-to-be-pretty face. "Is Hannah okay?"

"Yes, she's fine. I'm here about something else."

An unshaven, shirtless man stepped up behind Jackie. "What do you want?" His tone was less than friendly.

"Are you Fritz Eastland?" JP asked.

"Yes. Not that it's any of your business. I repeat, what do you want?"

"I'm here about the death of Jim Nicholson."

"He's dead?" Jackie appeared to be genuinely surprised.

"I'm afraid so. Do either of you know anything about that?"

"No," Fritz said. "How would we know?"

"It was on the news."

"News is not my thing," Fritz said.

JP would have guessed that.

"What happened to him?" Jackie asked.

"From outward appearances, it looks like a suicide, but it's also possible someone killed him. The police don't know yet."

"That's too bad," Jackie said. "He seemed like a decent guy. He treated me right."

"Have either of you received any calls or texts about Nicholson since his death?"

"No, why would we?" Fritz asked.

"I guess you wouldn't." JP handed Jackie his card. "But if you do in the future, will you please call me?"

JP checked his phone. It was almost three o'clock. He had just enough time to meet Sabre at Hannah's. He hated that she was out there on her own. He worried about her anyway, but with a crazy person sending her photos of dead bodies, he now wanted to keep her constantly by his side. He knew Sabre would never stand for that; she was too independent. All he could hope for was that she would be careful and aware of her surroundings.

JP arrived before Sabre and waited in his truck. When he saw her drive up, he got out and walked toward her. When she opened her car door, she wasn't smiling.

"What's wrong?" JP asked.

Sabre sighed and handed him her phone. "I got an email just before I left the office."

"About Nicholson again?"

"No."

JP read the email.

I don't know how you live with yourself. You go about acting all sweet and innocent while you ruin children's lives. I will never forget what you did to me and my family.

Todd Lynch

CHAPTER 22

Thursday, p.m.

The Baxter Case

"Lynch is the guy from Pasadena, right?" JP felt the muscles in his jaw tighten. "The one who came to your office and threatened you?"

"Right," Sabre said.

"Was Nicholson ever on his case?"

"Not that I know of."

"Sabre, I don't like this one bit."

"I don't either, but I don't think it has anything to do with Nicholson," Sabre said dismissively. "Let's go in and see Hannah and her grandmother. We can deal with this message when we're done."

JP nodded.

Hannah's grandmother greeted them at the door and invited

them inside. She explained that the girl had just gotten home from school and was having a quick snack. They sat down in the living room and chatted until the six-year-old came in. Sabre introduced her to JP, then followed Hannah to her room to see her new hamster.

"Did you hear what happened to Jim Nicholson?" JP asked the grandmother.

"Hannah's new social worker came by yesterday and told me what happened. I'm sorry to hear about Jim. He seemed like a nice person, but I'm surprised he committed suicide."

"The police are still investigating," JP said. "Do you know of anyone on Hannah's case who might be angry enough to kill him?"

The grandmother's eyes opened wide. "Do you think that's what happened?"

"I don't know. I'm just trying to stay ahead of things."

She looked pensive for a moment, then said, "I can't imagine."

"What about Hannah's mother?"

"Jackie has her problems. She's my daughter-in-law, you know. She's made a lot of bad choices in her life, and marrying my son was one of them." She touched her hand to her heart. "Don't get me wrong, I love Nicky. But he's not good husband material, and he's made even worse choices than she has. But I don't think Jackie is a killer."

"How does she feel about Jim Nicholson?"

"She thought he was great, right up until the trial. Then she accused him of not having a backbone, but she mostly blamed the supervisor and County Counsel."

"And her boyfriend, Fritz Eastland? What's he like?" JP had a pretty good idea now, but he wanted to get her take.

"He's a creep, and I never trusted him with my granddaughter, but I doubt if he would kill anyone. Frankly, I think he's too big of a coward. Why else would he take advantage of a young child?"

JP didn't have an answer. Sexual abuse of children mystified him. "Anyone else you can think of who might want to harm the social worker?"

"Nicky is the only other one involved, and he's in prison. And if he wanted to kill someone on this case, it would've been Fritz Eastland."

Sabre walked into the room with Hannah following and carrying a hamster.

"What you got there?" JP asked. "Is that a reindeer?"

"No, silly," Hannah said. "It's a hamster."

"Oh yeah, I guess it would have antlers and a red nose if it was a reindeer."

Hannah grinned. "You're funny."

Sabre thanked Mrs. Baxter for her time, and they said goodbye. Before she reached her car, Sabre called Maxine Quinn.

"Hey, Max. Do you remember the Lynch case? Mother was a druggie, three boys, and Todd Lynch was the non-offending parent. We ended up placing the minors in a home in Pasadena and transferred the case to L.A."

"How could I forget? That man was a menace."

"I just received a disturbing email from him, and I wondered if he had any connection to Jim Nicholson."

"I don't believe so, but let me check." There was silence for a few minutes. "Jim was never on the case, but he had a run-in with Lynch one day when he came to the office looking for a supervisor."

"That's interesting. So, he did have some connection to him. Thanks." Sabre hung up and relayed the information to

JP. "It could be he's trying to even the score with everyone." Sabre paused. "But sending messages doesn't seem like his style."

"What do you mean?" JP responded, almost cutting her off. "He just sent you an email message."

"I know, but he signed his name. He's more of an in-your-face guy."

"I suppose that makes sense," JP said, a little less agitated. "It seems unlikely he would do some things anonymously, then send a signed email. But either way, I'm not letting Lynch get away with harassing you."

"I'm not afraid of Lynch." Sabre tried to sound braver than she felt. "He's been mouthing off all along. This isn't the first time I've heard from him since the case transferred."

JP looked startled. "What do you mean? Has he threatened you before?"

"Not really, but he sent me a letter a week after his case here wrapped up and said I was a horrible person and everyone in San Diego sucked. Then about six months later, I got an email from him saying he checks the obituaries every day for my name."

JP kicked the dirt with his boot. "Dang it, Sabre. Why didn't you tell me about this before?"

"Because I knew you would react like this. I won't let him bully me. The guy is all talk."

"You don't know that," JP said, raising his voice.

CHAPTER 23

Thursday, p.m.

JP waited for Sabre to pull out, then followed her as she drove away. As soon as they were on the highway, he used his navigation system to make a hands-free call, pleased that he had finally been able to make it work. Sabre had shown him how several times, but he still got confused occasionally. His call went through to Sabre's brother, Ron, on the first try. JP had been training Ron in the investigative business for the past six months because Ron had lost his job and wasn't sure what he wanted to do with his life. JP gave him work whenever he could.

"I have a job for you," JP said.

"When do I start?"

"Don't you want to know what it is?"

"I'm sure you'll tell me, but I need the money, so whatever it is, I'm your guy."

"I want you to keep an eye on Sabre."

"What? Are you two having trouble? Because I'm not going to dog my sister."

"No," JP said. "It's nothing like that. She has apparently received several threatening emails from Todd Lynch or someone pretending to be Todd Lynch. Remember him?"

"I sure do."

JP told him about the Jim Nicholson's incidents. "Sabre's being stubborn again, so I don't know how cautious she'll be."

"When do I start?"

"I'll let you know, but I'll be with her the rest of the day, so I'll call you later tonight or tomorrow morning with a plan."

JP hung up and called Bob. "I need your help."

"You've got it."

JP explained his concerns about Lynch. "Did you know about the new email?"

"No, but she usually shares those sort of things, so I expect she will when I see her."

JP had a flash of jealousy. "She didn't tell me she'd received messages from him in the past because she knew I'd be upset. So, I'm counting on you to keep me abreast. I know you don't want to violate her confidence, but I'm really worried. These things usually escalate."

"Do you think Lynch sent her the photo of Nicholson?"

"I have no idea, but it's possible. Otherwise, we have two crazies after her."

"What do you want me to do besides gather intel?"

"Please keep an eye on her when she's at court and whenever you can. I talked to Ron, and he'll pick up where you leave off. Between the three of us, we should be able to shadow her at all times."

"Ohh ... Sabre's not going to like that. Have you told her?"

"Of course not. She wouldn't have any part of it, but I'm not going to let anything happen to her."

JP followed Sabre until she pulled into his driveway. He already felt better knowing she was home. He approached her car and opened the door.

"I'm sorry I got a little gruff back there," JP said. "I just worry about you, honey."

"I know. I'm sorry too. I'll let you know if I get any more messages from Lynch." She squeezed his arm. "By the way, I called Maxine, and she checked the disposition of Lynch's case in Los Angeles County. The children were in the LaFiura foster home until three months ago. They have since been returned to the father, and the case closed yesterday. I'm guessing that's what prompted his email."

As they walked toward the door, Morgan ran out to greet them. "Hi, Sabre. Hi, Uncle Johnny. I had a befuddling day at school," Morgan announced.

"Befuddling?" Sabre asked. "Your word of the day?"

"Yup."

"What was so befuddling about it?" JP asked, as they entered the house. He and Sabre set their files on the table and listened to Morgan's account of her day.

"First, the teacher was doing science, and I always get confused—I mean, befuddled—in science. Did you know there is iron in our breakfast cereal?" Her expression was so earnest, JP repressed a smile. "Real iron, you know, the metal stuff," Morgan continued. "We did an experiment with a magnet and pulled the iron right out of the cereal. We worked in five groups, and we each had a different cereal. The one with the most iron was Raisin Bran, and Cocoa Puffs had the least. Our group did Rice Krispies. They were somewhere in the middle. Pretty amazing, huh?"

"Yes, that sounds amazing, Munchkin," JP said.

"And then, my friend, Olivia, decided she likes Anthony, but Anthony likes Reyna, and Reyna likes Quincy, but Olivia told Anthony she likes him anyway. And he told Reyna, and then Reyna got mad at Olivia and told Quincy that Olivia likes Anthony and that made Quincy mad because he likes Olivia."

"Now that's befuddling," JP said with a grin.

"That's what I said." Morgan smirked back. "By the way, I have signups for gymnastics at five o'clock today."

"That's right," Sabre said. "I knew that. I'll take you."

"I'll go along," JP said.

Sabre shifted her eyes toward him. "You don't have to go. I don't mind taking her."

"I'd like to go too."

"Well, if you're taking her, I can stay home and get something done."

"No, I want us both to go."

Sabre furrowed her brows and tilted her head to the side. "Why?"

"I...I don't feel that well, so I thought you could drive."

"You want to ride with me? While I drive and you're a passenger?"

"Yes."

"What is wrong with you? You always insist on driving."

"Nothing's wrong."

Morgan left the room, and Sabre said, "You're afraid to let me go somewhere by myself because of Lynch and Nicholson, aren't you?"

JP sidled up to Sabre and pulled her close. "Please, just humor me."

~

JP drove Morgan to her gymnastic signups, and Sabre sat in the passenger seat, as always. She considered driving and making him stick to his word but decided to not make him suffer. She knew how much JP hated being a passenger. The fact that he had offered to do it made her realize how worried he was. At the school, Sabre took care of the paperwork, and they were done in less than thirty minutes. On the way home, Sabre's phone beeped with a text message. She read it and looked up, wide-eyed at JP. He shook his head but didn't say anything until they were home and Morgan was out of sight.

"What is it?"

Sabre handed him her phone. The text displayed a photograph of a woman standing by her car with a flat tire. The background looked like the juvenile court parking lot.

"Do you know her?" JP frowned.

"Yes, it's Linda Farris, County Counsel."

"If that was taken today, it must have been just a few moments ago because the lighting is about the same as now."

"And that's the blouse she wore today." Sabre took her phone and called Linda. When she picked up, Sabre asked, "Are you at juvenile court right now?"

"Yes, why?"

"Do you have a flat tire?"

"How do you know?"

"You're not alone, are you?"

"No, there are still a few people here. We just finished a trial. What's going on?"

Sabre told her about the bizarre text photo. "I don't know who sent it or why, but I wanted to make sure you're okay."

"I'm inside the courthouse, and a bailiff is here with me. We're waiting for Auto Club to change the tire. But I don't get it. Why would someone take that photo, let alone send it to you?"

"I wish I knew." Worried that Linda might be in danger, Sabre summarized the other texts she'd received that week and encouraged her to be careful. Then she hung up and forwarded the photo to Detective Marlow.

CHAPTER 24

Friday, a.m.

The next morning, while Sabre took a shower, JP checked her car thoroughly for loose wires, fluid levels, and battery function. Satisfied that no one had tampered with her vehicle, he asked Sabre to drop Conner off at school on her way to work. JP then walked Morgan across the street to her school. On his way back, he received a text from Bob saying that Sabre was safe at court. He hated having to keep such a close eye on Sabre, but he couldn't bear the thought of anything happening to her.

JP settled in to work with his computer on and his white-board ready. He used the board to list the cases he was investigating and added Lynch to the bottom. Then he checked through each file to see if Linda Farris had been County Counsel. That wasn't fruitful since Farris had been on every case at one time or another.

On impulse, he reordered the list and put Lynch at the top

because he didn't like or trust him. Second was Baxter, because it was the most recent and the biggest battle between Sabre and Nicholson. Third and fourth were Fisher and King because they both had volatile parents. He followed with Cadle and Anderson, also unlikely suspects. That left only four cases to concentrate on, making it workable—if he was even on the right track.

Frustrated, and trying to figure out what he could do next, he called Detective Marlow.

"I just talked to Sabre," Marlow said. "I have no idea what the perpetrator is trying to do, but I'm sure it's meant as either a threat or a scare tactic. Apparently, Farris is on most of Sabre's cases because they're assigned to the same courtroom, so her inclusion doesn't narrow anything down."

"I know, I checked the files, and Linda Farris was on every case Nicholson handled," JP said. "Have you learned anything new you can share with me?"

"Not much. The mother on the Fisher case is in prison in Chino. So, unless she's somehow pulling strings from inside, we can probably rule her out. She's actually doing pretty well in a rehab program, making her more unlikely as a suspect."

JP reciprocated with the little information he'd gathered from his visits to Mrs. Baxter and Kelsey Anderson. His gut told him neither was involved. "What about the King case?"

"What do you want to know?" Marlow asked.

"Isaiah Banks, the Kordell kid's stepfather, is he in prison?"

"No, he's been out for three years now. We have reason to believe he's the head honcho in the Piru street gang. He's always on our gang-unit's radar, but they haven't been able to nail him. He'll make a mistake one of these days."

"Any chance he was involved in Nicholson's death?"

"Maybe, but my chief is pushing for suicide on this one. He doesn't want us wasting resources without more evidence." Marlow paused. "Here's an interesting detail. We checked into Nicholson's finances. He had nearly fifty thousand dollars in the bank."

"So, he wasn't broke?"

"Not exactly, but two months ago, he had two hundred thousand."

"Wow, that's a lot of money to save on a social worker's salary, but I suppose since he didn't have a family, it's not that unbelievable. But where did the money go? Is he being blackmailed?"

"We don't think so. He's been spending a lot of time at Viejas Casino and other such places. His sister in North Dakota said he had a real gambling problem when he was younger, but she thought he'd overcome it."

"What did she say about his health?"

"She said he seemed fine. He didn't get sick much. She did remember one time, recently, when he said he had a migraine and had to hang up." Marlow's tone shifted. "Truthfully, JP, if it wasn't for the text and package to Sabre, this case would be a slam dunk."

CHAPTER 25

Friday, a.m.

The Hendrickson Case

Child: Unity Hendrickson, Age 11 (F)
Parents: Father—Harvey Hendrickson & Mother—Vicki
Hendrickson
Issues: Dirty Home, Alcohol Abuse, Domestic Violence
Facts: Returning case, new to Sabre, same issues each time.

Sabre drove in silence to the receiving home with Bob as her passenger.

"You're awfully quiet, Sobs. What's on your mind?"

"I think my new cases are getting to me."

"Come on, you've been down this road before. You know you can handle them."

"I guess it's everything. The new cases, the email from Lynch, the whole Nicholson thing. And now the photo of Linda's flat tire. Why would someone send that? They had to be hanging around the court. It all bothers me more than I want to admit." She glanced at Bob. "Please don't tell JP what I said. He's worried enough." She pulled into a parking spot. "And another thing, you didn't need to come here with me."

"I told you, I have a client I need to see." Bob climbed out.

Sabre followed him toward the building. "Yeah? What's the name?"

"It's not a case you're on. You wouldn't know him."

"Just as I thought," Sabre said. "I know JP put you up to this."

Bob didn't respond.

Once inside, Sabre asked for her client to be sent to an interview room, and Bob waited in the lobby.

When Unity Hendrickson entered, Sabre wasn't surprised by her looks. She bore quite a resemblance to her mother. Both were overweight, and Unity had the same long nose. But the girl was short for her age with pale skin, in contrast to Vicki who stood five-eight. Unity had brown hair, probably close to her mother's natural color, and the same sad, angry eyes. She also had a birthmark on her left shoulder that extended up to her neck.

"Hi Unity. I'm your attorney, Sabre Brown."

"My mom says you're mean," she retorted.

"I certainly don't try to be mean. Your mother and I both want the same things for you. We want you to be safe and happy."

"I want to go home," she demanded. "That would make me happy."

"We're working on that, but in the meantime, can I ask you a few questions?" Sabre explained that anything she said would be confidential, but she didn't expect it to matter to this girl. Nor did she expect to get much information from her. Her mother had already planted the seeds to keep her daughter from trusting anyone else.

"What do you want to know?" Unity growled.

"For starters, I'd like to get to know you a bit, so I know how to represent you."

"You already know what I want. Just let me go home."

"So, tell me. What's it like at home?"

"It's fine."

"What kind of things do you do at home when you're not in school?"

The girl tipped her head and spoke in a sugary voice. "I read a lot, do my homework every night, and keep my room spotless. Oh, and I volunteer at the homeless shelter."

Sabre smiled. "Okay, that was cute. Now, tell me what you really do."

"Are you calling me a liar?" She spat the words.

"Unity, I already know that your grades are terrible, your room is a mess, and I rather doubt that you work at a homeless shelter. I also know that you've been down this road enough to say what you think we want to hear. But that's not what I need. I genuinely would like to know what your life is like."

"You know what it's like." A little less venom this time, followed by a flash of shame.

After a few seconds, Sabre asked, "Do you watch much television?"

"Yeah."

"What's your favorite show?"

Unity shrugged, but after a few seconds said, "I've been binge watching the *Friends* series on Netflix. It's pretty cool." For the first time, she sounded like a normal young girl. Then she rolled her eyes. "But I can't do that here. I hate this place. Why can't I go home?"

"Because your house isn't fit. Your mom can't live there either. We're trying to find a relative you can stay with for a while. Speaking of which, do you know your Aunt Yvonne very well?"

"Mom hates her."

"That's what I heard, but what do you think of her?"

"She's nice. She comes to visit me sometimes and takes me to the movies." Her eyes clouded over. "But she doesn't come around as much as she used to."

Sabre ached for the poor girl. "Do you know why?"

Unity took a breath and exhaled. "Mom says she doesn't like us anymore."

"You sound like you're not sure of that."

"It's because Mom hates her. I heard them arguing on the phone, and I don't know what Aunt Yvonne said, but I know Mom told her she couldn't come over. She'd never let me live with her. My auntie probably doesn't want me there anyway."

"If your aunt wants you to live with her, and the court orders it, your mother won't have a choice. I'll see what I can do."

CHAPTER 26

Friday, p.m.

When they left the receiving home, Bob asked, "Where to now, Sobs?"

"I need to see Vicki's sister, Yvonne. I'll drop you back at your car, then be on my way."

"Just stop there first. I'd like to see Yvonne again. I haven't checked in with her since this case came into the system the first time."

"I'd better do this alone. Yvonne might not be as open with you there because you represent Vicki." Sabre tipped her head and looked at Bob. "I'll be fine. I can't stop doing my job properly because of a few ugly messages."

Bob finally acquiesced. But he started texting on the way back, and Sabre was pretty certain he was notifying JP.

"I understand you've tried to keep a relationship with Unity," Sabre said, after she and Yvonne settled at the dining table. Sabre was pleased to see that the home was clean and suitable for a child.

"I have," Yvonne said. "But Vicki doesn't really want me around. I went to her house a week ago, and she wouldn't let me in. I got a glimpse of the living room and could smell the stench from the door." The pretty, slender, composed woman let out a deep sigh. Sabre was struck by what a complete contrast she was to her sister. "So, I called social services. I hate that Unity has to live in that squalor."

Sabre agreed, but kept her opinion to herself. "What was your sister like as a child?"

"She was fun to be around, but even as a kid, you could tell she had problems."

"Like what?"

"She was very moody and quick to anger," Yvonne said. "She hated when our mother gave me any extra attention. And she was deathly afraid of balloons."

"In what way?"

"She would cover her eyes and scream whenever she saw one. We didn't get to attend many birthday parties when we were kids because they usually had balloons. Or sometimes we'd go, but we'd have to leave because Vicki wouldn't stop screaming."

"Do you know what caused the phobia?"

"No idea. And I don't know if she still has it." Yvonne stood. "I need some water. Can I get you something to drink?"

"No, thanks. I'm fine."

The kitchen was only a few steps away, so Yvonne quickly returned and sat back down.

Sabre pressed forward, wanting to know more. "What was Vicki like as a teenager?"

"I didn't see her much. We had different fathers, and when I was eleven, I went to live with my dad. So, we went to different schools and didn't have a lot of contact. After high school, I tried to keep in touch, but it was a one-sided effort. I kind of gave up until Unity was born, then I wanted to know my niece, so I started coming around again."

"How did Vicki react?"

"At first, she was good about it. She allowed me to spend time with Unity and take her places. I think Vicki welcomed the break back then. But the last few years she seemed to grow more and more angry. I made the mistake of telling her she should keep her house a little cleaner. I even offered to help, but that just made her madder."

"I noticed Unity has some of that anger as well," Sabre said.

"She's had a rough life. This is the third time social services has gotten involved."

"Were you considered for placement before?"

"I spent a lot of time and money fighting to get Unity with me, but the social worker thought she should stay with her mother. They helped Vicki get different housing, sent her to parenting classes, then closed the case."

"And the second time around?"

"Vicki told them I was evil, and I just didn't have the time or strength to fight it. I was transitioning jobs and fighting pneumonia and lacked the energy."

"Would you like to be considered for placement now?"

"Absolutely. I know the older Unity gets, the harder she'll be to handle, but I love my niece, and I think I'd be good for her. She needs some stability in her life."

"Her case worker is lining up some therapy for her, and hopefully that will help Unity work through some things."

"I know you saw her angry side, but she also has a loving and witty side," Yvonne said. "I hope you get to know *that* Unity because she's pretty special."

After a few more questions, Sabre thanked her and left. When she pulled away from the house, she realized she was only a few miles from where her clients on the King petition had lived. JP wanted answers on that case too, so she decided to stop in—even though the last time she'd been shot at. *That was four years ago,* she thought. *Besides, what were the chances ...?* She pulled out and headed to see Mrs. Walker, the children's grandmother.

CHAPTER 27

Friday, p.m.

The King Case

Social Worker: Jim Nicholson
Children: Devon King, age 6 (M), Kordell King, age 16 (M)
Parents: Father of Devon—Isaiah Banks, Father of Kordell—
Clay Walker & Mother—Brenda King
Issues: Physical Abuse
Facts: Isaiah Banks beat his stepson, Kordell, with a belt and
his fist.
Status: Case closed, children living with grandmother, Mrs.
Walker, under a guardianship.

When Ron received the text from Bob that Sabre was going out on her own, he drove to the courthouse and waited until Bob dropped her off. Then he followed her to Yvonne's house and waited until she came out. She drove to Federal Boulevard and turned east as he expected her to do. But when she got to

Euclid, she went south. She obviously wasn't going home. He kept his distance, making sure she didn't see him, but he wasn't so far back that he would lose her. She drove into a well-known, gang-ridden neighborhood and stopped in front of a small house with a chain-link fence around a yard full of weeds. Ron held back until she exited her car and walked up to the front door. Then he drove past her to the end of the cul-de-sac and turned around. He was able to park across the street where he could see her come out, but she'd be unlikely to notice him.

Ron was nervous, partly about the neighborhood, but more concerned about how angry Sabre would be if she knew he was following her. She'd be furious with both him and JP. Ron called JP and checked in, explaining his location.

"Dang that girl," JP said. "She's gonna get herself killed."

"It's pretty quiet here," Ron said, glancing around.

"A few blocks over is a lot worse, but I still don't like her in that neighborhood."

"Do you want me to go in?"

"No, she's probably fine as long as she's inside." JP hesitated. "Although, the last time she was there, she got shot at."

"What?" Ron's anxiety escalated.

JP gave him a brief account of the gang shooting that had gone down.

Ron wanted out of there, and he wanted to take Sabre with him. "Are you sure you don't want me to go get her?"

"Just keep an eye out and watch your surroundings. She won't stay long, but keep me posted."

～

Sabre looked for a doorbell but didn't find one. Seconds after she knocked, a heavy-set, African-American woman opened it.

"Hello, Mrs. Walker," Sabre said. "Remember me?"

"Of course I do. Lordy, Lordy, come on in."

Sabre walked into the tiny living room. Everything looked the same as it had four years ago.

"Is something wrong on the guardianship?" Her dark eyes looked worried.

"No, not at all. I was in the neighborhood and just thought I would see how the boys are doing." Sabre's gaze landed on the antique Brazilian rosewood cabinet made by Mrs. Walker's father. The old TV it held had been replaced by a flat screen, but it was still surrounded by photos of Mrs. Walker's son as a child. New photos had been added of Devon and Kordell, mostly centered on sports. "I'm glad to see you still have your father's cabinet," Sabre said, gesturing. "It's so beautiful. If you ever decide to get rid of it, I better be your first call."

"You will be, but I don't expect that to happen. I'm hoping someday it'll be in Kordell's home."

"Are Kordell and Devon around?"

"No, sorry. Devon is at a friend's house, and Kordell is at football practice. He's become quite the star. He's the top running back for his high school team. We're hoping he'll get a scholarship and end up at UCLA or Michigan State."

"Does he have the grades for that?"

"He sure does. That boy is a bright kid. He's been on the honor roll every year, and he's earned every bit of it. He works hard at whatever he does. I'm so proud of him." She stopped talking for a second, then said, "Lordy, where's my manners? Would you like some lemonade?"

"Yes, please."

While Mrs. Walker was in the kitchen, Sabre eyed the

photographs on the credenza, studying the new ones of Kordell and Devon.

Within minutes, Mrs. Walker returned with two large glasses of lemonade. She handed one to Sabre and smiled. "This one doesn't come with gunshots."

Sabre chuckled. But the fiasco that happened four years ago during a home call flashed in her mind. She'd just been handed a lemonade when a drive-by shooter opened fire. The drink glasses had gone flying as everyone hit the floor. It was terrifying at the time, but no one had been hurt, and she was glad they could laugh about it now.

"Good to know. If it did, I think I'd give up lemonade forever." They sat down. Sabre took a sip, then glanced around sheepishly. "So far, it looks like we're safe."

"So far."

"I was looking at the photos of Devon and Kordell. They sure have grown, and Kordell really resembles his father."

"Yes, he does. He reminds me a lot of him too, the kind parts."

"And Devon's dad, Isaiah Banks, do you see much of him?"

"Not often, but it's still too much. A few times a year, he decides he needs to see Devon. It's hard on the boy because he admires his father so much, which is worrisome. Everybody knows Isaiah leads the local Piru gang. I hate for Devon to have him as a role model." She shuddered. "There's not much I can do about it though. Isaiah has the right to visit Devon as long as I'm supervising. I don't think Isaiah would intentionally hurt him, but he's not ashamed of his gang affiliation, and I don't want Devon exposed to it. He'll see all that soon enough in school and around the neighborhood."

"Isaiah doesn't fight you about the visitation being supervised?"

"No, but Devon is only six. I'm sure it'll be harder when he's older. I just wish he didn't admire the man so much. I pray every day that Isaiah will go back to prison."

"When was the last time you saw him?"

"Last Sunday. Before that, it had been four months, but he promised Devon he'd be back real soon. I doubt if he will. He's been breaking those kinds of promises to the kid all his life. Devon hasn't figured it out yet, though, and he watches and waits for him for weeks, sometimes months, before he realizes he's not coming."

"I know that's real hard on kids. I see it all too often."

"Isaiah has never been very responsible. Another thing, he just drops in. He's supposed to call and set a time, but he never does."

"You could refuse him when he doesn't call ahead."

"I know, but that would only cause problems. There's no point in poking the bear."

"You're right." Sabre took a sip of lemonade. "And their mother, how is she doing?"

Mrs. Walker looked solemn. "I guess you didn't hear. She overdosed a few years ago. It was hard on the boys, especially Devon. It was tough on Kordell too, but I think he kind of expected it."

"I'm sorry to hear that." Sabre set down the glass and said, "I'd better be going."

"I'm sorry you didn't get to visit Kordell."

"Me too, but please tell him I'm proud of what he's doing with his life."

As soon as Sabre left the house, she checked her phone for

messages. She had three missed calls from JP and one from Ron.

She contacted JP first.

"Where are you?" he asked without a greeting.

"Hello to you too," she said. "I'm just leaving Mrs. Walker's house. I stopped to see the children on the King case."

"Why?"

"Because you needed information, I was in the neighborhood, and I wanted to see how the boys were doing."

"Sabre, why didn't you tell me? I would've gone with you."

"No, you had to pick up the kids from school, and I was already close by."

JP sighed.

"Look, I know you worry, but I can't stop doing my job because some weirdo is sending me pictures of dead people." She waited for a second, expecting him to chew her out. But he didn't respond, so she continued. "Look, I'm sorry. I should've at least told you where I was, but I think it's safe to take the King case off your list. Isaiah Banks doesn't seem to care enough to want revenge, and the mother overdosed two years ago."

"Okay, please just come home."

"I'm on my way."

Sabre hung up and before she could call Ron, her phone rang. The screen read, UNKNOWN. When she answered it, she could hear someone breathing, but got no response to her greeting. After several attempts, she hung up. *Probably a bad connection or a bot call,* she thought. At least, she hoped so.

Sabre put her cell in her pocket and walked toward her car. A cherry red 1967 Chevy Impala pulled up behind her vehicle and a tall, muscular, African-American man stepped out. She moved around the back of her car and toward the driver's door, but the man hustled over and blocked her before she could get inside.

She took a deep breath and tried to sound calm. "Hello, Mr. Banks."

CHAPTER 28

Friday, p.m.

"What are you doing here?" Banks demanded.

"I came to see Mrs. Walker and the boys."

He moved closer, leaving just enough space so as not to touch her. "I thought this case was closed."

"It is."

He leaned in. A musky smell combined with citrus from his cologne filled the air, and she could feel his breath on her cheek. Sabre shuddered.

"Then you have no business here," he said in almost a whisper.

She tried to turn and open her door, but he was too close. He placed his hand on the door, holding it shut but backed up slightly. "Stay away from here, Sabre Brown, or you'll wish you had." He finally took a step back.

Ron jumped out of his car and started toward Sabre, his heart pounding. Abruptly, the big man turned and headed toward Mrs. Walker's house, so Ron got back in his vehicle and called JP.

"Where is Sabre now?"

"She's in her car, just sitting there, probably collecting herself. Do you want me to check on her?"

"Only if she stays much longer. I don't suppose you recognized the man?" JP asked.

"No, but I got photos."

"Send me one."

Ron sent the best frontal photo he'd taken. "Sabre's leaving. Do you want me to follow her?" Before JP could answer, he added, "The man just left the house and is moving toward his Chevy."

"Yes, follow her. Sabre said she was coming home. Make sure she does," JP said. A moment later, he yelled, "Damn! That's Isaiah Banks. Don't follow Sabre. Instead, keep an eye on Banks in case he goes after her. And Ron…"

"Yes?"

"Be careful. Don't get too close. Banks is a dangerous man, a well-known gang leader."

"You got it, boss."

Concern for his sister made Ron want to stick around, but he also felt out of his element. Ron watched as Sabre pulled away. He could see her until she turned right onto Euclid Avenue. Isaiah Banks remained in his car for several minutes. Ron wondered if he had been spotted. Banks obviously wasn't going to follow Sabre, or he would've already left. Ron got nervous just waiting there and thought about leaving, but he feared Banks would follow him. He'd rather be behind the thug than in front of him. He waited.

The longer he sat there, the more he felt like he needed to get a real job, something he loved doing. His mind wandered to the job he once had at the forestry department and wished he could do that again, but it wasn't in the cards now.

Another five minutes had passed when three young boys, ranging from six to ten, walked up the street. When they reached Banks' car, the man stepped out. Ron couldn't hear what they said, but they all spoke to him. Ron took photos of the boys as they chatted. A minute later, the two older boys walked away, and the younger one got into the car with Banks. Ron's first reaction was panic, but the kid didn't seem scared at all, and Ron was able to get a few good camera shots of the boy in the front seat.

Banks made a U-turn and drove towards Euclid Avenue. Uneasy about the little boy in the car, Ron followed Banks, keeping his distance. He continued behind him as he turned south on Euclid, traffic filling in between them. But the flashy red Chevy made it easy to keep in his sight. Ron stopped in a parking lot and waited as Banks drove through a fast-food place. Ron couldn't see what he bought, but it didn't take long, so he surmised it may have been sodas.

A few minutes later, Banks made one more stop in a Walgreens parking lot. He and the boy got out of the car and mingled with several other men standing near a black SUV. Ron was close enough to get some good photos, but he couldn't hear the conversation.

While he waited, Ron sent a message and the boy's photo to JP.

Shortly after, JP called. "The kid got in the car willingly?"

"Yes. He seemed happy to see Banks. I'm sure it was someone he knew."

"I expect it's his son. He's about the right age. Where did he take him?"

"They stopped at a fast-food place, and now we're in a Walgreens parking lot. He and the kid are standing by a black SUV. They're talking to three other black men. Wait, hold on. Banks just pointed toward his car, so the kid walked away." Ron paused. "Now he's getting inside."

"Where's Banks?"

"He's still with those guys, and he looks upset. I can't tell what he's saying, but his body language says he's not a happy camper."

"Maybe you should get out of there."

"Not while he has the kid. What if Banks kidnapped him?"

"That's possible, but please be careful. If something happens to you, I'll have to answer to Sabre," JP said, obviously trying to make light of the situation.

"He's leaving. I'm going to follow."

"I'll stay on the line for a while, and you can tell me where he goes."

"Okay." Ron let Banks drive away, then left by a different exit. "Banks is about a block ahead of me, and he's turning right onto Market."

A few blocks later, JP asked, "Are those sirens I hear?"

"Yup, sure are, but they're getting fainter, so they must be behind me. Banks just turned left on 36th Street, alongside Evergreen Cemetery." Ron paused. "Now we're passing the Home of Peace Cemetery. There sure are a lot of cemeteries here."

The traffic was lighter, and no cars turned onto 36th behind him, so Ron slowed down to leave a bigger gap between him and the red Chevy. When Banks reached Imperial and turned left, the traffic picked up and Ron was able to blend in better.

"We just turned east onto Imperial. We're passing Mt. Hope and Greenwood now. A lot of dead people in the area." They drove for another mile. More sirens wailed in the distance, and they were getting louder as they moved east.

"I hear the sirens again," JP said.

"We must be headed into them now."

Banks picked up speed as he passed over the 805 freeway but continued on Imperial until he reached Euclid. He slowed down to a cruising speed and turned left, heading back in the same direction he'd come from. Ron gave a blow by blow to JP.

"Banks is stopping again, so I'm pulling over."

"What's he doing?"

"He's in front of a pawn shop. Banks just got out and approached a guy standing near another car, but the boy stayed put."

JP said something, but the sirens were so loud Ron couldn't hear it. "Police cars are flying past, and there's an ambulance. Something serious went down."

"It's time you leave there," JP said sternly.

"Soon." Ron watched the two men talk for a moment; then Banks climbed back into his Chevy. "He's leaving now. He just pulled out onto Euclid." Ron followed. The traffic was nearly at a stop as the police cars whipped into a nearby parking lot.

"There must be ten cop cars at the Walgreens where Banks stopped earlier," Ron reported.

"Leave, now." JP's voice was harsh.

"Banks is headed back toward the house. I want to see if he takes the kid home. Then I'll go. I'll call you back." Ron hung up.

Banks kept moving, picking up speed once the traffic

cleared. When he reached the street where Mrs. Walker lived, he turned right and pulled over.

Ron was able to park about a hundred feet away. He hoped Banks wasn't about to walk back and shoot him or something. He had a good visual on the driver's side door, and it never opened. Instead, the little boy got out and walked up the street. Banks pulled away from the curb, made a U-turn, and drove back onto Euclid. He didn't look Ron's way as he drove past. Ron breathed a sigh of relief, then turned to see where the little boy went. He watched as the kid trudged up to Mrs. Walker's house and went inside. Ron headed home, calling JP as he drove.

"Are you okay?" JP asked.

"I'm fine. Banks took the kid home," Ron said. "What do you make of all that ruckus at Walgreens?"

"I'm not sure, but it's quite a coincidence that it happened right where Banks had just been. Whatever went down probably had something to do with him. I'll see what I can find out." JP's voice tightened. "Sabre knows Banks has supervised visits with his kid, but apparently he's been doing more than that. He could be angrier at Sabre about losing custody than we thought."

CHAPTER 29

Saturday, a.m.

The kids were still asleep, and they sat in the kitchen, Sabre with her herbal tea and JP with his coffee. Sabre always woke up ready to take on the world, but JP didn't get his voice until he'd been awake for a while. She'd learned to wait until he was ready. That was usually after his first dose of caffeine. So, they sat in silence for several minutes.

"I'm sorry I've been so on edge lately," JP said finally, "but I don't like you out of my sight with all this craziness going on. Between the creepy texts, the email from Lynch, and now the run-in you had with Banks yesterday, I worry about you all the time."

"I know. It bothers me too, but we just need to figure out who's harassing me, so our lives can get back to normal. As for Banks, I don't know what that was, maybe pent up anger, I guess. But the texts just don't seem like his style. And there's a good chance it's not Lynch. He's done this before, and nothing ever came of it."

"I think I'll do a little more legwork on Lynch anyway. I may even pay him a visit. And I'm not letting go of Banks yet either. He's a hardcore gangster, and he's smart. He may intentionally be trying to make it look like a childish prank."

"What good will that do?"

"I don't know, but I have to do something. Marlow is checking with social services in L.A. County to see if anything unusual is happening on Lynch's case. He's also checking with L.A.P.D. He said he'd try to get back to me this morning. I'll decide what to do after that." JP pushed his coffee cup aside. "By the way, I'm taking the Anderson case off the board. There's just no motive. The one who got hurt the most is Kelsey, and she has landed very well. She announced her engagement yesterday to a top film producer. Now she'll be in the movies. I don't think this little bump in the road is worth her time."

"Good. Anything else?"

"Did you get any information about the drug-baby case with the eighteen-year-old mother?"

"Yes. Mom is doing great. All of her tests have been clean, and she hasn't missed any at all. She completed her parenting class, and she's active in Narcotics Anonymous." Sabre had checked her files on Friday. "She and the grandmother seem to be doing well. There's a good chance the case will close at the review hearing in two months."

"So, I'll take that one off the board too, and follow up on Fisher and Cadle."

"In the meantime, you need to bring me reports on my new cases. I have hearings coming up."

"I'll get right on it."

"By the way," Sabre said, "Wendy Spencer finally named her baby. Are you ready for this?"

"Oh no, what is it?"

"Ecstasy."

JP shook his head and sighed. "After the drug?"

"Probably. You can't even imagine how many babies born on drugs are named Crystal."

"That's sick."

"So, have you learned anything about Wendy's parents?"

"The only address I can find for either is five years old, and they lived there only a few months. It appears they've been homeless most of Wendy's life."

Sabre stood. "Would you like more coffee?"

"Yes, but you don't need to wait on me."

"I know. I'm adding a little water to my tea. I can do it while I'm up." When she returned with the cups, she asked, "What's on your calendar today?"

"I plan to do some follow-up on your current cases, write a few reports, and maybe take a drive to Pasadena, depending on what Marlow says."

Sabre drew back and shifted in her chair. "You're going to see Todd Lynch?"

"I thought I might. Want to go? We could make it a family trip."

"Why would we want to do that?"

"Actually, I thought we could all take a ride. I'll drop you and the kids off at a mall, go see Lynch, then pick you up. Conner needs some new clothes. His pants are all too short for him cuz he just keeps getting taller."

"I know, and he never asks for anything. But we have perfectly good stores here in San Diego. Besides, Morgan has her first gymnastics session today."

"That's right. I forgot. What time is the class? I'll work it into my schedule."

"It's at ten, but I can take her."

"I'm the one who signed on for this parental thing, and I don't expect you to run the kids around. I'm sure you have work to do."

"I agreed to help you, so I'll do what I can." Sabre sat back down. "Besides, I love Conner and Morgan, and I think it would be fun to watch her first gymnastics class. I'll take my laptop and get some work done while I wait."

"What else is on your plate today?" JP asked.

"I have to see Unity Hendrickson and Miguel at Polinsky."

"I thought Miguel was in a foster home."

"He was, but the foster mother had a heart attack, and the children had to be removed."

"Boy, that kid can't catch a break."

"I know, and he seemed to like it there too. Why do you ask about my schedule?"

"I was hoping we could spend the day together. How about if we both go?"

Sabre raised her eyebrows. "Do you want to spend time with me? Or are you just worried because of everything that's going on?"

JP looked at her sheepishly. "Both."

"I'll be fine, but if you're that concerned, maybe I shouldn't take Morgan anywhere." Sabre glanced at the time on her phone and jumped up. "Either way, I need to wake her up so she can eat and get ready."

As Sabre left the room, she heard JP making a call. A minute later, Sabre's phone rang.

"Hi, Sis," Ron said. "Whatcha doing today?"

She told him her plans, and he asked if he could join her.

Sabre walked back into the kitchen, put the phone on speaker, and glared at JP. "Did JP put you up to this?"

"What are you talking about? I just want to spend time with my sister."

"And you want to do that at Morgan's gymnastics class and on home visits with me?"

"You're so busy I never get to see you. We can go to the class, then take Morgan with us to the home visits. I can stay with her, and you can get your business done."

Sabre thought for a second. She wasn't really worried for herself, but if JP was concerned, she would do it for Morgan's sake. "Both kids I need to visit are at Polinsky, and it isn't far from her class."

"See, it's serendipity."

"Okay, come on over. If you hurry, you can have breakfast before you go. I'm sure JP would be glad to fix it for you."

"I'm on my way."

"Ron."

"Yes?"

"Don't think for a minute that I don't know what you guys are up to."

"I learned at a very young age to never underestimate you, Sis."

CHAPTER 30

Saturday, a.m.

After Morgan's gymnastics class was over, Ron, Sabre, and Morgan pulled out of the parking lot. Sabre had already put the address into the GPS and called Polinsky to let them know she was coming to see Unity and Miguel.

"Did you have fun?" Sabre asked, looking back at Morgan.

"Yeah. It was stimulating."

"That's an interesting choice of words."

"Yeah, it's my newest word for the day, but I'm not sure it quite fits. It was enjoyable."

"You seemed to be having a good time," Ron said.

"Yeah, I did."

A few minutes later, Ron pulled into the parking lot of the receiving home, and Sabre got out.

"I'll be back soon. I'm sure you two can entertain yourselves."

Sabre went inside, checked in, and waited in the interview

room for Miguel. Within minutes, the curly-haired boy walked in. He smiled when he saw Sabre. She smiled back but felt a pang of sadness because she knew she'd already become one of the more consistent people in his life. She thought about how many times that was the case with her minor clients. Life shouldn't be like that for children.

"I'm sorry about your foster mother getting sick."

"Me too. She was a nice lady."

"How are things back here?"

"Good. Antonio and Manuelito are still here, and they still have bananas."

Sabre laughed. "Miguel, I have something for you."

"You do?"

Sabre took out the photo of him and his mother and handed it to him. The boy's eyes opened wide as he stared at the picture. Then he clutched it to his chest, and tears rolled down his cheeks. "Mamá," he said. "Mamá. My mamá." Sabre reached out and hugged him, and he cried hard for a few minutes. Then he pulled back, looked at the photo, then at her, and said with a quivering lip, "It's not broken anymore."

"No, it's not. I replaced the glass, but I kept the frame because you got that from your mama."

He hugged the picture again, his face sad. But he had stopped crying.

"Miguel, we're trying very hard to find your mama. In the meantime, you keep this by your bedside, and you can see her anytime you want. I know she's thinking of you and trying to get back to you."

Miguel was smiling again before he left the room. He was such a good-natured child. She really hoped they could find his mother, but it wouldn't be easy.

A few minutes later, Unity came into the interview room.

The scowl on her face made it evident she didn't want to be there.

"Hi, Unity."

"Hey," she responded, as she flopped down in the armchair, flinging one leg over the side. When Sabre didn't speak right away, Unity snapped, "What do you want?"

"I have some questions, and—"

The girl cut her off. "Mom says I don't have to talk to you."

"That's true, but you need to know that I'm the one person you can talk to who can't tell anyone what you say without your permission. I work for you, and I want to ensure that you are treated fairly and that we find the best solution to this problem."

"The problem is that I hate this place. Just let me go home and everything will be fine."

"Unity, I told you before. Your mom doesn't have a house right now, so there is no *home* with her. But I spoke to your Aunt Yvonne, and she wants you to live with her."

"Really?" Her eyes opened wider with a glimpse of hope.

"Really," Sabre said. "She misses you a lot."

"Mom'll never allow it."

"If the court orders it, your mother won't be able to stop it."

Unity seemed to relax, and her tone lightened. Sabre made small talk for a while, then asked, "Do you remember your father?"

"Not really. The only dad I knew was Paul, but Mom says he left us for some floozy bartender."

That was husband number two. "What was he like?"

"He was nice to me. He was good to my mom too, but

sometimes she wasn't nice to him. She always accused him of looking at other women."

"Did he?"

"I didn't think so, but Mom said I didn't understand. She'd get real mad if he even talked to another woman. She would yell awful things at him." Unity sighed. "I wish he was still with us."

"Do you remember the last time you saw him?"

"He and Mom went out and left me with a babysitter, and I was in bed when they got home. Mom came in by herself and told the sitter Paul was getting something out of the car."

"How do you know that?"

"I got up when I heard the car, so I peeked out."

"Did you see Paul?"

"No. Mom came to check on me, so I hopped in bed and pretended to be asleep. The next morning, Mom said Paul had left for work. He never came home after that."

"Did you hear him come in that night?"

"No." Unity sat quietly for a few seconds, then blurted, "Mom doesn't always tell the truth." She paused again. "There's something else you should know."

"What's that?"

The girl swung her leg down and sat up straighter. "My mom poisoned Wayne, her last husband. She put a bit of poison in his food every day, and he kept getting sicker and sicker. He thought something was wrong, but he was too weak to do anything about it. One day, Mom told him she was poisoning him. He begged and begged, but she would just laugh and call him a loser."

Sabre tried to hide her surprise. If Bob hadn't warned her about Vicki, she would assume the girl was making it up. "How do you know about the poison?"

"She told me her plan."

If that was true, Vicki might be insane. "Did Wayne call anyone for help?"

"Mom took away his cell phone. At first, she would answer his phone and say he wasn't well enough to talk. She was trying to catch his new girlfriend."

"Did he have a new girlfriend?"

"Probably not. If he even looked at a woman in public, Mom would go all crazy." Unity's shoulders tightened. "After a while, she shut off his phone and teased him with it."

"How?"

"She would show it to him, then say he couldn't call anyone." The girl lowered her voice to a whisper. "Wayne started foaming at the mouth and begging for water. She hadn't given him anything to drink in a long time. Then she laughed like someone out of a horror movie."

"And then?"

"He died. But Mom didn't call the ambulance for a while. She wanted to make sure he was dead."

Sabre didn't know what to believe. "And you saw all this?"

"Yes."

"Why didn't you tell anyone?"

"Because Mom threatened to kill me if I did. I didn't want her putting poison in my food."

CHAPTER 31

Saturday, p.m.

JP had just started an online search when his phone rang. *Sabre.* "Hi, kid."

"Hey." She took a quick breath. "I just had a disturbing talk with Unity Hendrickson, and before I report it, I need you to do something for me."

"Sure, what is it?"

"Find the death certificate for Wayne Iaconna. There should be a medical examiner's report too, because he died at home and was pretty young."

"Who's Wayne again?"

"Vicki's third husband. Unity says her mother poisoned him, and she gives a rather gruesome account. But the social worker's report says he died of a heart attack."

JP's cop instincts kicked in. "I'll get right on it, but if there's a medical examiner's report, I can't access it without a court order."

"We'll do that if we have to."

"Detective Marlow might get it for us, unless you don't want him involved."

"Update him if you need to. If what Unity says is true, homicide will have to know."

Sabre hung up, and before JP could start his search, his phone rang again. The caller ID read: *Curt Marlow.*

"Good to hear from you," JP said. "Do you have information for me on Lynch?"

"I spoke with social services in L.A. County and learned that the social worker was reluctant to close the case, but she had no factual basis to keep it open."

"What was her hesitation?"

"Just a bad feeling. But there's pressure to get cases off the books as soon as possible. I also spoke with a police officer who knows Lynch. He says he's a real jerk, but the guy hasn't committed any crimes that he's aware of."

JP was skeptical. "How does he know him?"

"The cop lives next door to Lynch and knows the whole family. Apparently, the father was a nice guy, but Lynch is cut from the same cloth as his mother. They're both volatile."

"Yeah, I've met his mother. She's a real peach." JP paused. "I just want Lynch to stop stalking Sabre. If he's the one who sent Sabre the photos, who knows what he might do?"

"If you're thinking about paying him a visit, I'd be careful. He's an angry man, and he's quick to sue. Anything you do could easily be seen as harassment."

"He's the stalker."

"Still, you know we can't do anything other than obtain a restraining order against him, and we both know what good that'll do."

"It might stop the notes from coming."

"It might, but if he sent the images of Nicholson, or maybe even killed him, then a restraining order isn't worth much."

Frustrated, JP snapped, "I know that."

"By the way, I don't think the perp is Lynch. It just doesn't make sense that he would send a message with his name on it if he was guilty." Marlow scoffed. "But I've seen crazier things." He paused for a second, and JP heard his toothpick click. "And just so you know. We ran a prison check on all the parents in the cases Sabre had with Nicholson. Both parents on the Fisher case are incarcerated. The father's in Donovan, and the mother transferred to Chino. As you know, Nick Baxter is still inside. And, of course, we know Isaiah Banks has been out for a while. Thanks for the information on him, by the way. It may prove to be very helpful."

"Speaking of which, what went down yesterday on Euclid?" JP asked.

"It was a drive-by shooting, killed two gangsters and put another in the ICU."

"Any leads?"

"I'm sure it was gang related and probably ordered by Banks, but he obviously wasn't the shooter. He keeps his hands pretty clean, but we know he's calling the shots. He's the shot-caller for the San Diego Pirus. His dad was a Compton Piru, so he has OG status. Being an original gangster is a biggie for the Piru gang."

"Are you handling the homicides?"

"No, the gang unit has them, but they're keeping me informed because of the connection to Nicholson and Sabre."

"Do you think Banks might have killed Nicholson?"

"He's my number one suspect." Another pause, another click of the toothpick. "I also discovered that the last attorney Mrs. Walker hired to fight Banks met an early demise."

"How?"

"He fell from his third-story office balcony downtown."

"That's quite a coincidence." JP shook his head. "Do you think Banks gave him a shove?"

"I'm saying you need to tell Sabre to stay away from that family and don't put any more surveillance on any of them."

"I hear ya. Thanks."

"I'm not sure you do. We may have made things worse for Sabre."

"How?"

"We visited Mrs. Walker. She was not aware that Devon had gone for a ride with his father, and she was pretty upset. When we talked to Devon, he admitted it had happened three or four times before. He said they mostly go for a ride. Sometimes they get food, and they talk to his homies. Mrs. Walker was livid, but she's also afraid of Banks. In addition, Devon told us about the meeting at Walgreens."

"Did he know the men they spoke to were later shot?"

"I don't think so, and we didn't bring it up."

"Does Banks know the kid talked?"

"I'm afraid so. We brought Banks in for questioning regarding the shooting. We tried to pressure him about taking his kid out without supervision. Of course, he denied everything, but hopefully, he won't take the kid anymore. He knows we'll be watching him, but I'm guessing Sabre will get the blame for that."

"Did he say anything about her?"

"No, and I didn't expect him to. But since he had an encounter with her that same day, I would imagine he thinks she reported him."

CHAPTER 32

Saturday, p.m.

JP hung up and got back to his whiteboard list. The Fishers, although locked up, could have someone working for them on the outside, but it was highly unlikely. The harassment against Sabre appeared to be more personal, like whoever was doing it had a real grudge. It didn't seem likely it was done by a third party. He crossed off Fisher. That left only the Cadle and Baxter people, none of whom seemed likely, although JP hadn't ruled out the father, Nick Baxter. Before continuing, he looked at the death certificate he had obtained from Marlow for Wayne Iaconna. It seemed straightforward—he'd died of a heart attack. Yet, because he was only thirty-eight and had died at home, the ME had conducted an investigation. JP wanted to see the report, so he called Marlow again.

"That was fast," the detective said. "You have something new?"

JP summarized what Sabre had learned about Vicki Hendrickson's late husband.

Marlow made a low whistling sound. "We may have to question the daughter. Do you think Vicki is the stalker?"

"Highly unlikely. Sabre didn't even get that case until after the texts started, but if what Unity is saying is true, that woman needs to be investigated."

"For sure. I'll get the report and make sure someone follows up. My caseload is pretty heavy right now, so it probably won't be me, but I'll let you know what I find out."

JP went back to work, searching online for the Cadle parents. An hour and a half later, he found contact information in Elko, Nevada. He made a fake sales call and verified their address. Then he crossed them off the whiteboard list.

JP's phone dinged. The text from Marlow read: *Sent report to your email.* JP thanked him, opened his mail, and downloaded the report. He read through it and called Sabre.

"I think Unity has quite the imagination, or she's been watching too many movies," JP said. "They did a complete toxicology screen and found nothing. The autopsy didn't show any foul play either. Wayne apparently worked out and was in good shape physically. One of those cases where the first heart attack is all you get. His father died the same way at fifty-five, so there was family history."

"I'm not surprised," Sabre said. "After I left her, I realized Unity's story reminded me of a detective show plot I saw recently. She must have watched the same show. I'll have another talk with her."

"Do you want to go back and see Unity now, Sis?" Ron asked. He eased off the gas, as though preparing to turn around.

"No, I'll give her a day or two, then I'll confront her. In the meantime, I'll make sure she's in therapy." They were already a few miles away from the receiving home, and Morgan was still with them.

"So, where to now?"

"My office. I need to pick up a file, and then we can head home."

Ron parked on Sixth Street in front of Sabre's building. Since the courthouse across the street was closed, there were plenty of spaces.

"Can I come in?" Morgan asked.

"Of course, you've been cooped up in this car for long enough."

They all three exited and started up the walkway.

"I like going to your office," Morgan said. "Is Elaine here?"

"No, she doesn't work on Saturday. We'll just run in and get the file."

"Can I shred something?"

"Sure, there's always a pile."

As they reached the steps, Sabre stopped, then held Morgan back before she darted up.

"What's the matter?" Ron asked.

Sabre pointed at a bouquet of dead roses tied together with a big red ribbon. They lay near the front door. To cover for Morgan, Sabre quickly added, "Elaine must've been throwing those flowers out yesterday and dropped them."

Ron stepped ahead and reached out his arm to stop Morgan from coming closer. Using a practiced Inspector Clouseau voice, he said, "I'm Detective Ron Brown, and I'll get to the bottom of this littering incident." He reached to his upper lip and made a fake mustache-twisting gesture, then took out his camera and snapped several photos. He looked at Morgan. "I have to gather evidence, you know." Then he carefully picked up the flowers by the tip. Sabre noticed the note attached to the ribbon.

"They won't bite you," Morgan said.

"They might. They have thorns, you know."

Morgan and Sabre stepped onto the porch. Ron checked the door. It was locked, as it should be. Sabre handed him her key. Before going in, he said. "You two wait here for a minute. I need to check for the perpetrator. She may be armed with more thorny flowers."

Morgan smiled at his antics. "What's he doing?"

"Just being silly. We'll humor him. He'll be out in a moment, still acting all detective-like."

Ron returned shortly without the flowers and announced in the same voice, "It's safe now. You may enter."

"You know you're bizarre, right?" Morgan tipped her head a little more to the left than usual.

Ron returned to his own voice. "Is *bizarre* today's word?"

"No, it's just what you are."

He put his arm around Morgan, and they followed Sabre inside. Once in the reception area, Ron looked at Sabre and nodded toward Elaine's desk.

Sabre glanced at the bouquet. Then she turned to Morgan. "Come with me. I'll get the file, and you can do a little shredding."

They walked to her office, and Sabre gave Morgan a stack of disposable papers. "Do what you can. I'll be right back." She returned to where Ron stood near the flowers.

"I'll put them in the trunk, so Morgan doesn't know we're

taking them," Ron said. "But first you need to see what the note says."

Ron held out the plain, white notecard, touching only a corner tip. Sabre stepped closer and read: *Everything beautiful eventually dies. Still LHO.*

CHAPTER 33

Saturday, p.m.

When they got home, Morgan said a quick "Hi" to JP and ran to her room.

"I'll get Conner," Ron said.

"What's going on?" JP asked.

"Marlow is on his way here," Sabre said. "So, Ron is taking Conner shopping, and Morgan will go along to make sure he looks fashionable."

Before Sabre could explain more, Morgan appeared. "I'm ready."

Conner and Ron came into the room. Sabre gave Ron her credit card. "No more than five hundred."

"Whoa!" Conner made a face. "I don't need that much."

Morgan looked him up and down, her little eyes tick-tocking as she gave him the once over. "Ah, yeah, you do."

"Take him somewhere decent," Sabre said. "He needs new

jeans and some shirts." She looked at his tattered sneakers. "And some shoes."

As the kids walked out, Sabre stopped Ron. "He doesn't need to go to Nordstrom's, but don't let him talk you into Walmart either. He'll do that just to save money. I want him to have a few nice things, but make sure they're what he likes."

"Yes, ma'am." Ron grinned and headed out.

"Now, will you tell me what's going on?" JP insisted. "Why is Marlow coming here?"

Sabre told him about the dead flowers.

"That's it!" JP bellowed as he paced the living room. "You're not going anywhere alone, and preferably not without *me*. I'll drive you to and from court." He locked eyes with Sabre. "I don't think you should work at your office either. And tell that bailiff, Mike Whatshisname …"

"McCormick."

"Yeah, him." JP lowered his voice. "Tell him what's going on, so he can keep an eye out."

"I think you're getting a little carried away. I don't want this to spill over into my work."

JP's voice rose again. "This came from your work. Whoever it is, you probably met at court."

"But they won't do something right there in court." Sabre lacked conviction.

"Do you *not* watch the news? Crazy people let loose wherever they happen to be. Court is the most likely place. And you could be followed from the courthouse."

The doorbell rang, and JP stopped ranting to let Detective Marlow inside. "Tell her, will you?"

"Tell her what?" Marlow's brow furrowed.

"Tell her she shouldn't be alone. Tell her crazy, revengeful people can act out anywhere."

"He's right, Sabre. You don't know where this stalker might strike," Marlow said. "Now, let's see what you've got."

Sabre led them to her car and opened the trunk. "I don't know if you can see the note, but it says, *Everything beautiful eventually dies. Still LHO.*"

"That sounds like a threat to me," JP said.

"Maybe." Marlow slipped on latex gloves and picked up the bouquet. "I'll run the card for fingerprints, but chances are we'll come up empty, just like the last time. Do you have a timeframe for when they were delivered?"

"Between five last night and an hour ago, but I'll try to narrow that down."

"You don't have any kind of security camera at the office, do you?"

"No," JP said. "But I'll talk to Ron tomorrow about installing one."

While JP and Marlow talked, Sabre called her three co-workers to see if they had been at the office that weekend. Neither Elaine nor Jack had been there since five the night before, but David had made his usual once-a-month trip there.

"One of my officemates stopped by the building this morn-ing," Sabre said. "He arrived about eleven o'clock and left by twelve-thirty, and the flowers weren't there."

"So, at best, the delivery was made less than an hour before you arrived," Marlow said.

JP looked at the detective. "Any chance you could call that cop neighbor and see if Lynch is home?" JP asked.

"Sure, I can do that." Marlow took out his cell phone and called. "Hi, Rick, this is Detective Marlow. We spoke a few days ago about your neighbor, Todd Lynch." He paused briefly. "We had another incident within the last two hours. Do you know if Lynch is home right now? Or whether he's been home for a while?" A pause. "Thanks." Marlow hung up, "Lynch's car is not in his driveway. Or at least it wasn't fifteen minutes ago when Rick left his house. He hasn't seen Lynch today, but that's not unusual. Many days go by that he doesn't see him, whether his car is home or not, and he doesn't have time today to go back and check."

"So, we still don't know for sure," JP grumbled. "But it doesn't rule him out."

Marlow looked at the note again. "Everything beautiful eventually dies. Still LHO," he read aloud. "Those aren't Lynch's initials, so that's strange."

"Maybe he has different personalities with different names," Sabre said.

"If that's the case, he's crazier than a peach-orchard boar," JP said.

"And even more dangerous," Marlow added.

The detective asked a few more questions, then took the flowers and left. As he walked away, Sabre thought his limp was more pronounced than usual. She wondered if he was just tired from the extra caseload he was carrying.

CHAPTER 34

Sunday, a.m.

"Are you sure this is the right thing to do?" JP asked Sabre, as they dressed to visit Gene in Donovan Prison.

"I think it will be good for Morgan and Conner. They love their father very much and have said it's what they want to do. They haven't once asked to visit their mother. So yes, I think it's the right thing."

"I know they love him. I just hate taking them to a prison."

"Me too." Sabre walked out to the living room with JP right behind her. Conner was waiting on the sofa. He stood when they came in.

"Wow, don't you look spiffy," Sabre commented.

Conner wore new jeans, a western shirt, a cowboy hat, and boots. "We went to Boot Barn," he said proudly. "They were having a big sale. I got two pair of pants, and the second one was half off, plus two shirts that were on sale. The boots cost the most, but they were marked down also. They're the nicest pair of boots I've ever had. But I made sure I left enough to buy Morgan boots too, 'cause she really liked them. I hope that was okay."

"Of course. It was generous of you to think of your sister."

Conner tipped his hat. "This was already mine. Dad got it for me a while back." He looked directly at Sabre. "Thanks again for the clothes."

Sabre was surprised by his comments, mostly because it was more than he'd said at one time since she met him. Morgan talked non-stop, but Conner was far more introspective.

"You're very welcome, and you look amazing."

Just then, Morgan walked out wearing jeans, a pink shirt, and her new pink boots.

"Well, don't you look cute." Sabre snapped a quick photo, wanting to preserve the moment.

"Do you think Daddy will like it?" Morgan fidgeted with her buttons.

"Of course he will, Munchkin," JP said. "But he'd be happy to see you even if you wore a gunny sack and clown shoes." JP squatted to be at the same level as Morgan. "Are you anxious about going?" he asked.

"A little, but I really want to see my dad," Morgan said.

JP stood. "What about you, Conner?"

"I don't like the idea of seeing him in prison. He's never let us do that before. But I still want to see him."

"It can be a little overwhelming at first," JP explained. "But once you're there a while, you'll start to relax. And it'll be easier next time."

Morgan started to say something, then stopped.

"What is it, Munchkin?"

"Uhh … Will Daddy be in a cell?"

"No, he'll be in a large room with other people. We'll sit at a table with him while other families visit with their loved ones."

"Will I be able to hug him?"

JP looked at Sabre. "That's a good question," she said. "Unless the rules have changed recently, you'll be able to give him a quick hug and kiss when you first see him and before you leave. He can hold your hand while we talk, but you can't sit in his lap and snuggle him like you would at home."

"That's okay. I didn't think I'd get to hug him at all."

The half-hour drive to Donovan seemed much longer. Sabre couldn't stop thinking about the dead flowers and the threatening note.

When they arrived and parked, JP instructed them to double check their pockets to make sure they were empty. Sabre carried the kids' birth certificates and her driver's license. JP carried a plastic bag full of quarters for the vending machines. The guys had left their hats in the car. Sabre glanced at JP, knowing he felt naked without his hat and gun.

As they walked through the gates, and past the guards, Sabre started to second-guess herself, wondering if this visit was a good idea. Morgan squeezed her hand so hard it hurt, but Sabre didn't let on. Once inside, Conner kept his head down, but Morgan seemed fascinated and gaped at everything she saw. She was particularly intrigued by the metal detector. While they waited in line, Sabre explained how it worked and reminded her that she'd gone through one at juvenile court.

"I was so nervous that day, I don't even remember it."

"Yes, but you were very brave."

"Can I see the screen? I want to see how it works."

"No, you can't do that here. But one day I'll take you to court and show you."

Once through, they walked down a long, stark corridor. Morgan continued to assess everything. "Did you notice there are no pictures on the walls? Everything is so plain."

They had to wait in a room with other visitors for about twenty minutes before they were taken to the hall. They were seated at a round table and told that the inmates would be along soon. They waited another ten minutes before Gene was brought to them. During that time, Sabre watched as Morgan looked around at all the tables and visiting families. Her eyes settled on the man sitting by a podium.

"Why is he there?"

"He keeps an eye on everything," JP said. "And those other men walking around are making sure no one breaks the rules."

"So, we're safe here?"

"Yes, Munchkin, or I wouldn't have brought you. You'll have your Uncle Johnny and your Dad with you, what could go wrong?"

"I can think of a few things," Connor mumbled.

A six-foot-two African-American inmate with a sculpted body approached their table. He stopped when he was within three feet and gave Sabre a long, studied look. He took another step, stopped and stared again. Then his eyes found the guard at the front, and he kept going.

"Who was that?" JP asked.

In the real world, it would have sparked jealousy, but in here, she knew it was concern. "I have no idea," Sabre said. "Probably someone from one of my cases.

"I don't like it."

CHAPTER 35

Sunday, a.m.

The family waited patiently for another five minutes until Sabre saw a well-built man with sandy-blond, wavy hair walk into the room. She'd forgotten how much Gene and Conner looked alike. They had the same eyes, mouth, and hair, but Conner was lankier.

"There he is," Sabre said pointing to Gene.

Without looking around, he walked directly toward them, aware of the table number where they were seated.

JP stood when he approached. "Hello, Gene."

To JP's apparent surprise, Gene reached his arm out and gave his brother a quick hug. "Thanks for coming and for bringing the kids."

Then he hugged Conner, who stood an inch or two taller than him. "I do believe you've passed me up, son." Gene knelt down and wrapped his arms around Morgan. She didn't want to let go, so he had to remove her arms from his neck. "I'm only allowed a brief hug, little one, but I'll get another before you leave. They're a stickler about rules here." He kissed her cheek and asked her to take a seat.

After they chatted for a while, JP took Conner and Morgan to the vending machines to buy sodas. While they were gone, Sabre said, "Have you considered applying for a family visit? Siblings, spouses, and children can participate if you're approved. Assuming the kids wanted to, they and JP would be here in an apartment-like facility with you for thirty or forty hours. It'll probably take several months before you get one, but I think it would be good for the kids. I won't be able to come, because it doesn't extend to your lawyer, but JP can bring Morgan and Conner."

"I've heard about other inmates having those, but I never wanted the kids to spend that much time here. And I sure didn't need to have their mother, Roxy, around. You can only get those visits every three to six months."

"That's right, so if you get one, it'll be about halfway through your time. You'll be out of here before a second one."

"I'll think about it."

JP and the children returned with sodas for everyone except Sabre, who had declined. They visited for another hour, mostly talking about the kids, their activities, and their growth. Gene knew how to engage them and seemed truly interested in what they had to say.

"Dad," Conner said. "I'll be sixteen soon, and I talked to Uncle Johnny about getting my driver's license. He said we needed to ask you."

Gene looked at JP.

"That's right," JP said. "We did have that discussion."

"The kid's a good driver," Gene said. "So, it's up to you, Jackie, since you're the one responsible for him right now."

"I know he's anxious to be able to drive, and he is a good kid." JP turned to Conner. "I'll think about it, but if we do this, there'll be a lot of rules."

"I know," Conner said, then added, "Like what?"

"You won't have a car of your own for quite a while," Gene said. "And you'll only drive when you have permission. And you won't drive with other kids in the car, except for Morgan."

"That's the law, Dad, in California."

"And you have to keep your grades up to show you're responsible," JP added.

"No drinking and driving either," Gene said.

"Dad, I don't drink."

"I know that, son." Gene's tone and expression were surprisingly serious. "But at some point, you might decide to have a drink, and if you do, no driving. That's a lifetime rule. Do you hear me?"

"Yes, Dad."

"So, get signed up for the driver's ed class in school and get your permit, then we'll figure it out from there."

When visiting time was nearly over, JP said he wanted a few minutes alone with Gene. After the others left, Gene said, "So, what's up, Jackie?"

JP frowned at the name. It always made him feel like a kid, Gene's little brother. He was pretty sure Gene knew that. But JP ignored it and got down to business. "There are a couple of guys in here that I'm investigating: Nick Baxter and Dale Fisher. Do you know either of them?"

"I know both. Fisher's temper always gets him in trouble.

He just can't figure out when to keep his mouth shut. Why do you ask?"

JP summarized the harassment directed at Sabre.

"Are my kids safe?"

"I believe they are, or I would've made other arrangements. I know I can protect them better myself than anyone else can. And I'm keeping watch on Sabre twenty-four-seven. I don't think Fisher or Baxter has anything to do with what's happening, but I'm checking all angles."

"What can I do to help?"

"Let's start with Nick Baxter. What do you know about him?"

"He's low key, tries to keep his nose clean, a short-timer. I think he has about four months left. I can't imagine he'd do anything to jeopardize that."

"Has he ever talked about his kid?"

"Oh yeah. He told me how his old lady's boyfriend molested his little girl. He's still pretty pissed at him. I'm not sure what he'll do if he ever runs into that jerk, but I know Baxter's determined to go straight for his daughter. We have a lot in common. He's the only one here I talk to about my kids."

"Does he ever say anything about the social worker who was on the case? Jim Nicholson?"

"He mentioned him just once and called him an idiot, but he's happy with how the case turned out. His mother is raising the girl, and when Baxter gets out, he hopes to get custody of her."

"Anything else?"

"No, don't think so."

"Tell me what Fisher is like in here. Do you think he might have some influence on the outside?"

"Fisher thinks he's a badass, but he also strikes me as more talk than action. Or, as Grandpa Pippin would say, 'All hat, and no cowboy.' I can keep an ear out for any scuttlebutt."

"Just don't do anything that gets you into trouble. It's not worth that."

"And he's heavily involved with the Peckerheads—the white prison gang."

"Yeah, I know who they are." JP tensed. "I believe our father is a proud member."

"So I've heard. But in all fairness to Dad—not that he deserves any—considering the length of his sentence, he probably had to join just to survive on the inside."

JP stopped talking. After about ten seconds, Gene said, "Dad's not here if that's what you're wondering. I checked. I can't be certain, but I think he was moved to San Luis Obispo some time ago. I have no idea why. I'm sure you could find out where he is." Gene paused. "Were you hoping to see him?"

"No," JP snapped.

CHAPTER 36

Monday, a.m.

The Spencer Case

Child: Ecstasy Spencer, newborn (F)
Parents: Father—Carlos Vega & Mother—Wendy Spencer
Issues: Physical Abuse, Drugs
Facts: Baby born positive for methamphetamines.

"Are you ready on Spencer?" Bob asked, walking up to Department Four.

"I just read the reports," Sabre said. "Mr. and Mrs. Vega are here, and I want to speak with them before the hearing."

"The paternity test confirmed that Carlos Vega is the father, so the grandparents want to take little Ecstasy home with them."

"Does your client object?"

"No. Wendy thinks it's what's best for her child," Bob said. "She's not ready to be a parent."

"According to the report, she hasn't even visited the baby. Is that accurate?"

"That's right. She hasn't, and she doesn't want to. Babies scare her."

"Is she here?" Sabre was worried about the girl.

"Apparently you haven't received the supplemental report." Bob opened his file and pulled out a one-sheet document. "You might want to read this, but in a nutshell, Wendy is in juvenile hall with prostitution charges."

"What happened?"

"The Waterfall was raided last night. Tallulah Waters was arrested on all kinds of charges, including contributing to the delinquency of a minor." Bob's eyes flashed with anger. "And Wendy wasn't the only teenager. They picked up three others."

"I noticed the father hasn't checked in. Was he arrested too?"

"Not that I know of. According to Wendy, she and Carlos split up, and he headed for Wyoming. I guess he wants to be a cowboy when he grows up." Bob shook his head. "Stupid kids; they don't have a clue."

"Is that what he said? That he wanted to be a cowboy?"

"No, I added that part. He wants to join the military, but he won't be eighteen for a couple of months. He's on the 'down-low' until then. Apparently, he's not aware that he'll have to drug test. And get this." Bob grinned. "Carlos wants to join the service because he's tired of people telling him what to do."

"You're right—stupid." Sabre laughed, but she didn't feel like her usual relaxed self.

Bob must have noticed, "Sobs, are you okay?"

"Yeah, I'm fine."

"Something's bothering you. Is it the flowers?"

"I can't keep from thinking about that ominous note. Who would send that? What does it all mean?"

"I know it must be hard, but you're safe here."

"That's what I said. But JP and Marlow reminded me that crazies let loose anywhere. Not only that, JP reminded me that the stalker is probably from one of my cases, so court isn't exactly a safe place." She glanced around again. "Normally, I don't let things like this get to me, but I'm kind of on edge this time."

"I think you're safe here right now. The bailiffs have been alerted, and they're keeping a watchful eye out. And the only cases you have on calendar this morning are new cases, ones you got after Nicholson died, so there shouldn't be a problem."

"That does make me feel a little better." Sabre looked up. "Oh, there's the paternal grandparents. I'll see you later."

She met Mr. and Mrs. Vega as they approached and walked them upstairs, so they could have a little privacy. Sabre was pleased to see they were both under forty. They all sat down on a bench in the mezzanine.

"Do you know where your son is?" Sabre asked.

"No." Mrs. Vega looked grim. "We heard he left the state."

"Do you know where he might have gone?"

"We have family in Utah, but I don't think he would go to them. The majority of the family lives in Arizona, but he has burnt most of those bridges already." She choked up. "Everyone has tried to help him, but he has to want a better life before he can get off the drugs."

"How long has it been?"

"We've been fighting it for years. He got mixed up with a bad crowd when he was fifteen, and he's never been the same since. I can't tell you the number of sleepless nights we've had over the years."

"I understand you want to care for Ecstasy. At best, her father will have supervised visits. Do you think you could enforce that?"

For the first time, Mr. Vega spoke up. "We will protect our grandchild. Carlos won't be allowed in our home unless he's been clean for a long time. He has to rebuild our trust."

"Do you have any other children?" Sabre asked.

"No," Mrs. Vega said. "Carlos was an only child. We were very young when he was born, and I know we made a lot of mistakes. We lived in a bad neighborhood because it was all we could afford. We became more financially sound and were able to move, but it was too late for Carlos." Her husband reached for her hand, and she continued. "Don't get me wrong. I'm not blaming it all on where we lived. We spoiled Carlos and probably gave him too much freedom. All I can say is that we're smarter now, and we want to give Ecstasy a good life."

"Do you think you want to keep her permanently?"

"Yes. We've already contacted an attorney in Tucson, and we've met with social services there. We hope to file for a guardianship or an adoption if the parents' rights are terminated. I understand our son has already signed forms giving up his rights, and Wendy plans to do the same. Or maybe she already has."

"That appears to be the case," Sabre said. "Do you have any questions?"

"When can we take our granddaughter home?"

"That's up to the judge, but your home has already been evaluated by social services in Tucson, and it was approved, so if there is no objection in court, you should be able to take her soon."

They walked quietly to Department Four, where they met up with Bob, Mike Powers, and the social worker. Once inside the court, with everyone seated, a bailiff brought Wendy in. The case was called to order, and the attorneys introduced themselves for the record.

"County Counsel, did you file a dependency petition on the father as a minor?" Judge Hekman asked.

"No, Your Honor," Farris said. "The father will turn eighteen in less than two months, so we determined it was futile. Also, he has given up his parental rights and fled the state."

"Is that correct, Mr. Powers?"

Mike Powers stood. "Yes, Your Honor, except I'm not sure *fled* is the proper word for my client's non-attendance this morning. I have full authority to appear for him and convey his wishes to the court. I was with my client when he signed the papers. I advised him of his rights and explained that this was a permanent decision. He assured me he understood what he was doing."

The judge turned to Farris again. "Was a petition filed on Wendy Spencer as a minor?"

"We have it ready to go, Your Honor, but a petition was already filed in delinquency court, alleging prostitution charges."

Bob stood. "Your Honor, I have spoken with my client's defense attorney, Mr. Leahy, and he's pretty confident he'll be able to get the charges set aside."

"Of course he is. Mr. Leahy is always confident about such matters." She paused. "But from what I've seen, dependency may be a better route for this child. Please file the petition, and we'll leave it, pending the outcome of the delinquency case. It might boost Mr. Leahy's confidence even more." She looked back at the file in front of her. "Has there been any contact with Wendy's parents?"

"No, Your Honor," Farris said.

The judge turned to Sabre.

"No. My investigator has tried to find them, but so far we have nothing."

Judge Hekman looked directly at Wendy Spencer. "I understand you signed forms relinquishing all rights to your daughter, is that correct?"

"Yes, sir."

Judge Hekman rolled her eyes, and Bob whispered something in his client's ear.

"Did your attorney explain what that means?" Hekman asked.

"Yes, s ...Your Honor. He said if I signed I wouldn't have any say in anything Ecstasy did, and I wouldn't have any right to contact her ever again."

"That's what you want?"

"Yes."

"One more thing." The judge locked eyes with Wendy. "Why did you name the child Ecstasy?"

Bob whispered in Wendy's ear before she could answer.

"Never mind," Hekman said. "I don't think I really want to know."

The judge asked a few more questions, then turned to the bailiff. "Please bring in the paternal grandparents."

CHAPTER 37

Monday, a.m.

JP read the Baxter file from beginning to end, looking for anything worth investigating, but he came up blank. He was about to get up and stretch when his phone rang. The ID indicated Gene was calling from the prison. JP had set up with Global Tel Link so the kids could talk to their father occasionally. The privately-owned company contracted with the California Department of Corrections to provide inmates with various outreach services. JP was surprised by the timing, since Gene usually called when the kids were home. "Hello," JP said.

After a few seconds of dead air, Gene responded. "Hey, Jackie."

JP rolled his eyes. The nickname annoyed him, but he couldn't get Gene to stop—because the more he asked him not to use it, the more his brother kept it up. "Is everything okay?" JP asked.

"Yeah, it's fine. I wanted you to know that I spoke with Dale Fisher."

JP pulsed with anger. "What are you doing, bro? I didn't want you to get mixed up in this or tip our hand. I shouldn't have said anything to you."

"Hold your horses. I didn't approach him. He came to me."

"Why would he do that?"

"Because he was in the visiting room when you guys were here, and he recognized Sabre. Actually, he just knew she looked familiar. At least that's what Fisher said, and he sounded sincere. When I told him she was an attorney, he just assumed he'd seen her in court. He didn't mention that she was on his case."

A brief memory surfaced. "I bet that was the guy who checked out Sabre just before you came in. She had no idea who he was. Since she only saw Fisher once four years ago, she wouldn't likely remember him."

"He's an angry son-of-a-gun," Gene said. "But I'm pretty sure he's not out for revenge on Sabre. He's obviously not the stalker, and I don't think he has put anyone else up to it. But I'll keep my ear to the ground."

"Don't get involved, Gene."

"Don't worry, I won't jeopardize my time here. But if Sabre's not safe, then my children may not be either."

"Maybe you should call once a day, if you can," JP said. "At least until we figure this out, just in case one of us has information for the other. It's not that easy for me to reach you."

Gene agreed and they hung up. JP retrieved the Fisher file. It still seemed unlikely that Dale Fisher had pulled strings from prison to kill a social worker four years after the fact, especially since he would be released in eight months. JP read through his criminal record. Even though Fisher was a volatile guy, his incarcerations didn't reflect that. They were all for drug-related charges. JP skimmed old police reports, expecting to find an officer-assault or resisting-arrest charge, but nothing. It appeared Gene was right; Fisher was all hat and no cattle. JP was reading the last police report when his phone rang. Sabre's photo and name flashed across the screen.

"You can stop any investigation on the Spencer case," Sabre said.

"What happened in court?"

"Just what I expected. Both teenagers relinquished their parental rights, and the grandparents are taking the baby back to Arizona, where they will pursue adoption. It'll take a while, but there's no need to find Wendy's parents."

"Okay, that one's off my workload. And I think we can take Dale Fisher off our suspect list for the Nicholson incidents." He summarized his call with Gene. "Although, it is quite a coincidence that he asked about you."

"That was probably only because he saw me. It's likely there are lots of others who recognized me too."

"Yeah, but he's the only one who said anything to Gene."

"It's a bit of a concern," Sabre admitted.

"I also followed up on the mother at CIW. She's been a model inmate, and I don't think we need to waste any time with her," JP said. "But I think I'll keep Dale Fisher on my radar for a while."

"So, who does that leave?"

JP looked at the whiteboard. "Baxter, only because it was the most recent case you had with Nicholson. Based on what I found out, there doesn't seem to be any real suspects in that file either."

"So, basically, we're at a dead end?" Sabre sounded discouraged.

"There's still Lynch." JP hung up, then made an appointment to see Brad Lawson, the Los Angeles cop who lived next door to Lynch. He texted Bob and told him to let Ron know when they were done in court so he could take over. Then he called Ron and asked him to make sure Sabre wasn't left alone.

"What are you going to do?" Ron asked.

"I'm driving to Pasadena."

CHAPTER 38

Monday, a.m./p.m.

The Lynch Case

Social Worker: Jim Nicholson
Children: Three boys
Parents: Father—Todd Lynch
Disposition: Case transferred to L.A. County one year ago.
Facts: Non-offending father with anger issues, stalking Sabre.

JP rang the bell on the house next door to Todd Lynch's. A man about five-eleven, with dark hair and blue eyes answered the door.

"Brad Lawson?"

"You must be JP."

"Thanks for seeing me."

"No problem. Come on in and have a seat. My wife and kids aren't home, so we can talk right here." He led JP into the living room, where they both sat down.

"How long have you lived here?" JP asked.

"All my life, except for two years of college. This is my childhood home." He gestured at a wall of photos. "I bought it from my parents when they retired. They wanted to downsize, and I've always loved this place, so here I am."

"It's a beautiful home and a nice, clean neighborhood."

"The only sore spot is next door," Brad said.

"It didn't look that bad."

"Not on the outside, but the personalities inside are scary. It wasn't like that when Mr. Lynch was alive." He paused. "That's not entirely true. Mrs. Lynch was always scary, but Mr. Lynch was a super nice guy. Todd was just plain mean. His brother Ian was my best friend. Todd would pick on him mercilessly, on me too, but even more on his brother. Ian was older, but Todd was bigger. I remember once when we were kids, Todd put a snake in Ian's bed, nearly scared him to death."

"Did Todd get in trouble for it?"

"He denied it, and his mother believed him. His dad talked to him, but it didn't do any good."

"Are you sure Todd did it?"

"Oh, yes. Todd made sure Ian knew he had done it. He always wanted his victims to know who hurt them. He seemed to get a perverse pleasure out of it. Of course, he didn't want to get into trouble, so he denied it to his parents."

"Did he always do that?"

"Always. He never admitted anything to his parents, but he definitely wanted Ian to know he was the torturer. Sometimes I think he might have taken credit for things he didn't even do, but I'm sure he put the snake in his bed." Brad thought for a minute. "Then there were times when he would do something right to Ian's face, then later follow up with more torture and deny that he did it. Almost as if he was trying to drive his brother crazy."

"Did Todd ever admit to doing evil things in front of you?"

"No, he was smarter than that. He never wanted a witness." Brad smiled, apparently thinking of something amusing, then said, "When I was thirteen, Todd came over to my house looking for Ian. My parents weren't home, so I took a butcher knife out of the kitchen drawer and went after him. I told him if he didn't leave me and Ian alone, I'd use it on him."

"Did it help?"

"Only for a few months, then things went back to normal." Brad smirked. "In my senior year, a few months after Ian left, Todd and I got into a fist fight. I had gained some weight and had been training for quite a while. I beat him up pretty bad, two black eyes, a bloody nose, and a swollen lip."

JP smiled. "I'm sorry, but I'm getting some pleasure out of that. It's always nice to see a wolverine-mean guy get his due. Did you get in trouble?"

"No, because I got the best of him. He didn't want to admit that, so he told his parents three guys jumped him."

"I know he has anger issues, as well as being a bully and a coward, but have you ever seen him with his kids?"

Brad tensed and his face twitched. "Those kids seem scared to death of him—*and* their grandmother. I don't see how that custody case was ever closed."

After a few more questions, JP thanked Brad and walked next door. One of the boys answered the door.

"Hi." JP tried to sound friendly. "Is your father home?"

"Dad," the kid yelled. "Someone's here to see you."

He left the door open and backed up. JP stepped into the house.

Just then, Todd Lynch walked up. "What do *you* want?"

179

"Just a few words with you."

Lynch turned to the blond-haired boy who seemed to be shaking. "Go to your room." The boy darted off, and Lynch spun around. "I don't need to talk to you. Get out of my house."

JP stepped back, keeping his foot on the threshold and his left hand against the door. "You better stop sending threatening notes to Sabre, you coward. You stay away from her. You don't text her or email her, or even think about her. If you want a fight, bring it on—to someone your own size."

"Like you?"

"Yes, like me. But fair warning, you'd be better off sandpapering a bobcat's ass in a phone booth than messing with me."

CHAPTER 39

Monday, a.m./p.m.

The White Case

Child: Suzie White, Age 7 (F)
Parents: Father— Thomas White, Jr. & Mother—Georgia
White
Issues: Neglect, Sexual Abuse
Facts: Suzie was molested by the paternal grandfather, a
member of their household. Parents continued to live with him.

"What do you have left on calendar?" Bob asked Sabre, as they sat together on the bench not far from Department Four.

"I have White and Hendrickson, both with you," Sabre said. "Do you have anything else?"

"Just a quick review. By the way, dear old Grandpa White is here again."

"Are you kidding me?"

"Just so you know, he didn't come with my client. He drove himself."

Sabre shook her head. "These people don't get it, do they?"

"Nope. Want to have lunch?"

"Sure, but you'll have to drive. JP dropped me off this morning." She watched Bob's face. "But you already knew that, didn't you?"

Bob smiled without comment.

"Where do you want to eat?"

"I found a new Vietnamese restaurant. A friend of mine, Jim Doyle, told me about it. It's called Kevin's Noodle House."

"Really? It doesn't sound very Vietnamese-ish." Sabre gave him a skeptical look.

"What the heck? We may as well try it."

"Do you think they'll have your number one-twenty-four?" She smiled. "Do you know what the dish is called so you can ask for it?"

"Yeah, it's bún thịt nướng."

"Are you sure you're pronouncing that right?"

"Probably not, but I have it written down so I can show the waiter."

They were interrupted when Vicki Hendrickson walked up, carrying her tablet. In a stern southern accent, she said, "Mr. Clark, I need to talk to you."

"Talk away," Bob said.

While Sabre gathered up her things, she heard Vicki drawl, "What is *she* doing here?"

"She represents your daughter. She has to be here."

"I want to fire her," Vicki said in a loud voice, obviously intended for Sabre to hear.

"I'm afraid you can't do that," Bob said. "And you need to calm down."

That was the last she heard as she walked to the courtroom, thinking about Suzie White. Sabre was frustrated that there wasn't a good family placement for the child. She had hoped the paternal aunt, Anita Gage, would come through, but she hadn't. Anita was the only one on the father's side that Sabre trusted to keep the grandfather away. There were no local relatives on the mother's side, and even though they were evaluating a maternal aunt in Idaho, it wasn't looking very hopeful.

Sabre went inside the courtroom and discovered a *pro tem* on the bench in place of Judge Hekman. Sabre was never sure what a substitute judge might do, but they usually followed the recommendations of the Department of Social Services. Since she and the department were in agreement today, Sabre wasn't too concerned.

After Bob arrived, the case was called. The parents were both present in the courtroom, and the grandfather had come in again. He remained in the back.

"Your Honor," Sabre said, "the alleged perpetrator is present in the courtroom. I object to his presence and request that the court ask him to leave."

The judge looked at County Counsel. Farris nodded. "I join in that request, Your Honor."

This time, the bailiff was already at the grandfather's side before the judge made the order. "Mr. White, you'll need to leave the courtroom. These are confidential proceedings."

"Why can't I stay?" Mr. White asked.

"Because I just ordered you to leave," the judge said sternly.

He left without further comment.

Sabre whispered to Bob, "That guy doesn't know when to quit, does he?"

"No, and I bet he's not too fond of you."

The father's attorney asked for a trial date for both jurisdiction and disposition of the case, and Bob joined in the request on behalf of the mother. They went off the record to pick a suitable date.

"Back on the record," the judge said. "That leaves the issue of detention for this child pending the trial."

The father's attorney argued for detention with him and his wife. County Counsel and Sabre both objected.

"It sounds like that's an issue for trial," the judge said. "In the meantime, where is the child now?"

"In a foster home," Farris said. "She was moved there yesterday."

"Are there no suitable relatives?"

"No, Your Honor, none that we are confident will protect this child. We have a home evaluation pending for a maternal aunt in Idaho."

"The minor will stay in foster care until the trial," the judge ordered. "Supervised visits for the parents."

The father's attorney stood and tried to argue for unsupervised visits, but the judge cut him off. "Those are the orders, counselor. You can deal with it at trial."

The Hendrickson Case

Child: Unity Hendrickson Age 11 (F)
Parents: Father—Harvey Hendrickson & Mother—Vicki Hendrickson

Disposition: Dirty Home, Alcohol Abuse, Domestic Violence
Facts: Returning case, new to Sabre, same issues each time.

After the White case, Sabre was called to Department One for a special hearing added at the last minute. It wrapped up quickly, and she waited in the courtroom while Bob finished a review hearing. Then she and Bob headed back toward Department Four, ready for the Hendrickson case. Another attorney stopped them along the way to discuss a case with Sabre. Bob kept walking.

A few minutes later, Sabre reached the bench where Bob and his client were sitting. She found Bob talking softly to Vicki. He had one hand on her shoulder as he often did with clients. She had calmed down and was smiling at him.

"I'm ready whenever you are," Sabre said, walking up.

"Can't you see we're having a private conversation?" Vicki jumped up, knocking her iPad to the floor. "Now, look what you done!" While Bob reached down and picked up the tablet, Vicki took a step closer, her large body dwarfing Sabre's. "Get out of my face, ma'am!" Vicki yelled.

Sabre took a step back, raising her right hand up, palm facing Vicki. Sabre spoke directly to Bob. "I'll be inside." When she reached the door, she looked back and saw Vicki smiling at Bob, her head tilted to the right in a seductive pose. The bailiff flung the door open just as Sabre got there.

"Everything okay out here?" Mike asked.

"Yes, it's the praying mantis. Seems she doesn't like me much."

Mike glanced over at the bench. "She apparently likes Bob. He'd better be careful, or he'll get sucked into her web."

Sabre watched as Mike walked over and asked Bob, "Are

you ready on the Hendrickson case? The judge would like to finish up the calendar."

Vicki looked up at Mike, tilting her head in the same seductive way. "You are one handsome man, Mr. Bailiff."

Mike turned and walked into the courtroom with a red face.

"Why, I do believe you're blushing, Mr. Bailiff," Sabre said in a mock southern accent. "Watch out, or you'll get sucked into that web."

"That woman is crazy." Mike shook his head.

"No kidding," Sabre said, dropping the accent.

"Are you sure she's not your stalker?"

"I wish; at least then I'd know who I was dealing with. But she can't be. I wasn't appointed on that case until after I got the first text. So, unless she's not only crazy, but clairvoyant too, it can't be her."

Bob and his client entered shortly after, and the case was called to order. Bob asked for a trial date, which was set for two weeks away.

Sabre glanced over and saw that Vicki was glaring at her. Sabre turned back toward the judge, avoiding further eye contact with the crazy lady.

Bob stood. "The mother would like unsupervised visits. As the court can see, the allegations in this petition pertain to neglect. My client has never hurt her daughter, and there is no reason to think she would."

"Counselor?" The judge looked at Sabre.

"I'm asking the court to continue with supervised visits and to advise the mother to not say derogatory things about me. She is making it difficult for me to represent my client."

"I want her fired!" Vicki shouted, forgetting her southern persona.

Bob leaned down to whisper in her ear.

"She shouldn't be on this case," Vicki said loud enough for everyone to hear. "She can't be fair because she's jealous of me."

Bob continued to soothe Vicki until he got her calmed down and she stopped talking.

"Mrs. Hendrickson," the judge said sternly, "you have your attorney, and your daughter has hers. I will not remove Ms. Brown from the case. And I'm ordering you to not say anything negative to your daughter about Ms. Brown. Do you understand?"

Vicki didn't say anything until Bob whispered to her again.

"Yes, ma'am." She folded her arms defiantly.

"I hope you're taking this seriously. There will be great repercussions if you interfere with Unity's right to counsel. Do you understand?"

"Yes."

"Your Honor," Bob continued, "we request detention with my client once she has found suitable housing."

Sabre stood. "I don't think that's appropriate at this time, Your Honor. This is Mrs. Hendrickson's third petition before this court. I think it would be in the best interest of this child for the mother to stabilize before we try another placement at home. In the meantime, DSS is evaluating the maternal aunt, Yvonne Dixon, which I believe would be a good ..."

"No! I don't want her there," Vicki blurted.

Bob spoke to his client, and she stopped talking. He looked at the judge. "My client objects to detention with her sister because she believes she wouldn't have access to Unity. They have not been getting along for some time."

"That seems to be a pattern with your client, Mr. Clark." The judge looked at her notes. "With Ms. Brown's approval, I'll give the social worker discretion to detain Unity with the maternal aunt, Yvonne Dixon. We'll revisit this issue at the disposition of this case."

"Thank you, Your Honor." Bob sat down.

"I'm also ordering a new psychological exam for the mother and the minor."

"I would object, Your Honor," Bob said, "until after disposition. According to *Laurie S. v. Superior Court*, the court cannot order a psychological evaluation until jurisdiction has been established. If DSS doesn't have the facts to support their petition, they can't order an evaluation, then use it to bolster their lack of facts."

"I know the law, Mr. Clark. And we have Ms. Brown to thank for that precedent." She turned to Sabre. "What do you think of the law now, Ms. Brown?"

"It's still good law, Your Honor."

"I will order an evaluation, but stipulate that it not be used until, or unless, jurisdiction is found. In the meantime, there is an earlier psychological evaluation that can be considered." The judge looked at Bob. "Perhaps you can explain to your client that a newer evaluation might be better than the previous one. However, as per the law, that evaluation will only be used for disposition of the case. You can make that determination before the trial."

"One more thing," Sabre said, as she stood. "I think Unity would benefit from counseling. She's having a rough time, Your Honor."

"No!" Vicki blurted again before Bob could stop her. He tried to calm her, but she insisted. "I don't want them screwing with her head. They'll fill it full of lies like they did last time."

"Your Honor." Sabre cut in, still on her feet. "This child has been traumatized by her living situation. She has had three different father figures in her life, and she's filled with anger and likely has abandonment issues. Regardless of what happens in this case, the minor needs professional help." Sabre sat down and watched Bob try to calm his client.

County Counsel agreed with Sabre, and the judge ordered the therapy.

Vicki continued to glare at Sabre throughout the rest of the hearing. When it was over, Bob escorted his client out of the courtroom. As Vicki reached the door, she turned back and raised two fingers to her eyes, then pointed them at Sabre and mouthed, *I'm watching you.*

CHAPTER 40

Monday, p.m.

Sabre and Bob took a seat at Kevin's Noodle House. As she opened the menu, Ron joined them. "Okay," Sabre said, "I know you all want to protect me, but I'm starting to feel claustrophobic with all this attention."

"I'm just here to have lunch," Ron said.

"Me too." Bob grinned.

"Sure you are." Sabre rolled her eyes. "I don't need to be watched every second. No real threats have been made, you know, just some silly sophomoric gestures."

"Look, Sis," Ron said, "I wasn't around the last time you had a stalker, and that one was all my fault."

Sabre interrupted him. "It was *not* your fault."

"Let me finish. It *was* my fault, and you could've been killed. You don't know what you're up against with this wacko, any more than you did the last one. I couldn't help you then, but I can now. So, please, just humor me."

"Okay, bro." She touched his hand. "Let's order some food."

They chatted through lunch, avoiding further discussion of Sabre's stalker. Mostly they talked about the new restaurant and how it did or didn't measure up to Pho Pasteur.

Sabre summed up their assessment. "So, the consensus is that the food is good, but we need to keep looking to find a number one-twenty-four that measures up."

"Yeah, I'll tell Jim it was close, but no cigar. He eats out a lot and loves Vietnamese, so I'll ask him to keep me posted if he finds anything else."

After lunch, Ron drove Sabre back to her office. He followed her inside, sat down, and started fiddling with his phone. Sabre shook her head. "You can't stay here and watch me. Go." She waved him away. "I'll call you when I'm ready to leave."

"I don't have anywhere to go."

"I don't care. Go see Addie or go shopping, just do something somewhere else."

"Nope. I'm staying right here. Boss's orders."

"I'm calling your boss." Sabre picked up her cell and tried to reach JP, but he didn't answer. "That's the second time he's been unavailable. Do you know what he's doing?"

"Maybe he's driving. You know he doesn't answer the phone when he's driving. He can't figure out how to use the system in his car, and he won't use a headset."

"Nice try, but I think he finally mastered that. He's been calling me on it for a week or so now."

"Yeah, but I don't think he's that comfortable on it." Ron continued to make excuses.

"Then he must be on a long drive."

Ron shrugged and went back to playing on his phone.

"Oh, no. He went to see Lynch, didn't he?"

"I'm not his keeper," Ron said.

"I know. Apparently, you're *my* keeper." Now Sabre was worried. She didn't like the thought of JP confronting Lynch. JP was calm and levelheaded most of the time, but when it came to someone he loved, he could be set off pretty easily.

Sabre knew she couldn't get Ron to leave, so she grabbed a file and started to work. She glanced over at Ron and thought about the years he'd been gone. She was so glad to have him back in her life, even though he could be annoying at times— like right now.

"Why don't you go into David's office so I can have a little privacy. These cases are all confidential, and I don't feel right with you sitting here."

"What if he comes in and wants his office?"

She snickered. "Yeah, that's gonna happen."

Ron reluctantly stood and left the room. Sabre continued to work, responding to emails and making phone calls. She heard a text message come in while she was on a call. When she hung up, she checked it. "Oh, no!"

Ron dashed into the room. "What is it?"

She held up her cell to Ron. Her stalker had sent a photo of a car, sitting alongside the road, with the side smashed. The caption read: *Don't mess with me.*

Sabre pulled the phone back and called Bob. When he didn't answer, she left a message: "Call me right away."

"Why did you call Bob?" Ron asked.

"Because that looks like Bob's car."

A few minutes later, Sabre's phone rang. "Hi, Bob. Are you okay?"

"Yes, but Marilee has been in an accident. I was talking to her when you called."

"Is she all right?"

"I don't know. An ambulance is taking her to Kaiser Hospital. I'm heading over now."

"I'll meet you there. There's something you need to see."

CHAPTER 41

Monday, p.m.

Sabre and Ron sat in the Kaiser ER waiting room. Sabre watched the door and spotted JP as he came in. She hurried to meet him, and he pulled her close and hugged her.

"How's Marilee?" he asked.

"We don't know yet. Bob said he'd come out when he knows something."

Before they had a chance to sit down, Detective Marlow arrived. He walked over, and Sabre introduced him to Ron.

"I was close by, so I thought I'd stop in. Have you shown the photo to Mr. Clark to see if it's his car?"

"No, we're waiting for him now."

Marlow and JP chatted, but Sabre didn't contribute to their conversation except when asked a direct question. Her mind reeled as she tried to figure out what this all meant.

They had been waiting approximately fifteen minutes when Bob came into the room, and Sabre asked, "How's Marilee?"

"She seems okay, but they're taking her for x-rays. Her neck is pretty sore, but other than that, she's not hurting anywhere. She was pretty lucky."

"Bob, this is Detective Marlow."

Marlow reached out his hand. "I'm sorry I have to deal with this now. I know it's a bad time for you."

Bob looked puzzled. "Deal with what?"

"Did your wife say how the accident happened?"

"Not really, just that someone hit her and kept going."

"I'd like to talk to her, but first, I want you to look at something." He brought up the forwarded photo on his cell. "Is this your car?"

Bob squinted, then reached out and enlarged the photo. "Yes."

"You're sure?"

"I can't see the license plate, but I recognize the decal on the back window. It's apparently a flower, not grapes like I thought when Marilee put it on there, but that's definitely our car."

"Thank you."

Bob finally noticed the concern on everyone's faces. "What do you all know that I don't?"

Sabre broke the news. "I received this text just before you told me about Marilee's accident. That's why I was trying to reach you."

"That doesn't make any sense."

"The caption read: *Don't mess with me.* Someone is obviously threatening me, and now they're coming after you too."

"I thought it was just some random driver." Bob rubbed his forehead. "But Marilee must have been targeted. That's insane. No, I switched cars with Marilee so I could fill her tank. The stalker probably thought it was me." He glanced around at

195

everyone. "And you think the accident is related to the other texts Sabre received?"

"We think so," Marlow said. "Whoever is doing all this knows you and Sabre have a close connection."

"Oh my God—CJ!" Bob blurted. "If he knew Marilee was driving the car, then he may know about my son as well."

"Where is he?" Marlow asked.

"At school." Bob started to pace. "I need to go get him."

"I can go," Ron said. "You stay here with Marilee. Call the school and tell them I'm coming."

Bob's hand shook as he pulled out his cell phone. "What if someone already has him?"

"CJ has a cell phone now," Sabre said. "Call him." She had never seen Bob so shook up that he couldn't think straight. Sometimes he got angry in court, but never flustered. This was different. This was personal.

"You call your son," Marlow said. "And I'll call the school and tell them to check on him."

Sabre gave the detective the school's name while Bob called CJ.

"Where are you?" Bob asked. He paused, and in a calmer voice, said, "Okay, go back inside and go directly to the office. When you get there, let me talk to the receptionist or the principal." A pause. "Yes, everything is okay, just go to the office now. I'll explain it when we get home. Ron is coming to pick you up because Mom and I got detained."

A long pause this time. "Ms. Sauer? The password is broccoli. Thank you. Ron will be right there."

"Now what?" Bob seemed to have regained his composure.

"Let's go see what your wife can tell us," Marlow said.

Sabre hugged Bob. "Give my love to Marilee. We have to check on Conner and Morgan. And we'll have Ron bring your son to our house. He and Morgan can hang out together until you're done here. Will that work for you?"

"Yes, that's good."

"Let me know when you're leaving here, and we'll bring CJ home."

"Or we can pick him up."

"We'll work it out. Go see your wife."

CHAPTER 42

Monday, p.m.

On the drive home, JP called Conner again. "Everything is fine, Uncle Johnny, just like the last time you called. Morgan is here with me, the doors are locked, and Ron is on his way. Maybe you should tell me what's goin' on."

"It's probably nothing, but Bob's wife was run off the road a while ago. She's fine, but whoever did it may be connected to a court case that he and Sabre are working on. We're just taking precautions."

"That doesn't sound like nothing," Conner mumbled.

"I'm only telling you so you can be careful and keep an eye on Morgan. Your father would go crazy if anything happened to you guys while you were in my charge."

"Like a loose mule in a corn patch," Conner said.

"Hey, now you're stealin' my lines."

"My dad says Grandpa Pippin said that one all the time."

"Indeed he did."

"Don't worry, Uncle Johnny. I'm used to looking over my shoulder, been doing it all my life."

JP hung up, thinking that wasn't what he wanted for these kids. He wanted them to have a normal life and be carefree for the first time. He had to make things better for them. They rode in silence for the next few miles.

Finally, Sabre broke it. "What do you think this means?"

"The caption certainly makes it seem like a threat. Like the stalker deliberately targeted someone you're close to as a warning."

"But if it was meant for Marilee, why her? We're not that close. I mean, I like her, but we're never together unless you and Bob are there. Why not Bob? Or you? Or, heaven forbid, one of the kids?"

"I don't know. I think it was meant for Bob; after all, it was *his* car. Maybe you and Bob were against him in court, and now he's targeting both of you. Maybe we need to start looking at cases you guys shared."

Sabre tilted her head and gave JP a wide-eyed look. "Do you realize how many cases we've had together?"

"I know it's a lot."

"My guess would be over a thousand."

"So, let's narrow it down. Which cases involved, you, Bob, and Nicholson?"

"Cadle, for one. That was the first case Bob and I had together. And a drug baby where Bob represented the mother, but nothing in that case raised any red flags."

"There was one more. Was Bob on Fisher?"

"I don't think so." Sabre thought for a minute. "No, Arroyo had the mother, and Serlis had the father. I remember, because Serlis had a hard time keeping Dale Fisher under control. She wasn't intimidated by him, but she couldn't get him to shut up when he was angry either."

"I know Bob was on another case."

"You're right, there was another tox-baby petition filed, where the mother showed up for one hearing and then disappeared. Bob was appointed on that, and that was the only case that County Counsel Farris was *not* on."

"I'll go through Cadle again to see if any cream rises to the top."

At home, JP went to his desk to work, and Sabre went to the bedroom to change her clothes. Ron arrived soon after with Bob's son. CJ and Morgan were close in age and were becoming good friends. CJ was a little shy, and Morgan seemed to bring him out of his shell. Plus it was good for Morgan to have a friend with a normal home life, where the parents got along, and their lives weren't filled with drama. Sabre intended to keep it that way and not tell either about the stalker.

After they all had dinner, Bob and Marilee showed up. The kids scattered, and the adults remained at the table.

"What happens now?" JP asked Bob.

"Marilee and CJ will stay with her sister in Santee for a few days. I'm not crazy about the sister, but her husband is a good guy—and a cop. They'll be safe there.

"I was coming from work when I was hit," Marilee added. "So, if the stalker was after me, he may not know where we live, but we're not taking that chance."

"But *you're* staying at home?" Sabre looked at Bob.

"Yeah, with my two friends, Smith and Wesson. If he

comes to my house, I'll blow his head off." Bob smiled. "Hey, JP, I need you to question a witness for me. It won't take long. Could you go with me sometime tomorrow?"

"I just need to work it out so Sabre isn't alone."

"I'll be fine," Sabre said.

"All I have on calendar is two reviews." Bob added. "And Sabre can cover those if you want to go in the morning."

JP frowned.

"Or not," Bob said. "We could go later."

Ron spoke up. "I can hang with Sabre at court."

"No." Sabre was adamant. "I do not need a babysitter at court. I appreciate the concern, but I'll be surrounded by bailiffs who don't let me out of their sight. There's nothing you could do that they can't."

"You're probably right." JP sighed. "I'll drive you to court and pick up Bob. Then I'll come back and get you when you're done and/or bring Bob back, depending on the time." JP looked at Sabre for approval.

"Sure," Sabre said. "I can deal with that."

After everyone left, JP and Sabre spent the rest of the evening reading every word in the Cadle file. Neither could find anything that might help. JP did what he could to trace relatives and friends involved in each case. Finally, he said, "We need to contact the parents on the Cadle case. Did you have a good relationship with them?"

"Yes, Bob and I both did. That's why it doesn't seem likely it would be either one."

"What about a relative or friend, maybe?"

"No one cared that much. The relatives were all a mess. They were far too concerned about themselves and their next fix. The grandmother was the only one interested in having the kids, and she was an alcoholic."

"Then you should be the one to contact them, instead of me," JP said. "Just make up some excuse. Say you're just checking to see how the kid is doing."

"I can do that. What's the number?"

"Do you want Laura or George?"

"Laura, she was my client."

JP gave her the number, and Sabre called. A woman answered and said, "Hello."

"Hi, Laura, this is Sabre Brown."

"What a nice surprise." Her voice was filled with genuine sincerity. "How are you?"

"I'm well."

Suddenly, Laura's voice changed to concern. "Why are you calling? Is something wrong?"

"No, not at all. I was cleaning out some old case files and came across yours. Bob and I think of you and your family often, and I wondered how things were going for you."

"They couldn't be better. Well, we could always use more money, but we're happy. We both work at the Gold Dust. George is a dealer, and I'm a cocktail waitress, so we make decent tips. We both stopped drinking, been sober for over six years. It took a while to get our act together but having that dependency case was a wakeup call."

"How's Emily? She must be in junior high by now."

"She will be next year. She's a good girl, likes school, and gets real good grades. So, we take her to a dance studio. She's been with them for three years now and loves it. So far, knock on wood, she hasn't started acting like a teenager yet."

"That's great to hear. I'm glad everything has worked out for you." Sabre hesitated, but she had to ask. "When was the last time you were in southern California?"

"Not since we got sober six years ago. We had to get away

from friends and family. It was too hard to fight the demons and them too."

Sabre thanked her and wished her a good life.

After she hung up, JP called the Nevada casino and verified that both parents had been working regularly the last two weeks. Although the texts could've come from anywhere, the stalker had been in San Diego for the flower delivery, the car accident, and for Nicholson's death. JP walked over to the whiteboard and crossed off Cadle again. That left Lynch and Banks, but with nothing concrete. They exchanged glances, both thinking the same thing—they had no solid suspects.

CHAPTER 43

Tuesday, a.m.

The next morning, they proceeded according to plan. JP dropped off Sabre and picked up Bob, who was waiting in front of the courthouse. As they drove to the meeting with Bob's witness, JP didn't say much.

"She'll be okay," Bob said. "I made sure McCormick knew Sabre was there alone."

"I'm sure you're right, but I'd never forgive myself if something happened to her. This whole thing is driving me crazy. It's worse than it was a few years ago when that judge was killed."

"Of course it is. The two of you have gotten a lot closer. Back then, you hadn't worked up the nerve to even ask her out. Now you're practically living together."

"Yeah, but Sabre wasn't the target then. The killer just happened to be connected to her cases." JP reconsidered. "But she sure has gotten herself into a couple of other pretty sticky situations. I can't help but be worried."

They reached the house they were looking for, and Bob and JP went inside. The interview didn't take long. They were on their way back to the courthouse within thirty minutes.

"How are you holding up during this mess with Sabre?" Bob asked.

"I'm frustrated that I can't get any closer to finding this crazy guy. Every time I cross someone off the list, I should feel closer to finding the perp, but instead, he seems further away. There must be something I'm missing."

"Or maybe it's not there to see. Some criminals cover their tracks very well."

A few minutes later, JP's cell phone rang. He glanced at the ID. "Excuse me, I have to take this. It's my friend from INS."

"Sure."

JP hit the button on the steering wheel, answering the call. "Hi, Pedro. Do you have good news for me?"

"Some. I haven't found Miguel's mother yet, but I think we've located the father. Tracing that pottery was a great idea. I have to give you credit."

"That was all Sabre," JP said. "She recognized it from trips she'd made to the region."

"Whoever's idea, it was smart. The father is in Tonalá. If we have the right guy—and I'm pretty certain we do—he doesn't know where Miguel's mother is. He thought she was in the U.S., but he hasn't heard from her in weeks."

"Will they send the boy back to his father?" JP asked.

"I'll do a little more follow up. I have a guy showing Miguel's photo around, and we're verifying with other relatives. I also want to take another shot at finding his mother. If she's here in the States, and she's seeking asylum, we'll deal with that or send them back together."

"I sure appreciate your help on this."

"My pleasure," Pedro said. "One more thing. You asked me to check on the illegal immigrant at the house where Miguel was living, a guy named Lorenzo. I did, and he was deported shortly after the bust. His last name is Ortega."

"Do you have a middle name or another surname for him?" JP asked.

"No, that's all I got. I hope it helps."

"Thanks, and please keep me posted." JP hung up and drove onto the freeway.

"Was that about the little boy from Mexico whose parents they can't find?" Bob asked.

"Yeah, his name's Miguel."

"I saw him at Polinsky one day with Sabre. He's as cute as can be, and such a happy little guy."

"He doesn't deserve this."

"None of these kids do." Bob paused for a moment. "So, one of the drug dealers in that home was Lorenzo Ortega, huh?"

JP glanced over at Bob. "Do you know him?"

"No, it's just that his initials are LO," Bob said, "like how the texts to Sabre are signed."

"Huh. Interesting."

"But that case didn't start until after Nicholson was dead. There's no way he would know Sabre would be assigned Miguel's case."

"And the guy doesn't speak English. It must be a coincidence."

JP's phone rang again. He glanced at it, then hit the button on the wheel, but it didn't connect. "That's Sabre; answer it for me."

Bob took the cell, put it on speaker, and said, "JP's phone."

"I just got a crazy text again."

JP blurted, "What did it say?"

"It was a cartoon, like picture of a bomb, and it read *Boom*. That's all it said, boom."

Suddenly, the background was noisy. They heard a garbled announcement over the speaker at juvenile court and lots of excited voices.

"Sabre," Bob said. "Can you hear me?"

"Something's going on, and I need to find out what. I'll call you back." She hung up.

JP swore under his breath and pressed the accelerator.

CHAPTER 44

Tuesday, a.m.

After hanging up, Sabre looked up and down the hall outside of Department One. The courtroom door burst open, and a group of people rushed out, all moving toward the front exit. A few bailiffs followed, herding everyone in the right direction. Sabre assumed the other bailiffs were escorting the judges toward the back door. That was their first priority.

The announcement came on again: "You need to leave the building immediately. Please do so in an orderly fashion." No explanation was given. Sabre moved with the crowd and heard someone mention a gas leak.

She joined a group headed toward the lobby. Some people were running and shoving others aside to get out quicker, but most were orderly. Sabre had an armload of files that she didn't want to leave behind, so she forged forward, holding them tight against her chest to keep them from being knocked loose. Toward the end of the hall, someone mumbled about an escaped prisoner. Just another rumor started out of midair, but Sabre knew what was happening. At least, she thought she did. What she didn't know was whether it was a real threat.

By the time she reached the main lobby, it had filled with people from the courtrooms emptying out, the hallways merging in, and the upper offices coming downstairs. She found herself shoulder to shoulder with strangers, and she still had thirty feet left until she reached the exit. Now the rumor was more embellished—an escaped prisoner holding hostages somewhere in the building, with possible snipers.

"Please evacuate the building now," the loudspeaker voice said again.

She heard someone ask, "Do you know what's going on?"

In the chaos and noise, it was hard to discern the voice. She turned and saw Attorney Collicott behind her. "I'm not sure," Sabre said. She wanted to say, *My guess would be a bomb scare,* but she didn't want to alarm anyone, in case she was wrong. There were enough rumors going around. *Was it just a scare, or did someone plant a real bomb?*

She thought about the way she'd ended the call to JP. He and Bob would both be freaking out but calling them now was pointless. There was too much noise. And she couldn't text while holding her files. She would call again as soon as she got outside. She felt a body press up against her, pushing her toward the door.

"Do you mind?" she snapped, turning to see who it was. The frightened look on the old woman's face was startling. She gasped and tried to speak, but the only words Sabre understood were "my medication."

Adding to the noise of the crowd and alarms, sirens began to blare as first responders approached the building. Sabre leaned toward the woman and shouted, "Where are your meds?"

"My husband …."

"Where is he?"

The woman pointed toward the exit.

Sabre saw an old man peering through the large windows, while a bailiff tried to get him to move away.

"We're almost there," Sabre said. "Hang onto me, so you don't get pushed aside."

The woman wrapped an arm around Sabre's waist, and they kept moving until they reached the door. When they finally stepped outside, the crowd dispersed, but the old man was gone.

"Where did he go?" The old woman's voice filled with panic. She clutched her chest and moaned.

"Are you having a heart attack?" Sabre asked.

"No, I don't think so. I need my pills."

Fire trucks, ambulances, and police cars circled the building. Firemen and cops ushered people across the parking lot. Patrol officers directed traffic and urged as many cars off the lot as they could. Only emergency vehicles were allowed to enter. Sabre wondered what JP would do when he arrived. She needed to reach him, but first she had to get this woman to her meds.

"Move it," a cop yelled, as they looked around for the husband. Sabre tried to explain, but the officer got involved with a different crowd. Then she tried to get the attention of a paramedic, but they were focused on a medical crisis in the parking lot.

"How are you doing?" Sabre asked the woman.

"I'll be okay if I can just get to my meds."

Sabre guided the woman, but she couldn't move very fast. "What's your husband's name?"

"John."

Sabre started yelling his name, but she was pretty sure it wasn't doing any good. She could hardly hear herself over the madness. They walked across the pavement, with people dashing past them, until Sabre spotted an old man, moving even slower than the woman. He stopped near a car, placed his hand on the trunk, and used it to support himself. Sabre pointed. "Is that him?"

"Yes."

"I'll go get your meds. You lean against this car and wait for me, okay?"

"Okay."

Sabre laid her files on the vehicle's hood. Then she ran and retrieved the woman's purse from her husband, instructing him to keep moving away from the building. She ran back, opened the purse, and removed the only pill bottle. "Is this what you need?"

The woman nodded. Sabre removed a pill and handed it to her. "Can you take it without water?"

She nodded again, then put the medicine in her mouth under her tongue.

Sabre glanced at the label on the pill bottle—Xanax—before dropping it back in the purse. She picked up her files, and they walked until they reached her husband, who was still resting. Sabre handed the woman's purse back to him.

"Are you going to be okay?" Sabre asked.

"I'm fine now, dear. I just had a little panic attack. The problem is I can't tell the difference between that and a stroke. If the pill works, I'll know what it was."

Sabre pointed toward the fence. "Just keep moving in that

direction until you reach the crowd. If you need medical attention, walk to your left. There are several ambulances parked
over there."

Sabre looked back toward the building. The only way to
drive out of the lot was past the courthouse, and only emergency vehicles were being allowed in or out. No one could
leave in their cars. But she knew a spot where the fence had an
opening she could walk through. She dashed across the
parking lot. Her load of files slowed her down, but she kept
moving. Most of the crowd had gathered against the northwest
side. Some were slipping through the buildings on the west
side and away from the grounds.

When Sabre reached the opening, she passed through and
dashed across the street. She kept hurrying until she reached
Children's Hospital. She sat down on the retaining wall, took
out her phone, and saw she had missed six calls and a text
from JP. She called him back.

"What is going on?" JP asked.

"I don't know for sure, but I'm okay," Sabre said.
"They've evacuated the courthouse."

"We can't even get close. Where are you?"

"I'm at Children's Hospital, on the east sidewalk. Come in
the back way and pick me up." Sabre hung up and called
Marlow.

CHAPTER 45

Tuesday, p.m.

The kids were in their rooms, and Sabre and JP stood in front of the whiteboard.

"I'm so frustrated," JP said. 'We don't have any viable suspects. I don't even know where to look, and Detective Marlow feels the same."

"What's the update?"

"He said he would check what time the bomb scare came in and compare it to when you received the message," JP said.

"We already know it was very close," Sabre said.

"Yeah, but if you got the message after the threat was called in, maybe the stalker heard about the bomb and sent you a message to scare you, after the fact."

"I thought about that."

"Well, whoever it was, knew you were at court today," JP said.

"I'm at court every day."

"That's true, but he may not know that. At least we know for certain that the threats are connected to your work."

"True enough." Sabre's eyes widened. "Until you said something just now, I never thought it wasn't work related, but it could've been some random thing, I guess."

"I considered that, but it doesn't seem likely. You have plenty of enemies, but none outside of your work. But whoever this is doesn't care about the chaos he causes just to get to you. He knows a lot about you, but we know very little about him."

"What does he really know though?" Sabre asked, shifting anxiously. "He knows I work in juvenile court, knows my office address, and my phone number. All very easy to obtain online."

"He also knows you have a connection to Nicholson and a friendship with Bob."

"Nicholson was a social worker, so the fact that we knew each other could have been a lucky guess," Sabre countered. "As for Bob, we go to lunch practically every day. They could have seen us together at Pho's."

"If that's the case, the perp could still be someone outside of your work, which puts us back at square one."

Her cell rang, and Sabre glanced at the screen. "It's Marlow," she said, answering. "I have you on speaker, Curt. I'm here with JP."

"That's good."

"What do you know?" JP asked.

"Your message came in at 11:43, correct?"

"That's right," Sabre said.

"The anonymous call for the bomb threat was received at 11:45, two minutes later. That was the official time according to the digital recording. And JP, if you're wondering, I compared Sabre's time with both mine and with dispatch. They were all in sync."

"Thanks, Marlow."

"And both calls came from a blocked number."

"So, the whole scare was aimed at me." Sabre felt herself tense.

"It appears so."

When Marlow hung up, JP was silent for a moment, then suggested, "Maybe you should go away for a while."

"Where would I go?" Sabre shook her head. "Never mind. I'm not going anywhere. I won't run."

"Okay, I got it, but maybe you could stay at your mother's for a while."

"And put her at risk? No thanks." She looked wide-eyed at JP. "But I don't have to stay here."

"What are you talking about?"

"I don't want to put these kids in danger either. Maybe I should go back to my condo."

"No." JP was adamant. "You're not staying somewhere I can't protect you. As long as you're in my house, you'll be safe. I'll see to that."

Sabre was worried too, but she wanted to stay grounded. "So far, no real attempt has been made on my life, and the bomb scare was just that—a scare. No bomb. I've received dead flowers, a photo of Nicholson, and a couple of bizarre texts." She gave a casual shrug. "And the police still think Nicholson committed suicide. Maybe the stalker just took the photo and had nothing to do with his death."

"That's a nice spin," JP argued. "But the way I see it, those messages constitute threats. Every message you receive is related to death. As for Nicholson, it wouldn't be the first time a murder was written off as suicide." His voice gained volume.

"And what about Marilee being run off the road? She could have been seriously hurt or killed, and you received a text immediately after it happened."

Before Sabre could say anything, he added, "This nut job is obsessed with death and obsessed with you."

"You really shouldn't sugarcoat it like that."

JP took her in his arms and pulled her close, softening his voice. "I'm sorry, Baby, but I'm scared and angry as hell. I couldn't stand to lose you."

Sabre relaxed into his arms. For the first time that day, she felt safe.

But it didn't last long. Her phone rang. Sabre pulled away and looked at the screen. An unknown number. JP took the cell and answered it. There was an obvious silence, then a click. JP tensed and handed the phone back to Sabre.

Within seconds, it beeped with a text. She read it, and her stomach churned.

"What is it?" JP asked.

"Just some letters. S-R-S-L-Y."

CHAPTER 46

Tuesday, p.m.

"What do you suppose the text means?" Sabre asked, repeating the letters. "S-R-S-L-Y?"

"Seriously," Conner said, as he walked in.

"What?" Sabre turned to him.

"The letters in your text are short for *seriously*."

"That's not very threatening," Sabre said.

"Should it be?" Conner scowled in confusion.

"No, of course not." Sabre caught herself before she said anything more.

"Is there something wrong?" Conner asked.

"No," JP said. "It's just someone being silly."

Sabre focused on Conner again. "Do you abbreviate a lot when you text?"

"I don't that much, but I have some gamer friends who do it a lot. So, I've learned to recognize most of it."

"Do the letters LHO mean anything?" Sabre asked.

"Yeah, it stands for *laughing head off.* You know, like LOL, laughing out loud, only stronger."

JP and Sabre both burst out laughing.

"What's so funny?" Conner asked.

"We thought it was someone's initials," JP explained. "And we wasted a lot of time on it."

Conner gave them a curious look. "I'm hungry. Is there anything to eat?"

"There's leftover chicken in the refrigerator," Sabre said. "Help yourself."

Conner went to the kitchen, and JP said, "That boy has a hollow leg. He'd eat a horse, then chase the rider."

"He's a growing boy."

"You got that right. He's already taller than his father, and he's going to pass me up soon."

Conner came back carrying a paper plate with three pieces of fried chicken. "Thanks," he said, nodding at Sabre. "And let me know if you need more text abbreviations translated."

JP's phone rang. "Hold on, Conner. It's your dad." He picked up the cell. "Hello, Gene. Conner's right here." He handed the phone to the boy, who walked away with it.

Sabre and JP sat on the sofa, and Sabre turned on the television. She searched for something they would both like and finally settled for a *M*A*S*H* rerun, hoping it would get their attention off the events of the day. But both kept glancing at the whiteboard. Finally, JP stood and turned it around so they couldn't read it.

Morgan came into the room. "Dad talked to both of us, and now he wants to speak to you." She handed JP the phone.

"Thanks, Munchkin. I'll be in there in a bit to tell you goodnight."

JP put the phone on speaker. "What's up?"

"Fisher asked about Sabre again," Gene said.

"What exactly did he say?"

"He said something like, 'You know that woman who came to see you on Sunday?' And I said, 'Yes, what about her?'" Gene paused to shout at someone in the background. "Sorry. Then Fisher said, 'I think she was on the case with my kid when social services took him away.' I acted like I didn't know anything about it."

"Did he say anything else?"

"Yeah, he wanted me to find out if Sabre was the one who handled the case."

"How did you respond?"

"I acted nonchalant. I shrugged and said, 'Sure, if I see her again.'"

"Do you really think he didn't know for certain?" JP asked.

"He seemed to be genuine, but who knows?" Gene scoffed. "Maybe it's his way of sending a message. Anyway, I thought you should know."

"Thanks, Gene." Sabre leaned toward the phone to be heard. "I really appreciate it."

JP cut in. "Hey, if I pass this on to Detective Marlow and he pays Fisher a visit, will that come back on you?"

"I'm sure it will. I doubt if Fisher talked to anyone else about Sabre, so he'd know it was me." Gene was silent for a second. "But if that's what you have to do to protect Sabre and my kids, then do it."

"Maybe I'll hold off for a while."

"Okay, just give me fair warning, so I can cover my back."

CHAPTER 47

Wednesday, a.m./p.m.

Sabre's phone lit up. She was in court, so the ringer was turned off, but she could see the screen. Another unknown caller who left no message. It was only eleven o'clock, and that was the fourth call this morning. She was starting to get irritated. She finished her morning calendar, then called Ron to let him know. JP had dropped her off, so she was once again without a car. She would be so glad when this was all over.

Bob had a trial that afternoon and needed to stay at court. She told him she was leaving and went outside to wait for Ron. She'd only been out there a few seconds when Jerry, a bailiff, walked out and started chatting with her.

"I'm fine," she said.

"I know, but JP is a buddy of mine. We did jail duty together when we were rookies. He'd kill me if I didn't keep an eye on you. Besides, you're pretty cool, so I wouldn't want anything to happen to you."

"Thanks, Jerry, I like you too." A car pulled up in front of the courthouse. "There's my brother now. I'll see you tomorrow."

Sabre got in Ron's car, and they drove off. "I'm so sick of this. I feel like I'm living in a glass cage. Everyone is watching me. Don't get me wrong, I really appreciate that. I just hate that I feel so vulnerable."

"I know, Sis, but we can't let anything happen to you. We'd all fall apart. You're the glue that holds us together."

Before Sabre could answer, her phone rang. She looked at it and tossed the device on the floor.

"Dropped call?" Ron asked with a smirk.

Sabre chuckled in spite of her frustration. "If the window had been open, I would've tossed it out. I'm so sick of these calls."

"We're headed to JP's, right? Or do you need some lunch?"

"I have stuff for sandwiches at home—I mean at JP's. We can eat there." Sabre picked up her phone and checked the time. "I have a home visit scheduled with Unity this afternoon, but not until after school. Are you my assigned chauffeur?"

"Probably." After a few seconds of silence, Ron started talking about their mother and her relationship with her boyfriend, Harley, a nice change from the usual *stalker* conversation.

"She's happier than I've seen her in years," Sabre said.

"They've been having a ball traveling and are taking another cruise next month."

"Where to this time?"

"Panama, I think."

They chatted about their mother until they arrived at JP's. Once they had lunch, they gathered in front of the whiteboard to get Ron up to speed and get his input.

While JP wrote on the board, Sabre opened up the discussion. "What do we know about this jerk?"

"We know he has some connection to Nicholson," JP said.

"Are you using the word *he* in a general sense or do you have some reason to believe it's a man?" Ron asked.

"Elaine was positive it was a man's voice on the call to the office," Sabre said. "The one where the guy told her to watch the news. So, unless the perp had someone else make that call, we're dealing with a man. And it's easier to just say 'he,' so that's what we've been doing."

"We know he started on Monday before last," JP said. "And he knows Sabre's office address and phone number. But he also knows about Bob's wife, Marilee, and probably where she works."

"Unless he was targeting Bob," Ron said, "in which case, he may not know anything about her, other than what he stumbled upon."

"Something strikes me as odd about his messages," Sabre said.

"What do you mean?" Ron asked.

"I don't know exactly, but he sounds young or immature."

"Maybe because he uses text abbreviations," JP said. "And Conner knew what they meant when we didn't."

"Maybe, but I think it's more than that," Sabre said. "The overall tone, the silly gestures like the dead flowers, the constant phone calls. It's so junior high."

"Do you think the perp might be a kid?" JP seemed skeptical. "Maybe a delinquency case?"

"That's not likely because Nicholson worked with dependency issues only, and so does County Counsel Farris." Sabre had been giving this thought. "The guy's use of text abbreviations makes me think he's our generation or younger, but he must be old enough to drive. And if he has access to a car, it's not likely he's in foster care. If he's a dependent, he's probably at home or with a relative."

"What about that Lynch guy?" Ron asked. "He's pretty childish."

"I haven't given up on him," JP said. "In fact, I think he's a real good candidate. But he's clever. I'm just waiting for him to slip up. Meanwhile, we have someone keeping an eye on him in Pasadena." JP informed Ron about Lynch's neighbor, the cop.

"I have to get going," Sabre said. "So, whoever is taking me to see Unity, we have to roll. Or, I can just drive myself."

Ron jumped up. "Let's roll, Sis."

CHAPTER 48

Wednesday, p.m.

When they arrived at the temporary foster home, Ron waited in the car. Sabre walked toward the house and chatted on the porch with the foster mother, Cara Yates, a tall, toned woman in her early fifties.

"How's Unity doing?" Sabre asked.

"Could be better, but we're coming to an understanding."

"What's been the problem?"

"Come on in. I'll explain." Cara led her inside and they sat down on the sofa. "She's not getting along with Tiffany, another foster child. We've had Tiffany about two months, and we never had any trouble before, but she and Unity argue a lot. They're pretty close in age, and Tiffany has only had to deal with younger children before, so I'm not sure who's at fault. But we're working on it. And …" The foster mother hesitated.

"And what?"

"I've caught Unity in a couple of"—she paused again

—"should we say, exaggerations. She likes to embellish things for effect. Sometimes, the stories are pretty outlandish."

"Like what?"

"They had a drill at school and had to evacuate. Unity came home and said they had a shooter, and two kids were killed. Tiffany called her on it and said it was just a drill."

"How did Unity react?"

"She stuck to her story. So, I called the school to make sure, and it was just a drill. We had another incident where my husband accidently bumped into her, and Unity claimed he pushed her. I'm keeping a record because that sort of thing can get out of hand. I know families who have lost their foster-parent license over a kid's lies."

"Are you concerned about that?"

"Not really. We've been doing this for twenty-five years, and we have a good reputation. But we're not ready to give up on her. She's an angry little girl, and she's had a rough life. But I'll keep reporting everything that happens to the social worker."

"Did Unity get started in therapy?" Sabre asked.

"She had her first session yesterday. Good therapist. I've had kids with her before."

"What's her name?"

"Dr. Jamison."

Sabre didn't know her. "Did Unity say anything after her visit?"

"No, and I never ask. I figure the girls will share if they want to."

"I appreciate that. Could I see Unity now?"

"Of course." Cara led her to Unity's room so they could have some privacy.

They talked briefly about her new school, and Unity

expressed her displeasure. When Sabre asked about the foster home, the girl rolled her eyes.

"It would be okay here if Tiffany would just leave me alone." Unity's voice was tight with anger.

"What does she do that bothers you?"

"She comes in my room when I'm not here and messes it up, then I have to clean it, or I'll get in trouble."

"Have you talked to her about it?"

"She denies everything, and no one believes me about anything."

"Why do you think that is?" Sabre asked.

"I don't know."

"Is it better here than in Polinsky?"

"Not really."

"Let's think about some of the good things about this home."

"Like what?" Unity snapped, still edgy.

"Your foster mother seems nice."

Unity rolled her eyes.

"And you have your own room."

"Which would be fine if Tiffany stayed out of it."

Sabre couldn't get Unity to say anything nice no matter how she tried, so she changed the subject completely.

"Your mother is contesting the allegations in the petition, and …"

"And I'm supposed to know what that means."

"It means she has set a trial. And you have been subpoenaed to testify."

"What if I don't want to?"

"The court has ordered it, so you'll have to go."

"They can't make me talk."

"They kind of can." Sabre explained her legal rights, and

the consequences if she didn't answer the questions, but Unity argued with her. Sabre was certain it was just an attempt to be obstinate, more than any real feelings about what she had to do. "Before the trial, I will take you to court, show you around the room so you can see where you will sit, and we'll go over a few procedural things. It'll make it less scary for you when we go to trial."

"I'm not scared. I just don't want to do it."

"I'll let you know when I get the time set up for your walk-through."

Unity shrugged.

Sabre continued to question her about her everyday life but made little progress. Finally, she got to the question about Wayne's death.

"Unity, you said Wayne was poisoned, but when I checked the medical examiner's report, nothing indicated that he was. Why do you suppose that is?"

"I don't know. Maybe they don't know what they're doing."

"Really?"

"Now you're calling me a liar?"

"That's not what I said."

"But it's what you meant. I told you, no one believes me. My mom killed Wayne, but if no one else cares, neither do I." She crossed her arms.

Sabre gently probed some more, but Unity stuck to her story. Sabre finally left, frustrated that she had a client she couldn't trust.

CHAPTER 49

Thursday, a.m.

The next morning, while waiting for a case to be called, Sabre thought about the discussion she'd had with Ron and JP. When she finished the hearing, she met with Bob and told him what they'd discussed. Then she suggested her new theory. "What if this involves an old case with an angry or mentally ill minor who is now an adult?"

"But you checked all the cases that were connected to Nicholson." Bob seemed skeptical.

"Yes, but even though he wasn't the social worker of record, the minor could've had dealings with him along the way. Social workers cover for each other just like we do."

"I know you have something in mind," Bob said. "What's your plan?"

"Come with me." Sabre starting walking.

"Where?"

"Maria Sanchez is working today," Sabre said over her shoulder. "I hope to get some information from her."

Bob followed Sabre upstairs to the clerk's office.

"Twice in one day," Maria said. "Nice to see you again, Sabre. And I see you brought your partner in crime. Hi, Bob."

"Hi, Maria."

"What can I do for you?" Maria asked.

"This may sound weird, but how would someone go about viewing their own juvenile dependency records?"

"They would need to file a *Petition to View Records* form. And they would have to show ID, of course."

"Do those get filed very often?"

"Most requests come from agencies that don't need a court order. For example, an Indian tribe of which the child is a member, or the District Attorney in special cases. But seldom, if ever, from an individual."

"Who handles those forms?"

"I do. There's just not that many."

"Maria, I know you can't disclose certain information, but I've had some strange—possibly life-threatening things—happen recently, and they appear to be related to an old case." Sabre paused to let her process. "The problem is, I don't know which case. I figure whoever sent the threats probably viewed or even copied their old file."

Maria nodded. "Correct. If a petition had been filed, I couldn't reveal which case."

"I knew it was a long shot."

"But I can tell you this. In the decade I've been here, I've only handled three such forms filed by individuals. And the last one was over two years ago. But ..." Maria hesitated.

"But what?"

"I did get a call from someone a few days ago inquiring about the process."

"Who was it?" Sabre didn't expect Maria to violate the rules and tell her, but she asked anyway.

"I don't remember the name, but he said he had three boys and needed all three files, and that his case had been transferred to L.A. County a few months back. He was very rude and snapped at me when I told him he needed the form. Then he hung up before I could tell him he could do it over the phone and sign the form when he got here."

"Thanks," Sabre said. "You're a peach."

CHAPTER 50

Thursday, p.m.

Ron drove Sabre home from court, and they all had lunch together again. Afterward, Ron volunteered to stay with the kids while Sabre and JP went to her office. They planned to search her files on the outside chance that the stalker had been a minor from a past case. Sabre had set up a chronological numbering system, starting at 100 for her oldest case. Her newest was 2,242. She kept an alphabetical list on her computer too, so she could cross-reference if she needed to.

"Wow!" JP seemed stunned. "You've had over two thousand cases. That's a lot of abuse and neglect."

"And I'm only one attorney. There are a hundred more of me. Most don't carry as heavy a caseload, but still, it's way too much." She sucked in a breath, not wanting to think about all those tragic lives. "So, do you want to start with the most recent case or the oldest?"

"Most recent. And will you print a case list so I can check them off or make notes?

"Sure."

"What age would the oldest child be now?"

"I've been practicing in juvenile court for eight years. So, if an early case had a seventeen-year-old, the oldest they could be now is twenty-four."

Sabre printed the list and handed it to JP. Then she opened a file drawer and started perusing. When she reached the eleventh file, she pulled it out. "This one has a sixteen-year-old girl. Do you want the girls too?"

"Sure. If the stalker is a young person, it wouldn't be unusual for them to have a friend make a prank call."

Sabre handed the file to JP. He started through it, asking occasional questions, as she continued to search the cabinet.

Sabre stopped when she reached a case with a twelve-year-old boy. "What's the youngest age we should be looking at? I mean for how old the client would be now."

JP gave it some thought. "The perp has access to burner phones, or at least knows how to use the programs online. And they must know how to drive, because they ran Marilee off the street without wrecking their own car. So, I'd say fifteen."

"Okay. That narrows it down, but not much." She would have to calculate the current age of each minor.

The first two drawers went quickly. Sabre handed only three files to JP, but the further back in time she went, the less familiar she was with the cases. She often had to spend a few minutes perusing the file to familiarize herself with the issues, but it didn't take long before a child's face came to mind, especially the cases that were more involved. She had spent a lot of time with these kids, and she knew them all pretty well. She couldn't help but wonder where their lives had taken them.

The next drawer produced another three possible cases, which she handed to JP. "You know, most of these kids don't ever come to court," Sabre said. "That only happens if they have to testify at a trial, and that's not very often."

"What's your point?"

"Most wouldn't have any idea who Linda Farris is. Why would they slash her tires?"

"Unless he or she didn't care whose tires they were. Maybe he just needed to show you he was at court, and Linda was the unlucky one."

Sabre thought for a second, then pulled out her phone and looked at the photo of Linda with the flat tire. "No, I think she was a target."

"Why?"

"Because this photo doesn't show the courthouse. I'm so familiar with the parking lot that I immediately knew the location. But if the car was random, the perp would have made sure to include the building as an identifier. Instead, he waited for Linda to reach her car, and then he took the picture."

"Well, aren't you just the little detective?" JP looked at her with love. "I agree. So, how do I know if the child has been to court?"

"Check the different colored hearing sheets. I always list who is present in court."

"You are so... so... efficient."

"You really meant *anal*, didn't you?"

"Maybe a little, but I give you credit. You are very good at your job," JP said. "Isn't it possible the stalker got a copy of his records and saw Linda Farris' name?"

"It's possible, but it didn't happen."

"And you know that how?"

"Because I already checked with the clerk, and she said no

one has filed a records petition in the last two years. But I did learn something else while I was there."

JP tilted his head as if he was weighing what she was about to say. "What did you learn?"

"A man called the clerk a few days ago and asked about getting his file. She didn't remember the name, but he had three boys and the case was transferred to L.A. County. And he was rude."

"Lynch," JP said with obvious anger.

"That was my guess."

"I think I need to make another trip to Pasadena."

"Please don't. It still doesn't mean anything. He has always had an agenda and spouted about suing everyone. That could be why he wants his file."

"Okay, where were we?" JP asked, but Sabre knew he wasn't done with Lynch.

"The kids who didn't go to court are less likely to be my stalker."

"Right. We'll spend very little time on any minor who didn't go to court."

"And since Linda Farris has only worked there five years, let's only go back that far. We have to place parameters around this search, or all my clients will be adults before we're done."

"Good point."

Sabre continued through the file drawers and handed JP another one. "What are you looking for exactly?"

"Mental illness, an angry kid ..."

"Angry fits most of these minors. They had parents who didn't care enough to put their children's needs above their own. Of course, they're upset."

"I'm looking for something more over the top. You're so used to seeing this stuff that nothing shocks you anymore. If it hits me in the gut"—JP held up a file—"like this one." He shook his head. "This kid had his hands held over a flame and suffered third-degree burns. That's more than the average reason for anger."

It took nearly three hours, but they finally narrowed their search to five files, plus a list with lots of JP's notes.

"It will be very difficult to track most of those kids," Sabre said.

"I know, but I'll start with the criminal system."

Sabre scowled.

JP gave her a half smile. "I'm not saying the perp is incarcerated, but that'll be the easiest thing to check."

"I suppose that makes sense."

Several moments of silence passed before JP said, "I still think I need to go see Lynch."

"What good will that do? He's not going to admit anything, and I sure don't want you losing your temper and punching him."

"I won't need to punch him, although I'd love to. He's a bully. Bullies can be intimidated. Maybe I can stop the harassment."

CHAPTER 51

Thursday, a.m./p.m.

Sabre was at court, it was early morning, and the sun was shining. JP didn't relish the idea of staying inside and perusing cases, but he had five files sitting on his desk waiting for him to do just that. Three were fairly small, but one consisted of two volumes and the other was three volumes. He hoped he wasn't wasting his time. He decided to go through the easy cases first, so he could feel some sense of accomplishment.

The first file involved a fifteen-year-old male whose stepfather beat him almost daily. The dependency petition closed a year later when the boy burned down his parents' house with them inside. His stepfather survived; his mother did not. The teenager would be nineteen now. Sabre was thorough and had noted that Jerry Leahy was the attorney of record in the delinquency case.

JP called Jerry and gave him a brief rundown, then waited while Jerry perused the file.

"I remember this kid." Jerry's tone was solemn. "I tried to get him into a psych ward, but I failed. I think the judge knew that's where he belonged, and that's why he let us try him as a minor instead of an adult. But there was a lot of political pressure to give these kids *real* sentences, and so he ended up serving time in California Youth Authority, which in my opinion is just a training ground for adult prison. He'll be there until he's twenty-five."

JP thanked him, glad to get one file off his desk. He had just started into the second, when his phone rang. It was from the prison.

"I'm just checking in," Gene said.

"I'm glad you did. We're at our wits end here." JP told him about Marilee's accident. "We don't know how it's connected, but Sabre received a text photo of the accident right after it happened. I'm searching old cases like a madman, but I keep hitting dead ends."

"What's your next step?"

"I can't help but wonder why Fisher asked about Sabre. If it was a scare tactic, it's working."

"And you want to sic the cops on him?" Gene asked.

"I was thinking I'd go talk to Fisher myself."

Gene was quiet for a second. "That would be better. Just handle him with finesse, Jackie. There's no place to hide in this joint. So, if I don't call you tomorrow, you'll know he didn't appreciate your visit."

"That's not funny, Gene."

"It is a little bit." He laughed. "I'm not worried. Really, do what you need to do."

JP hung up, closed the file he was working on, and called Donovan State Prison. He spoke to a friend in processing, faxed over the forms he needed for visitation, and made appointments to see Dale Fisher and Nick Baxter on Sunday. Since he had already been cleared to see Gene, the process was simpler. He just hoped the inmates would be willing to see him.

As JP mulled over which file to dig deeper into next, his cell rang. It was his buddy from INS.

"Pedro, good to hear from you. What's up?"

"I found Miguel's mother, Maria Luciana Bigotes. We have her on an INS hold. It appears she's been in custody for a while, but it's a long story. I'll tell you over drinks sometime. The important thing is that we found her."

"What happens now?"

"Have Sabre set a court hearing, and I'll get the mother there. I have to send her back to Mexico, and I'd like to send the child with her if possible."

"How much time do you need for notice?"

"A day. Just have her set it as soon as possible. There's a big push to get illegals out of the country."

JP hung up and called Sabre, then delved back into the new stack of files. In the second one, a thirteen-year-old girl had been repeatedly raped by her hooker mom's boyfriends. She was angry at the world and spent much of her time fighting with other foster kids until she landed in a group home at fifteen. The fights had continued until she was released from the system six months earlier, when she turned eighteen. No forwarding address.

JP started his search by contacting family members. After children aged out of the dependency system, they often had nowhere to go. This appeared to be the case with Sharna. It wasn't unusual for kids to go right back to the environment from which they'd been removed. Since the case closing wasn't that long ago, JP had high hopes that some of the addresses and phone numbers would be current. He tried the number for her mother, but it was no longer valid. There weren't many other family members listed, none for the paternal side, and only an aunt on the mother's side. JP tried that number.

"Hello," a woman answered.

JP explained who he was and said he was following up on Sharna. "Have you seen her?"

"No. I visited her a few times in the group home, but I didn't even know she was out."

"Could she be with her mother?"

"She could, I guess, but I hope not."

"Why's that?"

"Because her mother is working the streets again. At least she was the last I heard. I haven't seen my niece in over a year."

"Does her mother have a home?"

"Not that I'm aware of. She used to work the area around Kansas Street and El Cajon Boulevard, and I doubt that's changed. If Sharna was looking for her, that's where she'd go."

JP considered going out to look for Sharna, but the chances of finding her were pretty slim. He didn't know what she looked like, and he didn't expect to get much cooperation on the streets. Instead, he called a friend in vice to see if he knew Sharna and/or her mother. His cop friend was familiar with the mother but had no knowledge of her daughter.

JP picked up the third slim file and read through it. The case had been closed for three years. The boy had entered the system at twelve, after being severely beaten by his stepfather for years. He couldn't function in foster care because he fought with the other children. He'd spent the last three years of his dependency in group homes, where he bullied younger, smaller kids.

JP's check into the boy's criminal record showed that, shortly after his eighteenth birthday, he'd been arrested for felony assault on an officer. He'd been released on probation, assaulted another officer, and was serving time for both offenses in Donovan.

JP opened up the first volume of the fourth case and jotted down the name and the basis for the petition. This child had been left alone for long periods due to her mother's drug abuse. It continued for years, with the girl bouncing in and out of the system. By the time she was a teenager she was moving from one foster home to another. Then she entered a gothic stage and proclaimed she was a witch. She spent years in therapy. The one thing she maintained was good grades even though she didn't like school, or at least she didn't like the other students. At eighteen she aged out of the system.

JP ran a criminal check on her, but found nothing, at least not in California. He then contacted her last foster parents, and to his surprise found that she was living with them, attending college, and working part time in a drug rehab center for teenagers. He placed the file in the reject stack and moved on to the last case.

He had hoped to find something in these cases that might lead them to Sabre's stalker because it was his last shot. He was beginning to think the perp wasn't connected to Sabre's work. As much as he hated the idea, he needed to ask Sabre about past relationships. He shuddered at the thought. He couldn't stand to hear about other men Sabre had been involved with, and his jealousy frustrated him. He'd never been that way with other women. *Why was it so different with Sabre?* He knew he loved her more than anyone he'd ever met, but their age difference bothered him. Sabre was barely thirty, and he was pushing fifty. She could have anyone she wanted, and he often questioned why she was with him.

JP picked up his cell phone to make another call, and it rang in his hand. "Hello. This is JP Torn."

"This is Sharna's aunt. I found her. Can you come?"

JP drove to El Cajon Boulevard, about three blocks from Kansas Street, and parked in front of a 24-hour diner. Two scantily-dressed women were on the sidewalk. The one wearing a short leather skirt and high heels approached his car. He waved her on. He climbed out and found the aunt waiting near the diner, just where she told him she would be. They introduced themselves and walked to an alley where several homeless people lounged against the wall.

"Sharna," the aunt said, kneeling down in front of a spaced-out young girl.

The girl blinked, but she could hardly hold up her head. "Auntie?" She tried to sit up but couldn't. "What are you doing here?"

"I was wondering the same about you," the aunt said.

"I came to find my mother."

"Did you?"

"Oh, yeah. She's here." Sharna's eyes kept closing. "Did you bring me some money?"

"No, I did not, but I'll get you help if you want it."

"I just need some money. That's all."

"I'll tell you the same thing I told your mother. You know where I live. If you decide to get clean, let me know."

Sabre was already home when JP arrived. Ron and Sabre had

stopped at the high school and picked up Conner. Ron was waiting for JP to return, although he wouldn't admit it. Sabre had adjusted to being babysat and enjoyed Ron's company. So, she chatted with him until JP got there.

JP kissed Sabre. "Everything go okay?" he asked.

"Just fine. And I talked to your friend at INS. We have Miguel's special hearing scheduled for tomorrow morning. Pedro said he would get the mother to court."

"Good," JP said. "Where's Conner?"

"He went to Morgan's school to walk her home," Sabre said. "How was your day?"

"Some good, some bad. I researched and investigated all those files on the teenagers we pulled, and I don't think any of them are the stalker. I'll give you details later."

Sabre peered out and saw the kids coming across the street. "There they are," she said.

"If you don't need anything," Ron said, "I'll take off."

"Thanks, Ron," Sabre and JP said together.

Ron gave Morgan a hug on his way out.

Sabre's cell phone beeped. She glanced over and swallowed.

"What is it?" JP asked.

"It just says 1-8-2." She looked questioningly at Conner. "Do you know what it means?"

Conner glanced at Morgan, then back at Sabre. Sabre put her arm around the girl. "We've got Girl Scout cookies in the kitchen if you'd like, and there's milk in the refrigerator."

Morgan dashed off, and Conner read the text. "It means *I hate you*." His brow wrinkled. "Are you in some danger?"

"No," JP spoke up. "We don't think so, but we're being cautious. Don't you worry."

CHAPTER 52

Friday, a.m.

"Ms. Brown, you asked for this special hearing, correct?" Judge Hekman said.

"Yes, Your Honor. We found Miguel's mother, Maria Luciana Bigotes, who is present in court, accompanied by Federal Agent Pedro Torres from INS, as well as a Spanish interpreter."

"And you're asking for a dismissal of the case?"

"Yes, Your Honor. I'm asking that the child be reunited with his mother, at which time, they will both be deported back to Mexico."

"Does the mother have an attorney?"

"No, Your Honor."

Judge Hekman looked to the back of the room where Bob was sitting. "Mr. Clark, are you available to counsel this mother?"

"Yes, Your Honor."

"Please do that now, and we will resume as soon as you're ready." She looked at County Counsel. "Where is Miguel now?"

"We have him upstairs in the Voices for Children office, Your Honor."

"Good."

They returned to the courtroom fifteen minutes later, and this time the mother had Bob at her side. The court appointed him to represent her.

"Have you advised your client, Mr. Clark?"

"Yes, Your Honor. I did that with the help of Patricia Leahy, the court interpreter." Sabre and Bob both liked using Patricia as their interpreter because she was so good at her job. She was also married to their good friend, Jerry Leahy.

"And what is your position?"

"My client is in agreement with the recommendations by DSS to dismiss the case."

"Does she understand that she and her son will be deported?"

"Yes, Your Honor," Bob said.

The judge explained the ramifications to the mother again, while Patricia translated. "Do you understand that your son was in a home with known drug traffickers?"

"Sí, Señora," she responded, and the interpreter translated.

"Do you understand that you could have lost your son forever if it wasn't for Mr. Torres and Ms. Brown?"

"Sí, Señora."

"You have been given a one-time chance to get your son back. I realize that you came to America to make a better life, but you almost lost your son in the process." The judge shifted to a sterner tone. "Imagine what might have happened if Social

Services hadn't stepped in and found Miguel. I hope you're taking this seriously."

The mother choked up when she responded, and the interpreter said, "I'm taking it very seriously. My son is the most important thing in the world to me."

Judge Hekman stopped her lecture and turned to Sabre. "Ms. Brown, will you please go get Miguel?"

Sabre left the courtroom, walked upstairs to the CASA office, and held her hand out to Miguel.

"Where are we going?"

"To the courtroom. The judge wants to talk to you. And there's someone else who wants to see you too."

Back downstairs, Sabre opened the courtroom door and walked inside with Miguel, his little hand still cupped inside hers. But as soon as he saw the woman sitting at the counsel table, he let go and ran to her.

"Mamacita, mamacita!" he cried out. "You came for me. I knew you would." Tears rolled down his mother's cheeks, as they stood holding on to each other. But the smile on Miguel's face told it all.

The judge let the reunification take place, giving them both time to express their love for one another. When the excitement settled down, Judge Hekman started again. "Ms. Bigotes, I hope you know how lucky you are that Miguel was not hurt during this whole ordeal." The interpreter translated as the judge spoke. Maria nodded and hugged Miguel tighter. "I can't begin to list the many things that could have happened to him. I also hope you know that you are getting a big break here." Maria nodded again. "Thanks to Agent Torres, you are getting the chance to take your child home. I would strongly urge you to not return to this country unless it is by a legal means."

"I promise I won't, madam," Patricia Leahy translated.

"The child is returned to the custody of the mother, and this case is dismissed. The attorneys are relieved," the judged ordered.

Sabre watched the boy exit with mother, and her heart soared for the first time in a week.

She and Bob worked through the rest of their morning cases. Bob was done first and waited outside until Sabre came out. He was talking to one of the bailiffs when Sabre walked up.

"You ready?" he asked.

"I'm ready."

"Do you want to have lunch? We can try another Vietnamese restaurant. Jim told me about one called Pho Saigon Bliss. It's on Canyon Murphy Road."

"Let's try it. The name sounds more authentic than Kevin's Noodle House."

"Yeah, that was okay, but I'm sure we can do better."

They walked to Bob's car. "We're having a birthday party for CJ next Sunday. He'd like Morgan to come."

"Of course. She'd like that," Sabre said. She opened the passenger door and started to get inside, but she saw something lying on the seat. "Eww!" She jumped back. "Is that real? Because it's not funny."

Bob opened the door and saw the tip of the head of a dead mouse peeking out of a brown paper bag. Its eyeballs stared up at them. Sabre started to reach down. "Don't touch it," Bob said. "That thing looks real to me, and I didn't put it there."

"Then where did it come from?" She took a deep breath. "Why did he have to kill that poor little thing?"

Bob removed a pen from his shirt pocket, leaned inside, and poked the bag. The head rolled onto the seat, startling

Sabre. She jumped back, took a deep breath, and then bent forward to get a better look inside the car.

"There's a yellow sticky note attached to the bag."

"What does it say?" Bob asked.

"*Watch out, or you could lose your ...*" Sabre stopped. "I can't see the rest. Give me your pen." Bob handed it to her, and she leaned in further and used the pen to flatten the note. "*Watch out, or you could lose your pretty little head too. 1-8-2.*"

"This guy is wacko," Bob said.

Sabre put her files on the top of Bob's car and took out her cell phone. She snapped several photos, making sure the note was legible. She glanced around at the windows to see if anything was broken. "How did they get in your car? It doesn't look like they broke in over here. Is your side damaged?"

Bob shook his head. "I didn't lock it. I seldom do unless I have files in the backseat."

"You still don't lock your car? Even after it was broken into that time?"

"No, because if they want in, they'll find a way. And then I'll have to pay for a broken window or damage to the car door. This way, the damage is minimal."

"You're a nut."

Sabre sent a text with the photos and a brief note to Detective Marlow. Then she turned to Bob. "I assume this is for me, but maybe not. Maybe it was intended for you. You've had some pretty crazy clients too."

"Yeah, but you're the one getting all the sweet messages. Besides, I don't have a pretty little head. And the 1-8-2 is definitely meant for you. No one hates me."

Sabre called JP.

~

Detective Marlow took more photos, then placed the mouse and note in an evidence bag. "Is this your car?"

"No, it belongs to my friend, Bob," Sabre said. "But I was riding with him to lunch."

"Did you ride with him this morning to court?"

"No, JP brought me."

"How would anyone know you would be in this car at some point?"

"Because we always go to lunch together, or at least three or four times a week."

"And you always take Bob's car?"

"No, we alternate. But since I didn't have my car here, it's obvious I would ride in Bob's."

"But someone would have to know your patterns, either someone who has known you a long time or has been watching you very closely."

"That's true," JP said, walking up. "I'm not making headway with my investigation either. Do you have anything that might help me?"

"No," Marlow said. "I don't expect to get any fingerprints from this either. Except for the sophistication of not leaving any evidence behind, it seems almost childlike."

"That's what Sabre and I thought too, so I went through every file she has, looking for a minor who might be a suspect. I struck out. I must be missing something, but I can't for the life of me figure it out. If the perp hadn't killed Jim Nicholson, I would say it was all a prank, but I think we have to take him seriously."

"I agree, but the brass is calling Nicholson a suicide."

Marlow shifted his toothpick. "We can't find any indication there was foul play."

"That doesn't make it a reality."

"I agree. And personally, I think it was ordered by Banks. We searched every angle we could on him. It seems awfully suspicious that two people connected to Banks have fallen to their death from a third-story window. But if it's him, he sure has his tracks covered."

"I have to assume Nicholson's death could have been murder. When it comes to protecting Sabre, I err on the side of caution."

"For your investigation, you may want to look a little wider, because as far as my department is concerned, this is not a murder investigation. My captain only left it open because he's a good guy. But I don't have much time to work the case, and a dead mouse won't buy me more time." Marlow shifted, his tone more upbeat. "It helps now that the gang unit is investigating Banks and those drive-by murders, because they keep me in the loop. We may not have anything on Banks now, but he'll make a mistake one of these days, and we'll nab him."

CHAPTER 53

Sunday, a.m.

"Thanks for meeting with me," JP said, as he sat across from Dale Fisher. JP had never been this close to him and hadn't realized what a big man he was. He was glad Fisher wasn't meeting him in a dark alley somewhere.

"It's always nice to have a visitor, even if it's a stranger." Fisher narrowed his eyes. "What do you want?"

"I saw you last Sunday when I was here visiting my brother. You kept looking at my girlfriend."

Fisher raised his eyebrows and sounded agitated. "Are you here to call me out on some dimepiece?"

JP thought it prudent not to object to the term *dimepiece*. "Not at all. Sabre was the attorney on your son's dependency case four years ago."

"Oh, her. Yeah, she looked familiar, and a nice-looking woman like that is hard to forget. I finally remembered where I'd seen her. But I still don't know why you're here."

JP kept eye contact with him. "I'll level with you. Someone has been sending threatening messages to her, and I'm trying to find out where they're coming from."

"And you think it might be me?" Fisher glanced around the room. "Can you see where I am? I can't do much from here. And why would I? I never even had a conversation with the woman. I only remember her looks because she's hot. That's hardly a reason to harass her."

"You got a little volatile with her in court one day."

Fisher laughed. "I get a little volatile with everyone who gets in my way. But it couldn't have been a big deal, because I don't even remember that one."

JP thought he sounded sincere. "Is there anyone in your family who might be involved in targeting her?"

"Not that I'd tell you if there was, but no one in my family cared if that child was taken away. As for his mom, she's in prison too, but that bitch didn't want the kid. All she wanted was her drugs."

"Thanks for seeing me and for your honesty." JP felt a little better and hoped he hadn't been conned.

"Thanks for the visit." Before Fisher left, he added. "I only have eight months left in this place, and although I have trouble controlling my temper, I'm sure not going to do anything else that keeps me inside."

JP approached the guard and told him he had another visit scheduled. The guard sent for Baxter, and JP was pleased to hear that Baxter had accepted his request to meet. Ten minutes passed before someone brought the inmate out. He was the father of Hannah, the six-year-old girl who'd been molested by her mother's boyfriend.

JP was thinking about how he should approach the subject when a man in his early forties with a shaved head walked up.

"You're JP Torn?"

"Yes."

"I'm Nick Baxter." He took a seat. "You related to Gene?"

"His brother."

"Gene's good people. What can I do for you?"

"I'm the private investigator for Sabre Brown, your daughter's attorney. She's getting threatening messages connected to the social worker on your case, Jim Nicholson, who, by the way, is dead now."

"Whoa. I didn't see that coming. How did he die?"

"We think someone killed him."

"And what does that have to do with me?"

"You went to the trial when she was fighting to keep your daughter away from Eastland and your ex."

"That's right. So?"

"Do you think Eastland, or your ex, might be angry enough to go after Ms. Brown?"

"I would love to think it was Eastland and have you pin it on him. I wouldn't be surprised if he hid behind nasty messages, but I doubt he killed Nicholson."

"Why not?"

"Because the man's a coward, and he only cares about himself. He wouldn't go out on a limb for anyone, not even my ex."

"What about her? Did you ever see a violent streak?"

"Not really. She's an idiot, but not violent."

JP decided to come right out and ask. "What about you?"

Baxter half smiled. "I knew you would get there."

JP looked him right in the eyes. "Did you have him killed?"

"Hell no. I don't have a reason to go after Nicholson, and why would I harass Ms. Brown? She got me everything I wanted in that case." Baxter leaned forward and lowered his voice. "If I had any pull from in here, I would use it to kick Eastland's ass for what he did to my daughter." Baxter stood and walked away, the conversation over.

On the drive back from Donovan, JP called Sabre and left a message saying they could probably eliminate the Baxter and Fisher cases.

CHAPTER 54

Sunday, p.m.

After dinner, Sabre and Morgan cleaned the kitchen while JP sat on the sofa petting Louie. The six o'clock local news played in the background. An image of Donovan Prison popped up on the screen, grabbing JP's attention. The caption read: *Prisoner stabbed: Donovan on lockdown.* JP's heart revved. *I hope it's not Gene*, he thought. He knew he couldn't let the kids see it, and Morgan was just around the corner. He muted the sound and watched the images. They didn't display a photo of the victim, but they did show the ambulance taking him away.

As soon as the news changed to something else, JP paused it to watch again later when Morgan wasn't so close. His heart was still pounding, and he prayed the inmate wasn't his brother.

Just then Sabre and Morgan came into the room.

"Whatcha watching?" Morgan asked, reaching down to pet Louie on the head.

"The news."

"Boring. I'm going to my room."

"Do you have homework, Munchkin?" JP asked.

"Just a little math, but I don't need any help. I'll go do it. If you decide to watch anything good on TV, let me know." She bent down and kissed the dog. "Want to go with me, Louie? Come on."

Louie jumped down and followed her as she walked away.

"You need to see this, Sabre." JP rewound the program until it reached the Donovan story. He un-muted the sound but kept it low. "Someone was stabbed at Donovan."

Sabre's face lost color. She sat down next to him.

The announcer said, "Donovan Prison is on lockdown tonight after an inmate was stabbed with a homemade knife."

Just then Conner walked in the room, and JP hit pause again.

"Uncle Johnny, I just saw that someone was stabbed at Donovan. What if it's Dad?"

"I just saw that, but so far they haven't given a name. Sit down." JP patted the cushion next to him.

Conner remained standing. "No, I can't. I need to know." He stood next to the sofa, wringing his hands.

JP turned the news back on. "All we know so far is that an inmate was stabbed by another inmate, and the victim was rushed to the hospital. He's undergoing surgery, but we don't know his condition. We don't yet know the victim's name or who stabbed him. The prison investigators are trying to contact the family before they release the victim's name."

"That's it?" Conner's voice cracked. "Dad didn't call tonight, did he?"

"No, he hasn't, but that doesn't mean he was hurt."

"Then why wouldn't he call?"

"Because they're on lockdown. That means no one leaves their cell, so no phone calls."

"You have to do something, Uncle Johnny. You have to find out who it is."

JP had never seen Conner so upset, even when he was dealing with his own murder charges. JP wondered how much time Conner spent worrying about this very thing happening to his father. JP knew what that felt like, but it made him angrier with his brother for being in that position. Gene knew better. He knew what they had gone through as kids, always wondering if their father would get hurt in prison. JP's feelings were all mixed up with anger and fear. "I'll make some calls."

"Is there anything I can do?" Sabre asked.

"Just make sure Morgan stays in her room while I do this."

Sabre left, and JP called his long-time friend, Deputy Sheriff Ernie Madrigal and told him about the news report. "Do you know anything? I just want to make sure it wasn't my brother, Gene."

"Let me see what I can find out. I'll call you back."

JP tried making small talk with Conner but had little success. Sabre came out every ten minutes to see if there was any news. Conner kept pacing. He went to his room once but returned within five minutes. JP kept the news on in case there was an update. The weather report came on and then was interrupted.

The news announcer said, "We just got word that the victim of the Donovan stabbing is dead. He did not survive the surgery. We still have no name, nor do we know if the perpetrator was caught. Donovan remains on lockdown."

Half an hour went by before Ernie called back and said, "It's not your brother."

JP sighed and then told Conner, "It's not your dad. Can you go tell Sabre and ask her to come out here?"

Conner left, and JP finished his conversation. "I'm so relieved. Do you know what happened?"

"The victim was stabbed with a shank on the way to dinner. They think they know who did it, but I don't have details on that, so I'm not sure. The victim was a guy named Dale Fisher. He ..."

"Fisher?"

"Yeah, do you know him?"

"I just saw him today." JP took a deep breath. "Please let me know when you find out who the attacker was."

"Are you worried that it might be Gene?"

"I sure hope not, but I can't say that I know him well enough to be certain."

CHAPTER 55

Monday, a.m.

The White Case

Child: Suzie White, Age 7 (F)
Parents: Father—Thomas White, Jr. & Mother—Georgia
White
Issues: Neglect, Sexual Abuse
Facts: Suzie was allegedly molested by the paternal grandfa-
ther, a member of their household. Parents continued to live
with him.

"How was your weekend?" Bob asked Sabre as they walked
out of the attorney lounge on Monday morning.

"Morgan and I went shopping for CJ's birthday present.
She's pretty excited about what she bought for him." Sabre
smiled grimly. "And I received another text from my stalker."

"What did you get this time?"

Sabre opened her phone and showed Bob the photo she'd received. "I got this last night."

"It looks like a dead person," Bob said.

"That's right."

"Anyone you know?"

"No. Do you recognize him?"

Bob took a closer look. "Nope, but that's taken right out in front of this courthouse. That's disturbing."

"I think I'm getting numb to all this," Sabre commented. "It doesn't even bother me that much anymore. I'm sure if it was a picture of someone I knew, I would feel far worse." She paused, remembering her original reaction. "I was concerned that this guy was killed because of me. But Marlow said nothing happened in front of our courthouse, so that part must have been photoshopped. He's checking it out." Sabre took a deep breath. "Other than that, the weekend went well. We took the kids to the zoo on Saturday, and on Sunday we had a barbecue lunch after JP returned from his trek to Donovan."

"He was there yesterday during the lockdown?"

"No, he left before the stabbing took place. JP had just interviewed a couple of my stalker suspects. One was the guy who was killed, Dale Fisher."

"Oh no. Do you think he was your stalker?"

"No, because I got that text last night after he was already dead, but JP thinks it's somehow related." Sabre hesitated.

"You're concerned about that stabbing. What is it?"

"After our visit to see Gene, Fisher questioned him about me. JP's worried that Gene may have gotten more involved than he should have."

"Has he talked to him?"

"No, they were still on lockdown last night. I'm not sure

about today, and I know they've arrested someone and have him confined, but we have no idea who it is."

Sabre's phone beeped with another text. She looked at it and rolled her eyes.

"What this time?"

"It's another dead body. Nobody I know." She put her phone up so Bob could get a closer look.

"Me either."

Sabre sent a copy of the text to Marlow, and they continued through the lobby in silence. Finally, Bob asked, "Did you do any work this weekend?"

"I saw Suzie White, so I could be ready for this trial. JP went with me, of course. He won't let me out of his sight."

"How was Suzie?"

"She's in a foster home, but she's pretty lonely. She misses her brother a lot. Her Aunt Anita has been visiting her, and that's going well. She likes seeing her cousin Becky, and she's even had an overnight there, which helps some."

"Any chance Anita will take her in?"

"I don't think so. It's a struggle for her, having to fight with that family all the time. It might be different if Grandpa wasn't around."

Bob spotted JP standing next to the information desk and walked toward him. "Why is JP here?"

"Don't talk to him."

Bob looked at Sabre. "Don't talk to him?"

"Yeah, he's here to keep an eye on me and watch for anyone acting strangely toward me. Hopefully, whoever it is won't know we're together. It's a long shot, but we don't know what else to do, and JP is about to go out of his mind with worry." Sabre smiled. "So, humor him."

"Okay, ignore the guy it is. Let's take care of the White

case." Bob started down the hall. "With the new information, the judge hoped we could settle this. If not, we have to come back for trial this afternoon."

"I just got the supplemental report, but I haven't had a chance to read it all yet. I got as far as grandpa's 'accident.'" She made air quotes. "Did someone really try to kill him?"

"Yes, they did. My client said someone cut his brake line, and he crashed. He didn't get hurt badly though. Then the cops arrested him."

Sabre stopped. "For the accident?"

"No, for twenty-three counts of child molestation on three of his grandchildren, including Suzie."

"Good, I hope he rots in jail." She started for the courtroom again.

"Me too." Bob followed, still talking about the bust. "The cops found tons of child porn downloaded on his computer, and in the last year and a half, he took three trips to Thailand. What do you suppose he was doing there?"

"I can only imagine. Do they have any suspects for the attempted murder?" She was only curious, not particularly concerned.

"Not that I'm aware of."

"I wonder if it was one of his boys," Sabre mused. "He apparently helped them all financially. Maybe one wanted the rest of his money right away."

"If they did, the joke's on them. As it turned out, he was going broke. He had refinanced the house so there's no equity left. Also, his bank account was down to nothing, and he was in debt. The money all went to Thailand trips and porn. He didn't even have the cash for an attorney, so he's represented by the public defender."

"He's a sick man. How are his sons taking it?"

"According to my client, they're mad as hell." Bob laughed. "Not about what he did, but because there's no money left."

"Nice family."

Bob stopped this time and looked curiously at Sabre. "You didn't get a text on this one, did you?"

"No, at least not yet."

"Great. Can we settle this case since Grandpa is no longer a threat?"

"We still need to take jurisdiction and get these parents into housing," Sabre said. "They need to be monitored for a while even though Grandpa's not around. And even if I were willing to let Suzie go home at this point, which I am not, DSS will not go along with it." Sabre started for the courtroom again, worried about being late. "If Grandpa gets convicted and receives a sentence long enough for Suzie to reach majority, then I'll consider it. I'm not taking a chance on him getting out on bail or only a slap on the hand. I'm sorry, but I do not trust your client or Suzie's father to protect her from that man."

"I knew that's what you'd say."

"Talk to your client and see if the parents will enter a plea to the jurisdiction. We can set the child's placement over for about six weeks, and by then we may know what's happening with Grandpa." She stopped outside the courtroom. "Or maybe your client will go it alone without the father who is too influenced by his dad. However it shakes out, we should have a better perspective by then."

"I'll talk to my client."

"I'll wait inside," Sabre said. "Make sure Powers and the father are on board too. I really don't want to come back here this afternoon. And if we settle it this morning, Suzie won't need to testify. You know you can't win jurisdiction on this one."

"Oh, I know that, not with Hekman on the bench. But if my client wants her day in court, she can have it. I'll give her a good dog-and-pony show."

Within ten minutes, Bob entered the courtroom. Another hearing was in session, so he sat next to Sabre in the back and whispered, "If the department is in agreement, we'll submit on jurisdiction and set dispo over for six weeks."

"I already spoke with County Counsel, and she's fine with it."

"I'll make an argument for unsupervised visits."

"I'd expect nothing less. I'll oppose it, and you'll lose."

"I know, but expect a battle at the disposition trial."

"If Grandpa is out of the picture, you may not have one. Suzie really misses her parents and her brother."

"It looks like they're done," Bob said. "Let's do this."

The case went just as Sabre expected. The parents entered pleas, disposition was set over for six weeks, and visits remained supervised.

They left the courtroom and started down the hallway when Sabre felt her phone vibrate. She answered the call from Detective Marlow.

"We haven't been able to determine who the dead people are in those photos, but we do know that one is from a website called *Dreamstime*. They sell photos of just about anything you want."

"That's kind of creepy."

"Not really. Most are just everyday photos that people would use on their websites or graphic art. They're not all gruesome."

"So, it was just for effect."

"That's right, and the one in front of juvenile court is photoshopped. We don't know where the body picture came from, but it could've been from anywhere online."

CHAPTER 56

Monday, a.m.

JP waited outside the courtroom for Sabre to come out. He continued to follow her around the building, keeping enough distance to not draw attention to himself. He tried to keep his mind on the task at hand, but it was difficult because he was so worried about his brother. *Did Gene learn something about Fisher that made him realize he was a danger to our family? And, if he did, was he the one who killed him?* JP wanted to believe that Gene wouldn't go that far, but the truth was, he just didn't know.

JP shook his head and made himself concentrate on the people. He was no good to Sabre if he couldn't focus. He observed a couple, who looked homeless, intertwined and kissing near the patio door. *There's someone for everyone,* JP thought.

He watched people come and go from the crowded court-house, looking for anyone who paid attention to Sabre. He observed as David Carr, an attorney, flirted with her. JP took a step closer, feeling his cheeks flush. He wanted to step in, and normally he would've taken action, but instead, he just mentally added Carr to his suspect list. JP didn't want to blow his cover, and he wasn't there to make a scene.

He moved on and observed the bailiffs, the interpreters, the attorneys and social workers, but especially the lay people. Some were crying, some were laughing, and many were angry. The only thing suspicious he saw were a few glances from men as Sabre walked past, but they were nothing more than a quick look at a beautiful woman. He couldn't blame them. Every once in a while, out of habit, he would reach for his holster. He felt naked without his gun, but he couldn't wear it in the courthouse.

He followed Sabre from Department One, down the hallway and through the lobby until they reached Department Four, which sat two doors inside the east hallway. Standing at the entrance was a big, bearded man dressed in leathers—the word *Mongols* prominently displayed across the back of his vest. JP knew the Mongols to be one of the most tenacious motorcycle gangs in southern California. He had dealt with many of them as a young cop. JP kept a close eye on the Mongol, although the guy never paid any attention to Sabre, not even when she walked past him.

Sabre took a seat on a bench and looked at her phone, presumably at a text. JP glanced around to see if anyone was texting. He saw a woman staring at her phone as if she were waiting for a response. He walked over and sat down by her, but she didn't seem to notice. He looked over her shoulder to see what was on her phone screen—a grocery list.

Sabre got up and headed inside Department Four. JP waited in the hall, observing the masses. Ten minutes later, he felt his phone vibrate in his pocket. He removed it and read a text from Sabre: *On my last case. This one should be short.*

JP texted back: *When you're done, walk to Bob's car with him. I'll follow. If nothing suspicious, have Bob drive you to my truck.*

Sabre: *OK*

It wasn't long before Sabre and Bob exited the courtroom and walked outside. JP followed, keeping his distance. A man in his late thirties started across the street behind the two. JP picked up his pace and was within a few feet, when the man stopped at a car and got inside. JP sighed and walked on. He was getting too jumpy, but he had no idea who or what he was looking for.

He reached Sabre just as she climbed into Bob's car. He walked past her and said, "Meet me at the Shell station."

JP kept moving. His truck was parked two rows away. He looked around, but saw no one suspicious, and it didn't appear that anyone had followed Sabre. He left the parking lot and drove to the gas station two blocks away. Less than a minute later, Bob drove up, Sabre got out, and climbed inside his truck. Just as she did, JP's phone rang. Curt Marlow's name came up on the navigation screen.

"Hi Curt," JP said as he hit the receive button.

"We found Nicholson's suicide note," Curt said without any formalities.

"Does it seem legit?"

"We're still investigating, but so far it does. It was hand-written, and we're verifying his writing now. I'll let you know as soon as I learn more."

"Thanks." JP turned to Sabre and said, "That was interesting. But I'm still not convinced."

"I'm sure we'll know more soon." She paused. "So, have you heard anything more about the Donovan stabbing?"

"No, nothing."

"Did you learn anything today at court?"

"Not really, except there are a lot of strange people at your courthouse. But I guess I already knew that. I just hadn't paid that close attention."

Sabre's phone beeped with an incoming text. She read the message and said, "That's weird."

"What is it?" JP asked, not hiding his concern.

"Look." She turned the phone toward him. "It's a really old, dirty fedora. It looks like something out of the forties. Why would someone send me a photo of a hat?"

A second text came in. Sabre read it out loud. "He would want you to have it. 1-8-2."

"What does that mean?" JP asked.

Sabre didn't answer as she studied the photo. "JP, this was taken near the back door of my office. It's setting on the step."

"Maybe it was photoshopped like the other ones."

"Either way, he had to be at my office to take the photo, with or without the hat."

"Let's go see."

JP drove to Sabre's building and pulled around to the back parking lot. Before they got out of the truck, Sabre pointed. "There it is." She picked up her cell and called Detective Marlow. JP called Ron and told him to install cameras.

CHAPTER 57

Tuesday, a.m.

The next day, JP went to court with Sabre again. He watched her every move, but nothing unusual happened. At noon, Sabre rode with Bob to In-N-Out, and JP followed and joined them inside.

"This is a good day," Sabre said, as they waited for their order. "So far, I haven't received any bizarre texts."

"Have you been getting something every day?" Bob asked.

"Lately, I have. He has definitely escalated his text attacks. All the recent ones have the 1-8-2 message."

"He's making sure you know he hates you."

"I think he made that point perfectly clear."

"Well, don't be too disappointed. It's early yet," Bob said flippantly. "You can still hear from him."

JP had been sitting quietly, listening to the banter, but finally broke his silence. "I'm glad you two think this is so funny."

"Aren't you the grump today," Bob retorted.

"I'm sorry. It's just that I'm worried and frustrated, and I don't have any idea where to look next."

Sabre reached over and put her hand on his knee, squeezing it lovingly. "I'm not trying to make light of it. Well, I guess I am, but I don't know how else to handle it. I promise you, I'm being very watchful."

"I know," he muttered.

They ate their burgers in near silence, occasionally mentioning something unrelated. As they got ready to leave, Sabre's phone beeped. They looked at each other for a second before she checked her message. The blood drained out of Sabre's face.

JP grabbed her phone. It was another photo of a dead man.

"This is ridiculous," JP said

"What is it, Sobs?" Bob asked. "You're white as a ghost."

Sabre took the phone back and showed the image to Bob.

"That looks like Wagner."

"That's what I thought."

"Are you sure it's him?" JP asked.

"No, I can't be certain, but it sure looks like him."

Sabre found Richard Wagner in her contact list and called. It went straight to voice mail. She texted, asking him to call her as soon as possible.

"He's not answering," she said. She looked at JP, then turned to Bob. "I talked to Wags this morning, and he said he had a trial this afternoon. He probably has his phone shut off."

"Should we go to court and see if he's there?" JP asked.

"Yes, of course," Sabre said, her voice shaking. "In the meantime, I'll forward the photo to Marlow and tell him our concerns."

When they got to the courthouse, JP went in first so he

could keep an eye out for anything suspicious. She and Bob stalled, then walked in a few minutes later. The lobby was almost empty, except for a few witnesses waiting to be called. Sabre stopped at the information desk to ask where Wagner's trial was, then headed down the hall to Department Two. Just as they reached the door, Wagner came out. Sabre grabbed him and hugged him.

"I don't know what prompted that," Wagner said, "but don't stop now."

"I'm just glad to see you're alive."

"Am I supposed to be dead? Because I didn't get the memo."

They sat on the bench, and Sabre showed him the photo and explained what was going on.

"That's insane." Wagner looked stunned and tapped the image. "That's what I wore to court one day last week. I remember because my wife said the shirt and tie didn't match, but I wore it anyway."

"She was right," Bob said. "You should've listened to her."

Wagner ignored him. "I can assure you, I'm very much alive."

"Do you remember which day you wore that?" Sabre asked.

"It was later in the week, either Thursday or Friday. I'm not sure which. No, it had to be Thursday because I wasn't here on Friday. Maybe it was Wednesday."

Sabre's phone rang. "Hi, Marlow."

"I had a technician get right on this, and the last image you sent was photoshopped," the detective said.

"Yeah, I just figured that out. Wagner is sitting right here with me."

"Not much time or effort was taken to make it look real,"

Marlow added. "I don't know if that means he didn't care or didn't have enough time to do it right."

"The photo was taken last week, probably Wednesday or Thursday," Sabre said. "That's when he wore that shirt."

"So, it was your friend, Richard Wagner, for sure?"

"Yes. Do you think it was a warning?" Sabre put the phone on speaker so everyone could hear.

"I would tell your friend to watch his back. And please text me his phone number so I can ask him a few questions. If we can connect someone to him, it might help us figure this whole thing out."

"Will do," Sabre said.

"Now, if you'll take me off speaker, I have some other information about Nicholson, you and JP will be interested in."

"Better yet, we'll go outside, so we can both hear you." She said goodbye to Bob and Wagner, and she and JP walked to his truck.

"What've you got?" JP asked.

"We had the suicide note analyzed. It was Nicholson's handwriting. Of course, he could have been forced to write it, but there's no evidence of that. In fact, the expert said he didn't appear to be under duress when he wrote it. She explained how the lettering would be shaky and how some things would differ, but I don't give that a lot of credence. It seems that's very much an opinion on her part."

They heard the click of Marlow's toothpick.

"The note outlined his financial trouble. He said he had started gambling again and couldn't stop. He claimed that no one really loved him. We already know that he was somewhat of a loner, which gives credence to that statement. He also stated that his job was too stressful." The detective shuffled papers in the background. "His exact words were that he was 'tired of the molesters and druggies who didn't deserve to have children.' His last comment was that he didn't want to die a long, agonizing death."

"Do you have any idea what he meant by that? Was he sick?"

"We didn't find anything in his medical records, but we learned something when I finally reached Nicholson's brother. He said their father died of a brain tumor. He apparently suffered for months and went a little crazy from it. That would explain Nicholson's comment about a 'long, agonizing death.'"

"Are you closing the case?"

"We're officially calling Nicholson's death a suicide."

"One other thing," JP said. "We know it was Dale Fisher who was killed at Donovan. Have you been able to tie him into this whole stalker thing?"

"No, but I heard you had a chat with Fisher a few hours before he was killed. Is there anything you care to share with me?"

"He seemed legit. I was about to delete him from the list of suspects, but now I don't know what to think."

"They're still on lockdown, but it should lift soon, and I'll be able to get more information. They're confident they have the killer, but I don't know the motive yet."

"I heard he was a white guy. That's about all I have."

CHAPTER 58

Wednesday, a.m.

JP accompanied Sabre to court again the next day and kept a watchful eye on her. For the first few hours, nothing out of the ordinary happened, and he saw no one he could seriously consider a suspect. But just after ten, he glanced at the front door and saw a familiar blond man walk in and empty his pockets onto the metal detector belt.

After gathering up his things, the man glanced around, then strode down the east hall. JP kept an eye on him, glad that Sabre was in Department One, off the west wing. Todd Lynch walked to the end, turned around, and headed for the information counter. JP moved to the other side to stay out of sight. Lynch spoke to the desk clerk, then walked to the door leading upstairs.

JP hurried over to the nearest bailiff and said, "Please let Mike McCormick know that Todd Lynch is in the courthouse."

"Sure."

JP started for the stairs, texting Ron at the same time: *Come to court.*

Ron quickly texted back: *I'm at Sabre's office installing cameras.*

JP: *I need you right now. Lynch is here.*

Ron: *Be there in five.*

JP followed Lynch upstairs, giving him enough time to reach the next level, so Lynch wouldn't know he was following. When he reached the landing, JP saw Lynch walking along the mezzanine wall that overlooked the lobby. A moment later, Lynch entered the clerk's office.

JP sent a text to Sabre: *Lynch is here. Please stay out of sight if you can.*

She didn't text back. JP didn't know if she was in a hearing and couldn't respond, or if she hadn't seen it at all. His phone dinged with a message from Ron: *I'm here. What next?*

JP texted back: *Come upstairs to the mezzanine.*

A few minutes later, JP met Ron in the stairwell and explained where Lynch was. "Please keep an eye on him. If he sees me, he'll recognize me and get suspicious. He won't know who you are. You've never seen him, right?"

"Right."

JP scrolled for an image, showed it to Ron, then sent him the photo. "Lynch is wearing jeans and a black t-shirt with an American flag. He should be easy to spot when he comes out of the clerk's office. Very few people roam around up here."

"There's no other way out?"

"He has to go down these stairs." JP cleared his throat. "Unless you want to throw him over the wall. That would be fine with me."

"I'll leave that sort of thing to you."

"Another reason why *you* should follow Lynch instead of me."

"Where will you be?" Ron asked.

"Downstairs, to talk to McCormick. He's hated that guy since he first came to court, and now that it looks like he might be Sabre's stalker, he'll really want to put him in his place. Text me when he comes out."

JP left and ran into McCormick in the lobby. "Can we step outside? Todd Lynch is here, and I don't want him to see me."

"What's he doing?" McCormick asked, as they walked out.

"My guess is he's looking for Sabre."

"You think he's the one who's sending her those texts?"

"I considered him, then kind of let it go. But several things have happened to put Lynch back at the top of my list. Now that he's here, it's looking even more likely, unless he has a darn good reason to be in court. His case transferred a long time ago."

"Do you want me to find out?"

"Would you? I'm afraid if I confront him, he'll think I'm harassing him. And if I don't like his answers, I'm liable to punch the guy."

"Yeah, that wouldn't be good," McCormick said. "Let me do it." He smiled. "Does Sabre know he's here?"

"I sent her a text, but I don't know if she got it."

"I'll check in with her. She should stay wherever she is until we get him out of here."

"The last I knew she was in Department One."

"I'll notify the bailiff there."

"Thanks, Mike. In the meantime, I'll call Detective Marlow and let him know."

JP kept out of sight and waited.

Fifteen minutes passed before Lynch came out of the clerk's office. Ron texted JP, then followed Lynch downstairs. By the time he reached the bottom step, McCormick was standing there, waiting for him. Ron stopped where he could hear the conversation, but not be visible.

"Hello, Mr. Lynch," McCormick said.

"Hello," Todd said, trying to walk past him.

"We need to talk. Do you mind coming with me?"

"In fact, I do mind."

"Maybe you should come anyway."

"I have things to do."

"You can do them when we're done."

Another bailiff approached. "Need any help?"

"You can help me escort Mr. Lynch to the back for some questioning."

"All right, I'll go." Lynch put up his hands, palms out. "Just keep your hands off me."

CHAPTER 59

Wednesday, a.m.

Curt Marlow walked into a back office at the courthouse, escorted by a bailiff. He'd spoken briefly to JP out front, but his priority was Todd Lynch. Another bailiff stood from his desk and stuck out his hand. "Mike McCormick."

Marlow introduced himself and took a seat.

"You're just in time," McCormick said. "I was about to ask Mr. Lynch some questions about why he's here. You can do the honors, if you'd like."

"Who are you?" Lynch asked with a sneer.

"I just told you, Detective Marlow, San Diego PD." Then he added, "Homicide Division."

"Homicide!" Todd's voice pitched higher, and his eyes flashed with fear. "I sure as hell haven't killed anyone."

"I didn't say you did," Marlow responded nonchalantly, as he chewed his toothpick. "Please explain why you're here in San Diego at juvenile court."

"I came to get copies of court records, not that it's any of your business."

"Where are your copies?"

"They have to mail them." He rolled his eyes. "I guess they need time to copy the files."

"Why didn't you do it by phone?" Marlow asked.

"I tried that, but I didn't get very far. So, I thought I could just pick them up." Lynch's shoulders tensed. "Is there a law against being in this courthouse or something?"

"Before you went upstairs, you walked to the end of the hall." Marlow flipped his toothpick. "Who were you looking for?"

"You were watching me?" Lynch's anger mounted.

"Just answer the question, please."

"I don't have to answer that."

"You do if you want to get out of here any time soon."

Lynch was silent for a few seconds, then said, "I was looking for the entrance to the clerk's office."

"Right," McCormick said.

"Can I go now?"

Marlow leaned toward him. "Are you here to see Sabre Brown?"

"What?" Lynch jumped up. "I want no part of that woman."

"The letters and emails you've sent her say otherwise."

"I never threatened her."

"I didn't say you did."

"Is someone after her? Because I can understand why. That woman destroyed my life!" he yelled. "I hope whoever it is gets the job done."

Marlow waited, hoping the man would incriminate himself.

"Did she call the cops on me?" Lynch complained.

"Because I have every right to be here. And if she called the cops, she's harassing me."

Marlow kept his voice deadpan. "Were you looking for Ms. Brown when you walked down that hallway?"

"No!" Lynch yelled. "I was looking for the door to go upstairs, like I just told you."

Marlow questioned Lynch for another thirty minutes, but he got no admission. He escorted him out of the building without making an arrest.

JP met Marlow as he re-entered the courthouse.

"You let him go?" JP asked.

"I didn't have cause to hold him."

"Why was he here if it wasn't to harass Sabre?"

"He said he just wanted to pick up court documents."

"And you believed him?"

"McCormick checked with the clerk, and Lynch did have copies made of his old file."

"That was just a ruse."

"I'm sure it was, but I still had no probable cause to arrest him." Marlow flicked his toothpick. "JP, I know you're frustrated, but at least now we know who we're looking for and can keep an eye on him."

"He'd better hope you catch him instead of me."

"Don't do anything stupid, my friend."

CHAPTER 60

Thursday, p.m.

JP picked up Conner from school. As soon as the boy got in the truck, he asked, "Any word from Dad yet?"

"No, sorry, kid. I heard they lifted the lockdown this morning though. So, I expect we'll be hearing soon."

Conner sat quietly for a while, then asked, "Why do you suppose he hasn't called yet today?"

"I imagine there are a lot of people trying to make calls. He'll have to wait his turn."

"You don't think it's something else, do you?"

"Like what?" JP was pretty certain he knew what Conner was getting at, but he didn't want to put any ideas in his head.

"Do you think Dad might have killed him?"

"Do you?"

"No, I don't really. Dad isn't like that, but it's different inside. I know from that time I spent in the Hall. You have to protect yourself, and you start to think differently than you do on the outside. My dad is a good man. He has always been good to us kids, but he has a temper and sometimes doesn't think about the consequences."

"I expect we'll hear from him soon," JP said. But if Gene thought Fisher might hurt his kids, who knew what he could have done. Still, JP had to reassure Conner. And if Gene had done it, that meant he knew something important. He had to see his brother. Now that the lockdown was lifted, Sabre could get in to see him as his attorney.

When they returned to the house, Conner said hello to Sabre and went to his room.

"I heard they lifted the lockdown at Donovan this morning," Sabre said. "Have you heard from Gene?"

"Not a word. And the kids keep asking why he doesn't call, even though I explained there was a lockdown and that he can't."

"How's Conner handling it?"

"It's weighing heavy on him. Lots of crazy thoughts going through that kid's head."

"You can't blame him."

"I know. Conner is tougher than a two-dollar steak, but if it turns out Gene killed that guy, it's going to shatter him, and Morgan too."

After dinner, Sabre sat on the sofa and prepped for her upcoming trial. Conner and Morgan were both in their rooms, and JP was working at his desk. When the phone rang, he glanced at it: Global Tel Link. He grabbed the cell and answered it.

As soon as Gene came on the line, JP said, "It's about time you called. We're all going a little nuts here worrying about you."

"Oh, Jackie, I didn't know you cared."

"I care because your kids are freaking out."

"I was afraid of that, but I called as soon as I could. They just let us out of our cells this morning, and everyone and their brother lined up to use the phone."

"Let me get the kids. They need to hear your voice, but I want to talk to you afterward."

"Okay, Jackie."

JP covered the phone and called out, "Conner. Morgan. Your dad's on the line."

Conner rushed into the living room, with Morgan right behind. JP handed him the cell, but Morgan looked like she was about to cry. Conner gave the phone to her. "You talk to him first. I'm okay now."

Morgan chatted in her usual form, saying more than she heard. Then she said, "I love you too, Daddy. Here's Conner."

Conner took the device and went to his room. A few minutes later, he returned with a pleased expression. He smiled at JP as he handed over the phone.

Once both kids were gone, JP asked, "Did you have anything to do with Fisher's death?"

"I can't believe you'd ask me that, brother."

"That doesn't answer the question."

"No, I didn't. They already got the guy who shanked him."

"Do you know what happened?"

"Fisher got mad and mouthy with the wrong guy. I knew that temper would get him sooner or later."

JP sighed.

"Really, JP, I wasn't involved. I take it they haven't found Sabre's stalker yet."

"No, but I'm keeping a good eye on her and the kids as well. We're not leaving them alone until this is over."

CHAPTER 61

Friday, a.m./p.m.

The Hendrickson Case

Child: Unity Hendrickson, Age 11 (F)
Parents: Father—Harvey Hendrickson & Mother—Vicki
Hendrickson
Disposition: Dirty Home, Alcohol Abuse, Domestic Violence
Facts: Returning case, new to Sabre, same issues each time.

Sabre finished her calendar around eleven-thirty, then she and Bob rode together to lunch. JP followed, still acting as a lookout.

After they ate, Sabre turned to JP. "Why don't you get going? You don't want to be late for Morgan's parent/teacher conference."

"Maybe I should reschedule it. I hate to leave you alone."

"What am I?" Bob said. "Chopped liver?"

"I didn't mean that," JP said.

Sabre tried to ease JP's concerns. "Now that we know it's Lynch, we can spot him easily if he shows up. And every bailiff will be watching for him."

"We don't know for sure that it's Lynch," JP argued.

"You don't think it's him?" Bob asked.

"Yes, I do," JP said. "But I should be in court just in case."

"Either way, few people will be in the courthouse this afternoon, so there won't be many to watch," Sabre reasoned. "The only case I have is the Hendrickson trial, so I'll be upstairs in the DA's office talking to my client and prepping her for testimony. Then I'll go to one courtroom, do the trial, and I'll be done. By then, you'll be back to pick me up. Or Bob can drop me somewhere."

"I guess you're right," JP said. "I really shouldn't miss the teacher meeting."

"Besides, what's the worst that could happen? I might get another text. And truthfully, they don't scare me anymore. They've just become extremely annoying."

"That's my concern. You should be scared because you're more careful when you're scared."

"Okay, I'm scared." Sabre smiled.

JP kissed her and started to walk away. He stopped and looked at Bob. "You better keep an eye on her."

"I will."

Before he turned away again, JP said, "Maybe I should send Ron to be the lookout."

"Just go." Sabre waved him off. "I'll be fine."

"Okay. I'll be back as soon as the meeting is over. If you finish beforehand, let me know."

~

Bob and Sabre walked toward the courthouse from the parking lot.

"I have one other case this afternoon in Department Two, but it shouldn't take long," Bob said. "I'll do that first if I can, and then I'll be ready for our trial."

As they approached the entrance, Sabre spotted Vicki Hendrickson standing outside. "There's your lovely client now. I'll leave you with her. I have to pick up a report and check on Unity."

As Bob approached her, Vicki smiled coquettishly. Then she turned to Sabre, and her lips thinned as she bared her teeth slightly. Vicki turned back to Bob with a smile.

"Good afternoon, Ms. Hendrickson," Sabre said, as she walked by. She got no response and continued into the courthouse.

Sabre went directly to the attorney lounge to pick up supplemental reports. She found a social study and the psychological evaluation on Vicki. Sabre tucked them into her folder and went upstairs to see if Unity had arrived. At the top of the stairs, she turned right and headed for the DA's office. She heard a noise and turned around. At the far end of the hallway, past the restrooms, she saw someone enter the room that housed the San Diego Court Appointed Special Advocates chapter. No one else was in sight.

Sabre checked inside the DA's office to see if Unity was there, but the girl hadn't yet arrived, so she sat outside the office on a bench and commenced reading the report.

Vicki Hendrickson suffers from pathological jealousy, a disorder in which she is preoccupied with the thought that her partner is being unfaithful, without having any real proof, along with abnormal behavior regarding these thoughts. Some examples that she admitted to with her last partner were 1) questioning his phone calls, 2) checking his social media accounts, and 3) searching through his belongings, often finding things that she could use to "prove" he was being unfaithful. When questioned about the things she found, they did not appear to be proof of any kind, but rather normal behaviors. She continually denied that she was jealous, although she admitted to examining the bedsheets, his underwear, and his genitalia for evidence of infidelity.

In women, the strongest trigger for this disorder is emotional infidelity. This frequently leads to stalking and often violence, or as a final resort, to suicide or murder of whoever she has fixated on. Women are much less likely to kill their partner than men, unless it is self-defense, but it does happen. Also, there is the possibility of violence toward someone outside of the relationship if Vicki has fixated on one particular individual as the cause of her partner's infidelity.

Morbid jealousy can occur in a number of conditions, such as chronic alcoholism, addiction to substances other than alcohol, organic brain disorders such as Parkinson's or Huntington's, schizophrenia, neurosis, or personality disorders. The social study and Vicki's own admission indicate that she may have a problem with alcohol. Further investigation is warranted to determine if alcoholism, or any of the other disorders named, is present.

It is recommended that Vicki Hendrickson begin cognitive behavioral therapy immediately and be seen by a medical doctor for possible diagnosis of other physical disorders. Also, it is recommended that she be seen by a psychiatrist to determine if antipsychotic or antidepressant medication is warranted. The history of alcohol abuse needs to be addressed. If there is any indication of illegal-drug abuse, that issue needs *to be treated immediately as well, as the morbid jealousy may be a manifestation of the addiction.*

The actions of a morbidly jealous parent may put the children living in that household at risk. They may witness violence between the parents or overhear arguments that frighten them. They could be accidently injured if assaults take place. The parent with the disorder may employ a child to spy on their intimate partner or to share unnerving secrets. Often the child can become a witness to a homicide or suicide.

Sabre heard footsteps and glanced up to see Bob approaching. "Did you get the psych eval?" she asked.

"I just read it." Bob smiled. "I love the nutjobs. They sure spice up a case."

"You'd better be careful. I think Vicki is *fixating* on you now." Sabre used air quotes.

Bob sat down beside her.

"I'm not sure I want you that close to me," Sabre joked. "What if Vicki sees you? After reading that report, I'm afraid to give her a reason to come after me. I don't need two crazies hounding me. If I didn't know better, I'd think she was my stalker."

"That can't be," Bob said. "She didn't even know who you were when Nicholson was killed and you got that first text."

"I know. I wish she was the perp. At least then I'd only have one person who wants to kill me."

CHAPTER 62

Friday, p.m.

Sabre was still sitting on the bench when Unity arrived. The social worker left the girl with Sabre and headed into the DA's office.

"Hello, Unity," Sabre said.

"Hi." She didn't use her usual snarky voice.

"Are you nervous?"

"A little."

"Why don't you have a seat?"

Unity hesitated. "Can I look over the wall first?"

Sabre stood. "Of course. It's kind of fun." They walked over and peered down. "The people look a lot smaller from here, don't they?"

"They sure do."

"I know testifying can be a little scary," Sabre said softly. "Remember when I brought you here last week for the walk-through, and I showed you where you'd sit for the trial?"

"Yeah."

"That's the same courtroom we'll be in, and the judge is very nice." Sabre led Unity to the bench, and they both sat down.

"What if I don't know what to say?"

"All you have to do is answer truthfully. If you remember, please call the judge 'Your Honor.' But if you forget, that's all right too. This judge is very nice. The only thing you really have to remember is to speak the truth."

"What if I don't know the answer?" Unity sounded more like a normal eleven-year-old than a teenager with an attitude, like she had previously.

"Then just say, 'I don't know.' It's as simple as that. You don't have to have all the answers, but if you do know the answer, you must tell all of it."

The girl shifted uncomfortably.

"What is it, Unity? Is there something I should know?"

"When Wayne had a heart attack, he and Mom had been fighting. She was real angry, and she didn't call the paramedics right away."

"I thought you said your mother poisoned him."

Unity blushed. "I did say that, but I made that part up."

"Why?"

"Because no one believes me when I tell the truth anyway, so I just lie for fun."

"The problem, Unity, is when you tell lies sometimes, people don't know when to believe you. They don't know what part is the truth and what is a lie."

"The truth is my mom didn't poison Wayne. I made that up." The girl sounded upset now. "But when he had a heart attack, she just let him die. She could've helped him, and she didn't."

"What do you mean?" Sabre asked.

"Wayne kept begging her to call 9-1-1, but she wouldn't. He tried to get the phone, but he couldn't."

"How long did she wait?"

"Until he was dead."

"And you saw all this?"

"Yes."

"Does your mother know you saw it?"

"She knows I saw something, but she doesn't know how much. She told me if I said anything, I would join him. Then she apologized and said she didn't mean it." Unity shook her head. "She also claimed she had already called 9-1-1 before I came in the room, but I know she didn't."

"How do you know?"

"Because I was peeking around the door. She never touched her phone. I also checked her phone afterward, and she didn't call until he was already dead." The more Unity spoke, the more her eyes filled with fear and grief.

"Why didn't you tell someone?"

"Because I was afraid she might hurt me. I didn't really like Wayne that much, but I wouldn't have let him die."

"You've been very brave telling me."

"Is Mom gonna go to prison?"

"I don't know, Unity. Your mom is mentally unhealthy, and she needs help."

Unity looked down at the floor. Sabre had no good way to make the poor girl feel better about what might happen to her mother. If what Unity said was true, her mother was a lot worse than she thought.

"How are things at your foster home?"

"They're not so bad, I guess. But I miss where Mom and I

were living when they took me away. It was the best place we ever had."

"What did you like about it?"

"It was in a big circle."

"What do you mean?"

"The apartments formed a big ring, three stories high, and inside the circle was like a paradise. Lots of palm trees and a big pool. It was pretty and fun."

Sabre's mouth gaped.

"It's true," Unity said. "I'm not making it up. It's a big circle of apartments."

"I believe you. Were they the Carousel Apartments on Rue d'Orleans?"

"Yeah, that's it."

"You and your mom lived there until you were removed by social services?"

"That's right, why?"

"Just curious." Sabre took out her cell phone. "Give me a minute. I have to take care of something."

Sabre walked away, upset at herself for not seeing it before, but she never had a reason to check their old address. She looked at the time. JP was in his parent/teacher conference right now. She sent him a text: *Vicki Hendrickson lived at the Carousel Apartments. Isn't that where Nicholson was killed? Please check.*

CHAPTER 63

Friday, p.m.

Sabre turned back toward Unity, who had stepped up to the wall and was looking over. The girl pointed at someone in the lobby. "There's my mom."

Vicki Hendrickson was walking toward the stairwell door. "Maybe you can see her after the trial, but for now, let's get you inside. I need to check on something before the trial starts."

Sabre walked Unity into the DA's office and left her with the social worker—until she was called to testify. Sabre needed to use the restroom before the trial started, but she had to get another message to JP first. She started to type it and heard someone coming up the steps. She looked up and saw Richard Wagner.

"Hi, Sabre."

"Hi, Wags."

"Are you okay?" he asked.

"I'm fine. Just a little harried. I have a trial this afternoon that just morphed into something bigger than I expected."

He gave her a sympathetic look and said, "I see your friend is here. Is that who the trial is with?"

"Who?" Sabre asked.

He stepped up to the wall, and Sabre did the same.

"That woman down there." He pointed near the stairwell door. "I can't remember her name."

"That's Vicki Hendrickson." A shiver of alarm went up Sabre's spine. "What do you mean *my friend*? Believe me, she doesn't like me very much."

"I know. I represented her the first time she came into court. Bob has her now, right?"

"Yeah, he calls her the *praying mantis* because her partners keep disappearing."

"She's the perfect client for Bob. He loves the crazies."

"I know."

"Don't you remember the last time?" Wagner asked. "She was with a guy who was twenty years younger. I can't remember *his* name either, but he wore a suit and carried a briefcase, so you thought he was an attorney."

"What are you talking about?"

"It was about a year ago. Vicki's partner sat down next to you and started talking. Vicki became insanely jealous and started following you around. She got in your face, and I had to come between you two." Wagner paused and squinted. "Remember? The bailiffs stepped in and even walked you to your car because she was still stalking you."

Sabre felt the blood leave her face.

"I know you recall the guy," Wagner said. "He was tall,

good-looking, and dressed well, except for an old, dirty Fedora."

"The hat," Sabre said. "Oh my God, that was Vicki." She tensed. "So, she already hated me before I was assigned the case." Sabre took out her cell phone and showed the photo to Wagner. "Was this the hat?"

"Yeah, looks like it. Why do you have a picture of it?"

"I think she's my stalker. This was sent to me in a text, just like the photo of you." Sabre's hand shook as she put her phone away. "Wags, you be careful too. She may be after both of us. I've got to go. My trial is about to start, and I have to use the restroom first."

"I have to leave anyway. I have to meet a CASA worker. Good luck." He walked away.

Sabre hurried toward the bathroom, texting JP as she went. She finished her message, sent it off, and entered a stall. She heard someone come into the main bathroom, but she didn't think much of it.

Sabre stepped out of the stall. Vicki lurched, raised her iPad, and swung it full frontal at Sabre's face. She turned and tried to duck, but it wasn't enough. She took the blow on one side, the metal smashing into her eye and cheek. The impact knocked her against the bathroom door. She heard the iPad slam into the tile floor.

Sabre stumbled and tried to regain her balance, but Vicki grabbed her around the neck and started choking her. Adrenaline rushed through her body as Sabre realized she was struggling for survival. She tried to pull Vicki's hands away, but the woman was too strong. Vicki used her substantial weight to press Sabre's body against the door.

Sabre kicked and struggled to get loose, forcing Vicki to move closer and making it more difficult for her to keep her hold around Sabre's neck. Still, Sabre struggled to breathe. She tried to scream but couldn't. Vicki squeezed harder on her airway. Suddenly Sabre felt calm, and her body went limp like a ragdoll. The next thing she knew, she was on the floor and the iPad was coming at her again. Then everything went black.

CHAPTER 64

Friday, p.m.

JP left the conference, feeling like a proud *papa*. Morgan was doing excellent in all her subjects. She was also a class leader, and the teacher thought she was very personable. He strutted as he walked Morgan across the street and told her how proud he was. Conner was home, so he planned to leave Morgan there and check on Sabre. JP waited until he was inside before he turned his phone back on. He'd missed two texts, both from Sabre.

The first read: *Vicki Hendrickson lived at the Carousel Apartments. Isn't that where Nicholson was killed? Please check.*

JP didn't need to. He knew exactly where Nicholson was killed, so that meant there was a connection between Nicholson and Vicki.

The second text gave him a chill: *And Vicki knew me before this case started. We had an encounter in court I had forgotten about.*

JP called Sabre but got her voice mail. He tried Bob with the same result. He suspected they were both in trial, but he couldn't help but be concerned. He tousled Morgan's hair. "Good job, Munchkin. I'm very proud of you, and your dad will be too." He grabbed his keys, "Thanks, Conner. Hopefully, this won't take long, but Sabre has a trial so I can't be certain. I'll let you know if we're running late."

"No worries," Conner said.

JP jumped in his truck and drove to juvenile court. At a red light, he tried calling Sabre again and left a message, telling her that Nicholson did live at that apartment complex and to be careful.

Did that make Vicki the stalker?

If so, she could easily have taken a photo of Nicholson, perhaps even killed him. And if Vicki knew Sabre from an earlier case, she could've been holding a grudge for a long time. Sabre could be in danger right now. Bob had said the woman was crazy, so who knew what she might do. JP sped up. He was driving way too fast, but he had to get to court. He should have never left Sabre alone.

Bob finished his case and headed to Department One for the Hendrickson trial. County Counsel, the bailiff, and the social worker were waiting.

"Have you seen Sabre?" Mike McCormick asked.

"She was upstairs the last time I saw her," Bob said.

"I saw her outside the DA's office about twenty minutes

ago," the social worker added. "But she wasn't there when I left to come down."

"She's probably talking to Unity," Bob said. "She's here to testify this afternoon."

"Are you ready for trial?" McCormick asked Bob.

"As soon as I find my client. I spoke with her earlier, but I don't know where she went. Maybe she's in the bathroom. I'll check the halls again."

Bob walked out and glanced around. Fewer than a dozen people were in the hall, but not Sabre or Vicki. As he started toward the bathrooms, he heard an announcement on the speaker. "Ms. Brown, please report to Department One. Ms. Brown, Department One for trial."

A bad feeling rolled over him. Sabre was never late to trial. And where the hell was Vicki? Bob turned left when he reached the lobby and exited out to the patio. He hurried to the end, but only found another attorney speaking with a client.

Back inside, Bob made his way through the lobby, passing a few people and the information desk. No Sabre. No Vicki. Although he didn't expect to see either in the other hall, he stepped in and looked around. Two attorneys, a sign-language interpreter, and a deaf couple were communicating halfway down. The rest was empty.

Bob headed out the front door and didn't see either woman, but he heard a faint siren in the distance. He went back inside, looking for someone who could check the women's bathroom upstairs. He opened the door to the stairwell, and two bailiffs rushed past him and ran up the stairs.

The sirens came closer. Another bailiff hurried toward him. "What's going on?" Bob asked.

"A woman passed out in the restroom. That's all I know."

The sirens sounded like they were right outside, then they

stopped. Bob climbed the steps, wondering if something had happened to his client. When he turned the corner to the second set, he saw Wagner at the top.

"Bob, it's Sabre," Wagner called down.

Bob took the stairs two at a time. "Is she okay?"

"I don't know."

Three paramedics blew past them, carrying a gurney and headed for the bathroom.

"Do you have any idea what happened? Did she just pass out?"

"I don't know. I talked to her five minutes ago. Sabre seemed a little distraught when I reminded her about the incident with your praying mantis client."

"What incident?"

Wagner described the confrontation that happened when he was on the case. "I think Sabre had forgotten it, but then she showed me a picture of the hat Vicki's boyfriend wore. What was that all about?"

Bob didn't answer his question. "Did you see Vicki up here earlier?"

"No, but after I talked to Sabre, I went to the CASA office for a few minutes. When I came out, I looked down into the lobby and saw Vicki going out the front door. She seemed to be in a hurry."

"How long ago was that?"

"Maybe ten minutes."

"Can you do me a favor?"

"Sure."

"Go to Department One and tell McCormick what happened with Sabre. I've got to call JP, and I don't want to leave her."

"No problem."

"Appear for both of us and see if you can get a continuance until next week. And if Vicki isn't there, make sure McCormick knows you saw her leaving."

Wagner started down the stairs, and Bob called JP.

"I'll be there in five minutes," JP said. "Is she conscious?"

"I don't think so." Bob glanced over at the bathroom. Paramedics were headed inside. "I can't see much, but the door just opened, and she's still on the floor."

"She better be okay," JP said.

"I'm so sorry. I should've never left her alone." Bob felt a little queasy. "I was doing my other case, and I thought Sabre was with her client."

"It's not your fault, and I wasn't blaming you. I should've canceled the dang conference and been there myself."

After a moment of silence, Bob said, "You know, neither of us would've been in the bathroom with her, so it still would've happened."

"But we may have found her sooner."

The bathroom door opened again. "Hold on, they're carrying her out."

"Is she moving? Does she look okay?"

"She's not moving."

Bob heard JP's tires screech and his truck door slam.

"I'm here." JP hung up.

JP ran into the courthouse lobby just as paramedics wheeled Sabre through. He caught a glimpse and cringed. Her face had started to swell, and blood oozed from her eye and nose. It had soaked the front of her blouse too, and JP thought he saw red marks on her neck.

McCormick followed the gurney and asked JP to stand back.

"Do you know what happened?" JP asked.

"Not for certain, but it appears Sabre was assaulted. They smashed something into her face and tried to choke her."

JP clenched his fists. He wanted to hit something, anything. He tried to control his anger, but his face and chest pulsed with heat. "Do you know who did it? Was it Vicki Hendrickson?"

"We think so, but we can't be sure yet. She left around that time, and no one has seen her since. We have an APB out for her."

"Damn!"

"They'll find her," McCormick said. "It happened inside the courthouse, so it'll get a lot of attention. That scares judges, so action will be taken and quickly."

CHAPTER 65

Friday, p.m.

JP made it to the hospital before the ambulance did. When they wheeled her in, he was at the door to greet her. Sabre had regained consciousness, and her eyes were open. "I'm okay," she whispered, in a hoarse, nearly inaudible voice.

"Don't try to talk."

The paramedics kept moving, and JP followed. They wheeled her into a cubicle. A doctor came in before they had her parked. JP stood back while she was examined. The doctor checked her airway and breathing but didn't comment. He shined a light in Sabre's eyes and asked her a few questions. She responded with difficulty. JP asked her to squeeze his hand and make movements with her arms, but Sabre floated in and out of consciousness.

Finally, the doctor said, "Her breathing is good, and her airway is open, but she likely has a concussion. I don't think she has any broken bones, but she'll have a whopper of a headache. It looks like she took two blows to the head."

"What next?" JP asked.

"We'll draw blood and take her for a CT scan, possibly an MRI. That will take a while, at least an hour. You can wait here if you want, but you may prefer to get a cup of coffee. If you need to make a phone call, you'll have to go elsewhere. There's almost no cell signal in this area." He stepped toward the curtain to leave.

"Doc?"

He turned around. "Yes?"

"She sounds pretty bad when she talks. Will it hurt her if she does?"

"It's painful right now for her, and she'll be hoarse. If there is no permanent damage, she'll be much better by tomorrow." The doctor stepped out.

A technician came in, drew several vials of blood, and left. Sabre opened her eyes and tried to talk, but no words came out.

"Don't try to talk." JP held her hand.

"Vicki," Sabre muttered.

"Is she the one who attacked you?"

Sabre nodded slightly. "Yes."

"I just wanted to confirm it, but the cops are aware of what happened. They can get the details later. You don't need to worry about it for now. You can explain it all when you're feeling better."

An orderly came into the room. "Are you ready for a road trip?"

Sabre forced a smile.

"I'm taking you for a CT Scan. And I brought you a warm blanket." He laid the blanket over her. "It gets a little chilly in there." He started to wheel her out. "Wave goodbye to your buddy." The orderly turned to JP. "I promise I'll have her home by midnight."

~

He returned Sabre about an hour later. She tried to talk, but JP stopped her. She smiled gratefully. JP was sitting by Sabre's bedside when the doctor came in.

"You're looking pretty good, counselor," the doctor said.

Sabre tried to speak, but all that came out was, "… go home?"

"Not quite yet," the doctor said. "We did a complete blood count and a coagulation study and CMP. The blood tests were all within normal ranges. The CT angiogram showed the carotid and vertebral arteries were not damaged." He touched his own throat as he talked. "The non-contrast CT of the brain indicated there was no intracranial hemorrhaging, in other words, no hemorrhagic stroke. We did an MRI/MRA of the brain and ruled out any global or anoxic brain injury, or ischemic strokes as well. You have a concussion, but all in all, you were pretty lucky."

Sabre attempted to speak again. The doctor raised his hand. "We'll put you in a room and keep you overnight to watch that concussion. You should be able to go home tomorrow, if all goes well."

Sabre nodded and gave the doctor a meek smile.

He was only gone a few minutes when two orderlies came in to move Sabre to her room. While she was being admitted, JP called Ron.

"How is she?" Ron asked.

"She's doing well, no major damage. But she has to stay

overnight for observation because of the concussion. Did you pick up the kids from school?"

"Yes, they're home safe and sound."

"Would you mind staying with them tonight? I know Conner is plenty capable of taking care of his sister, but with Vicki on the loose, I don't want to take a chance."

"I fully intended to stay. Don't worry."

"Thanks, bro."

"Can I bring the kids to see Sabre if they ask?"

"I'm sure they'll want to see her, but tell them she should be released tomorrow and if she's not, they can come by in the afternoon. Morgan has gymnastics in the morning. Can you get her there?"

"Of course."

JP hung up and called Detective Marlow to update him.

"Do you think she can answer some questions?"

"Not yet. She has a hard time talking, and her throat is sore where Vicki tried to strangle her. If you could wait until morning, it would be better."

"Has she told you who attacked her?"

"Vicki."

"Then the details can wait. I'll see you in the morning."

CHAPTER 66

Saturday, a.m.

Sabre was restless to leave by the time Detective Marlow came into the room. JP met him at the door.

"Is Sabre up for conversation?" Marlow asked.

"She's doing a lot better," JP said, as they walked toward her bed. "She still sounds hoarse, but she says it doesn't hurt to talk."

"I'll go easy on her." Marlow looked at Sabre. "You took quite a beating, didn't you?"

"A bit."

"We haven't found Hendrickson yet, but we will. Please tell me exactly what went down."

Sabre explained the best she could. "It all happened so fast, but I had already figured out that Vicki had sent the texts and threats."

"How did you know?"

"Another attorney reminded me that a year ago Vicki was

in court and thought I was flirting with her boyfriend, Wayne. She became very jealous and followed me around the courthouse. Wayne always wore an old, dirty hat, the same one she dropped on my office doorstep. Wagner confirmed that it was his." Sabre swallowed and stopped talking for a few seconds.

"We also discovered that Vicki lived in the same apartments where Nicholson's body was found," JP filled in, saving Sabre's voice.

"Yes, I just discovered that myself, but we still haven't found any evidence that she killed Jim Nicholson," Marlow said. "We've already started investigating her connection to him." He paused, seeming puzzled. "Why would Vicki, all of a sudden, decide to send Sabre the picture of Nicholson if it had been a year since the incident?"

"Because," Sabre said, "she was at court on that Thursday before I was appointed on her case, and she saw me. That must have triggered old jealous feelings. Nicholson was also at court that day. She could've seen me talking to him." Sabre stopped and took a sip of water, soothing her voice. "I only had a brief encounter with Vicki that time, but she gave me a mean stare. I didn't recognize her and didn't think much of it. We get angry people at juvenile court all the time." Sabre took another drink. "Vicki was already mad at me before I was appointed to her case Monday. If you read her psychological evaluation, you'll get a better picture."

"I'll definitely do that."

"Curt," Sabre said, "There's one other thing."

"What's that?"

"I had a long talk with Unity, Vicki's daughter. She says that Vicki let her last boyfriend, Wayne, die of a heart attack. Unity said her mother just watched him and didn't call 9-1-1 until it was too late."

"The girl claims she intentionally let him die?"

"Yes."

"Is this the same girl who said her mom poisoned him?"

"It is, but for the first time, I think she may be telling the truth. Unity was adamant that her mom did it on purpose." Sabre swallowed, then continued to speak, her voice getting scratchier. "Vicki lied to Unity and told her she had already called for help, but Unity checked her phone and she hadn't."

"That'll be tough to prove, but it does show she's further over the edge than I thought." Marlow flicked his toothpick. "You need to rest now, but be careful. You should both know that Vicki drives a gray 2015 Toyota Sienna." He gave them the license plate number. "Have you received any more texts?"

"No," JP said. "Sabre's phone was off for a while, but I checked recently, and there was nothing."

"Good." Marlow turned to JP. "I'm glad Sabre's okay, but you should keep her out of sight for a few days. It might be best if Hendrickson believes she's dead."

"I agree, and I'll keep an eye out for the crazy lady's car."

CHAPTER 67

Saturday & Sunday

Sabre was out of the hospital by two o'clock that afternoon. Conner and Morgan were excited to see her and made a banner that read: *Welcome Home, Sabre*. Sabre had asked Ron to caution the kids so they wouldn't be too surprised when they saw her. Sabre's face was bruised, and her head was still bandaged. But other than a headache, she looked worse than she felt.

When Sabre walked in, Morgan hugged her, then stepped back. "Ron said you had a bandage, but your face is all jacked up."

"Morgonster," Conner chided, "that wasn't nice." He turned to Sabre. "You don't look that bad."

"I didn't mean anything wrong by it," Morgan said. She continued to jabber, asking lots of questions about what happened.

"A woman on one of my cases got pretty mad and attacked me," Sabre explained.

"Is that the same one who sent you weird text messages?"

Sabre frowned. "How do you know about that?"

"You may try to keep things quiet when something is wrong, but I hear things."

Sabre smiled. "Yes, it's the same person, but we know who it is now, so it's all going to be okay. Don't you worry." Sabre made a mental note to be more careful around Morgan.

"Is she in jail?"

"Not yet, but the cops will find her."

The rest of the day was uneventful. Sunday was the same. They all had a quiet day at home. When Conner asked to go out with one of his friends, JP sat down with him and explained more of what was happening. He also told him what kind of car Vicki drove so he could be aware.

"I'd rather you didn't go anywhere for a few days. Hopefully, they'll catch this woman before she does any more damage. I know that's not fair to you, but I need to keep an eye on Sabre, and I don't need to be worrying about you too."

To JP's surprise and satisfaction, Conner didn't give him any guff over it. JP placed his hand on Conner's shoulder. "Thanks, Buddy, I really appreciate it," JP said. "Hopefully, this will all be over soon."

JP and Morgan made pancakes for breakfast. Sabre headed into the kitchen to get a cup of coffee. When she walked past a small table in the dining room, she saw the wrapped present they had bought for CJ's birthday.

"I totally forgot about CJ's party." She looked at Morgan's sad face. "I know how much you were looking forward to going. I'll get dressed and take you."

"I can take her," Conner offered.

"I don't think that's a good idea," JP said. "And I sure don't want to leave you, Sabre."

"What if we call Ron and see if he's busy?" Sabre said, making the call before anyone else could speak.

"If he's busy, I don't have to go," Morgan said, but the disappointment was evident in her voice.

Sabre hung up. "He's on his way. You go get ready. He has something he needs to do this afternoon, so he may bring you back a little early, if that's okay."

"I don't care." She hugged Sabre. "Thanks. I really wanted to go."

"I know."

Morgan returned from the party about three o'clock, carrying a piece of cake and two red balloons.

"How was the shindig?" JP asked.

"It was fabulous. CJ had a plethora of balloons."

"A plethora?" JP asked. "Is that your word of the day?"

"Yes, cool word, huh? He must've had a hundred of them. Balloons were everywhere."

"Is that how many it takes to make a plethora? A hundred?"

"You're silly, Uncle Johnny." She handed the cake to Conner. "This is for you." Then she gave the balloons to Sabre.

"What am I, horse manure?" JP asked.

"Conner gets the cake because I know he would've brought me some if he went and I didn't get to go. And Sabre gets the balloons because she's been in the hospital."

JP tousled her hair. "Just messing with you, Munchkin."

Morgan continued to babble about the party, telling every

little detail. Finally, JP asked her to help make dinner. JP and Conner grilled hamburgers while Morgan prepared the lettuce, tomato, and onions.

No one let Sabre do a thing. "I'm really okay," she said. "I can help."

"Nope, not this time," Morgan said. "You can find us a good movie to watch later. Uncle Johnny said we can have popcorn and hot chocolate too."

Sabre smiled, took a couple of Tylenol, and sat back on the sofa where she'd spent most of the day. Her head hurt, and she was glad to just rest. She stayed there until their early dinner was ready.

They had just finished eating when Sabre's phone beeped. JP, Conner, and Morgan all looked at Sabre. Her phone was across the room on the coffee table.

"I'm sure it's nothing," Sabre said.

No one spoke for several minutes. Finally, JP said, "Maybe you should check."

Morgan and Conner both nodded. Then Morgan jumped up. "I'll get your phone for you."

Before anyone could object, she ran to the coffee table.

"Don't look at the text," JP said.

"Okay." Morgan picked up the phone and handed it to Sabre.

She took a deep breath and read the text: *You ruined everything. 1-8-2*

Sabre showed the message to JP.

"What does it say?" Morgan asked.

"It just says, 'You ruined everything. 1-8-2.'" JP shrugged. "No big thing."

"That means 'I hate you,'" Morgan said.

"How do you know that?" Conner and Sabre asked in unison.

"You don't even have a phone," Conner added. "How would you know the text abbreviations?"

"Kids still write notes and stuff, you know. We use them all the time. Everyone knows what 1-8-2 means."

"I suppose even the chickens under the porch know that. Right, Munchkin?"

"At least the *young* chickens," Morgan said, and everyone laughed.

Sabre typed a response and showed the phone to JP again. "How's this?"

JP read it to himself: *She's dead. Leave us alone.*

"That's good. Send it."

CHAPTER 68

Wednesday, a.m./p.m.

Sabre dressed for her first day back at work since her attack. She still had some bruising and plenty of aches and pains, but she was glad to get out of the house. JP drove her to court and left her in Bob's hands, fully backed by the bailiffs. Even though Vicki hadn't been apprehended, Sabre felt safe at the courthouse now that she knew who was after her. There was no way Vicki could get to her in this building. Besides, she really hoped Vicki thought she was dead. She hadn't received any more messages, so it was possible.

Sabre finished her morning calendar and called JP to pick her up. While she waited, she phoned Marlow to see if he had anything new on Vicki's whereabouts. He had nothing.

Bob finished his afternoon trial, stopped at his office, and then went home. After dinner, Bob went to his study to relax and read a magazine, glad to be home. He had just gotten comfortable when from the family room, he heard his wife call out.

"Bob!" She sounded odd.

"What?"

"Come in here, please." Her voice cracked.

"What is it?" Bob said, walking into the room, a little annoyed. He stopped suddenly and stared at the surreal scene. Vicki was in his house, holding a knife to his wife's throat. Vicki's back was against the wall, her left arm wrapped around Marilee's chest, and her other hand holding a knife under her chin. Marilee's lips trembled.

"Vicki," Bob said softly, but sternly. "What are you doing?"

"I came to get you. We can leave together as soon as I get rid of this little obstacle."

"Vicki, don't!" He pleaded.

"Why not? You don't love her. You love me. Tell me you love me."

Bob's throat was dry, and he swallowed hard.

Vicki moved the knife slightly. "Tell me you love me, or I'll cut her throat."

He had to appease this crazy woman. "Of course, I love you." He glanced at Marilee, who blinked in return. "Vicki, I don't want you to hurt anyone on my account. Put the knife down and let's talk."

"We don't have time to talk. We need to get out of here. We need to get rid of her and get out of here."

Bob saw Marilee's eyes search the room without moving her head. She was either looking for an escape or, more likely, for their son in order to warn him. Bob knew CJ was in his room, or he had been ten minutes ago. But if the boy heard a commotion, he might show up. Bob desperately didn't want CJ to see this or get caught up in whatever was about to happen.

"Why don't we just tie her up and gag her?" Bob said. Marilee shot him a disturbing glance. He hoped she understood his plan. "Marilee," Bob soothed, "You'll just let us go, right? I know you wouldn't want anything to get in the way of my happiness." Bob could hardly get the words out, but this was the only thing that might save her.

Marilee started to respond, but Vicki tightened her grip. "Don't talk. I don't want to hear any of your lies. Yours either," she said to Bob. "You've been cheating on me, just like all the others. Men!" she hissed. "They all cheat and lie. Are you a cheater? Like the others?"

"No," Bob said, raising his palms. "I would never cheat on you."

A cell phone, sitting on the coffee table, rang and startled them all. Vicki twitched, and Marilee sucked in a breath. The knife nicked her, and a thin line of blood appeared.

"I should get that," Bob said. "Whoever's calling will wonder why Marilee didn't answer her phone."

"People miss calls all the time."

"Not Marilee. She always picks up." Bob made a slight move toward the phone.

"Leave it!" Vicki bellowed.

CJ had heard his mother yell for his dad. She did that a lot, but this time her voice sounded different, scared. He thought maybe she'd seen a spider or something. CJ left his room and headed into the den. Just before he reached the main living area, he heard a strange voice. He peeked around the end of the wall, and his mouth dropped open. A big woman stood behind his mother and she had a knife. His dad was in the opening to the kitchen, begging the woman not to hurt his mother.

CJ's instinct was to help his mom, but he knew if his dad wasn't moving, he shouldn't either. He quietly stepped back so no one could see him. He listened for a while, and the woman sounded very angry. He peeked again. She still had the knife at his mom's throat. He eased away and tried to figure out what to do. His mind spun in too many directions, but he knew this was an emergency. *What to do in an emergency?* Suddenly, he knew he had to get help. He tiptoed quickly to his dad's office and picked up his phone. Then he quietly made his way out to the backyard and to the gazebo. He wanted to press 9-1-1, but the police would have sirens and his mom might die. He found the name he was looking for and made the call.

JP had just returned home from picking up dinner from El Pollo Loco when his cell phone rang. "Hi, Bob."

"I..I..it's not Bob. It's CJ."

JP could barely hear his voice. "CJ, can you speak up?"

CJ continued to whisper. "I'm af..af..afraid she'll hear me."

"What's wrong?" JP switched to speaker, hoping it would increase the volume and let Sabre hear the conversation as well. She'd walked over as soon as she heard CJ's name.

"There's a wo..woman here ho..ho..holding a kn..knife on my m..m..mom." His voice choked up, and his stuttering was the worst they had ever heard.

"What?" JP's pulse escalated. "Where are you?"

"I sn..snuck outside. I'm in the b..b..back by the gazebo."

"Where's your dad?" JP grabbed his keys, and he and Sabre moved toward the truck.

"He's try..trying to t..t..talk the lady out of hurting M..Mom."

"Is she alone?" JP asked. "I mean, did you see anyone else with her?"

"No, no, no one else."

"Does she know where you are?"

"She d..didn't see me. N..neither did my m..mom or dad. I..I can't t..t..talk right."

JP started the engine and handed the phone to Sabre as she jumped in the passenger side.

"CJ, listen to me," Sabre said. "Take a deep breath and blow it out, then concentrate on your words."

They heard him breathing deeply. "I saw them, and then I sn..snuck around without making any noise." The boy spoke more deliberately. "I g..got my dad's phone and went out the b..b..back door. I was very quiet."

"Have you called 9-1-1?"

"N..no."

"Look, CJ, we're on our way," Sabre said. "You stay right where you are unless you see someone coming, then hide if you need to. I'll stay on the phone with you until we get there, and JP will call the police. Okay?"

"O..okay."

CHAPTER 69

Wednesday, p.m.

When JP and Sabre started to approach the house, JP shut off his lights and drove a few hundred feet past Bob's home and parked up the hill.

"I don't see Vicki's car," Sabre said. "I hope we're not too late."

"There it is." JP pointed across the street. "Just up ahead."

They climbed out, ran to Bob's house, and snuck along the side to the backyard. It was dark, but they refrained from using flashlights for fear they would be seen. JP peeked in a few windows but couldn't see anyone. He prayed they had arrived in time.

When they got near the gazebo, they heard CJ whisper, "Psst, I'm b..back here."

They found him crouched down behind the structure. Sabre wrapped her arms around the shaking boy. "You're safe now," Sabre said. He laid his head on her shoulder and started to cry.

"Is the back door unlocked?" JP asked.

"Y..Yes," he sobbed.

"Where exactly was the woman?"

"In the f..family room by the opening to the k..kitchen."

"Right by the front door?"

"Yes."

"Where were you?"

"In the d..den on the other s..side of the kitchen."

"So, if I go in the back door, through the living room, and then the den, she won't be able to see me until I get to the kitchen, right?"

"Right."

"Where was your dad?"

"He was in the other h..hall, right where the k..kitchen starts."

"Okay," JP said. "You stay here with Sabre and wait for the cops. I'm going inside to help your mom and dad."

JP wanted to get behind Vicki if he could, but that would be difficult. He knew the house well enough to know what his obstacles were. If he came in through the den, they'd have at least ten feet of kitchen between them. If he tried to come through the front door, she might kill Marilee before he could get to her. He couldn't risk that.

He crossed the yard, snuck in the back door, and moved quietly through the living room to the den. He stopped to assess the situation and heard voices in the next room.

"Vicki, you know me. You know how much I care for you," Bob pleaded. "But I would have a hard time if you hurt Marilee."

"Why? Because you love her more than me?"

"No, because I'm a pacifist, and I don't like bloodshed."

Vicki didn't respond.

"If you kill someone, the cops will eventually find you and arrest you, and then we'll be apart. I don't want that."

Vicki chortled. "It's too late for that."

"What do you mean?"

She didn't answer. JP inched forward, hoping to sneak a glance at their exact locations.

Bob spoke softly. "Vicki, have you already killed someone?"

"I never killed anyone who didn't deserve it. Men are horrible human beings, you know. They say they love you, but they always want someone younger, or prettier, or skinnier. Are you like that?"

"No, I'm not," Bob said.

"Good. I'd hate to have to kill you too." She sounded detached.

"Vicki, did you kill Jim Nicholson?"

"Why would I do that?" She chuckled. "I hardly knew the guy."

"I don't know, but you sent a photo of his dead body to Sabre, right?"

"Yeah, that was lucky—for me—not so much for Nicholson. I bet that text shook her up."

JP inched forward, glad Bob was buying time.

Vicki kept talking. "Sabre wants you, you know. She wanted him too. She's an awful woman, with her petite little body and flirty smile. I see the way she looks at you. She looked at *him* like that too."

"You mean Jim Nicholson?"

"No, not Nicholson. *Him*, she wanted *him*, and he was weak, and I couldn't trust him."

"Who are you talking about?"

"It doesn't matter. I showed him. He won't ever do that to me again."

Keep her talking, JP thought as he peeked around the corner. He couldn't see Bob, but he had an excellent view of Vicki with the knife held tight against Marilee's throat. JP was afraid to take a shot for fear he would hit Marilee. He needed another plan.

The sound of a siren came from the direction of Jamacha Road. JP wondered if it was the police on their way.

"What is that?" Vicki shouted, pulling Marilee tighter. "If you called the cops, I'll kill her before they get me."

"How could I call? I've been right here with you the whole time."

The siren started to fade, and Vicki seemed to relax a little.

"He haunts me," Vicki said.

"Who haunts you?" Bob asked.

"Wayne. He comes to me in the night and stands at the end of my bed. He swears he'll get even some day."

"Who is Wayne?"

"My last husband. We didn't have a ceremony, but we pledged to each other. That's what makes a real marriage—a pledge of fidelity and love. But he couldn't keep his promises. He sure was a handsome man. Women all thought so, and he knew it. Sabre knew it. She tried to take him away from me when we were in court the last time."

"You mean the other day?"

"No, a year ago. I caught her flirting with him. It probably wasn't his fault. How could he resist the devil? That's what Sabre is—a devil disguised as an angel." JP thought he saw Vicki's brow wrinkle, as if she was contemplating. "Maybe he didn't have to die."

"Did you kill him?"

"No. God gave him a heart attack." She snorted. "I just didn't stop God." An eerie smile played on her face. "Do you think that's why he haunts me? Because I let him die? I didn't actually kill him, you know."

"How does he haunt you?"

"He comes to me, mostly in the night. It scares me when he visits from the grave." Vicki was quiet for a moment, then asked, "Do you think *she* will?"

"Who?"

"Sabre. Do you think she'll visit me from the grave too?"

"I don't know how it works." Bob sounded distressed.

"Maybe when you kill someone, they never leave you alone," Vicki mused. "Or maybe they stop after a while. I never see Paul anymore. He used to come, but he doesn't now."

"Who's Paul?"

"My second husband. He cheated on me too, just like the rest. They're all cheaters."

"Paul used to haunt you?"

"Mostly in my dreams. But I knew he was really there because I could smell his cologne."

JP assessed the room. This woman was totally wacko, but she'd given him an idea. He stepped back and texted Sabre to meet him in the backyard. He carefully made his way in that direction.

Sabre was waiting when he stepped outside. They moved further away from the house near the orange trees so they wouldn't be heard. Still JP whispered, "The front deadbolt is unlocked, so I'll go in that way. You can sneak in the back. If you stay to your right, you can get to the den where you'll be able to see Vicki and Marilee. Turn off the sound on your phone and watch for messages." JP paused. This was the iffy part. "When I text, I want you to appear in the kitchen. She thinks you're dead. Seeing you should distract her enough that I can get a jump on her. Just be careful that she doesn't see you until I'm ready."

"Shouldn't we just wait for the cops to get here?" Sabre asked, keeping her voice low.

"I'm afraid they'll spook her. And she's already edgy. I thought she might finish off Marilee when she heard that earlier siren. We have to do something quick before they get here."

Suddenly Sabre remembered something. "Go ahead. I'll be right there." She ran back to CJ. "Do any of the balloons from your party still have air?"

"Y..yes."

"Where are they?"

"In the d..den."

Sabre snuck into the house and tiptoed her way to the den. Three balloons were wedged against the ceiling, their strings hanging down. Sabre pulled one to her. Then another. She waited behind the wall for JP's text, her heart thumping.

When the text came, Sabre readied herself. Using a spooky voice, she called out Vicki's name, stretching the sound. At the same time, she stepped into the kitchen with one arm in the air, waving and moving her body as though she were floating.

"Vicki!" She elongated the name again.

Vicki spun toward her and raised the knife, pointing it at Sabre.

The front door burst open, and JP grabbed Vicki's arm. Marilee ducked down just as Bob charged forward, pulling

Marilee out of danger. JP tried to get his other hand on Vicki, but she was moving toward Sabre.

"Go away, ghost!" Vicki screamed in pain, moving in slow motion as JP tried to hold her back. "You're dead."

JP tightened his grip on the arm with the knife as she struggled toward Sabre. When Vicki tried to throw the knife, Sabre pulled out the balloons from behind her back. Vicki threw her hand up to her face, covering her eyes. The knife fell to the tile floor, making a loud clang.

Vicki flailed her arms and kept struggling to cross the room, her weight pulling JP off balance. Vicki was only a few feet from Sabre and swung at her with her free hand. Sabre ducked and Vicki missed. JP grabbed the top of Vicki's shirt and yanked, putting pressure against her throat. When he got his footing, he reached his arm around her neck in a choke hold.

Moments later, the police burst through the door.

CHAPTER 70

Friday, a.m.

Sabre walked into the attorney lounge and found Bob looking through the petitions "Hey," Bob said, "I have a case that may need another appointment on it. The guy is a little wacko, but—"

She cut him off. "No, thank you. I haven't recovered from the last *wacko* case you got me on."

"In all fairness, my client was already after you, so taking the case didn't make much difference."

"That's true, but I think I'll lay low for another week or so."

"But this guy thinks he can fly on a hair dryer."

Sabre rolled her eyes, opened the door, and started to leave.

Bob followed. "He also thinks his pillow can talk."

"I don't want to hear it," Sabre said, brushing him off with her hand. "I'm not getting on that case."

"Okay, I'll get someone else, but you'll miss all the fun."

"What a shame."

"By the way, your face looks a lot better. Most of the bruising seems to be gone."

"It doesn't hurt anymore, either." Sabre touched it subconsciously. "Did you hear that Vicki confessed to killing Paul, her second husband? They're still looking for his body. And she let Harvey, Unity's father, bleed out when they had the car accident."

"I told you she was a praying mantis. I wonder if she had sex with them just before they died. Or right after, maybe."

"Bob, you're sick."

He grinned. "Can you go to lunch today?"

"Sure. Then later this afternoon, I have a home visit scheduled to see Unity."

"She's with her aunt now, right?"

"Yes, but I haven't seen her since she moved in. I hope she's doing well."

Sabre left court and drove to Unity's new home. After greeting Unity's aunt, sat down in the girl's bedroom to chat with her. Sabre glanced around the room. "This is nice. How do you like having your own space?"

"It's pretty cool."

"Your room looks neat. Have you been keeping it clean? Or did you tidy up because you knew I was coming?" Sabre smiled.

"I straightened a little, but I've been doing pretty good. I don't ever want it to get bad like at Mom's house."

"Good. How are you and your Aunt Yvonne getting along?"

"We're doing great. I act up sometimes, but she calls me on it, and I'm learning. She gets pretty frustrated when I tell lies. That's the thing that makes her the most mad. I'm trying because I want her to trust me."

"How's that working?"

"I'm doing better. We used to get into fights when she tried to correct me, but now we have a code word, and it kind of makes us laugh."

"What do you mean?"

"If I say something and Aunt Yvonne thinks it's a lie, she'll say, 'fuzzy buggles?' And if I'm lying, I'm supposed to admit that it's all fuzzy buggles."

"Do you admit it?"

"Usually. Because the whole thing makes me smile, and I don't feel like I have to lie then. So far, it's working."

"I'd call that progress. What if she calls you on something and you were telling the truth?"

"That only happened once. Auntie is pretty good and knows when I'm lying. But that time I just said, 'No—real buggles,' and she believed me."

"That sounds like a good system. I'm happy you have Yvonne."

"Me too." Unity suddenly looked sad and stared at the wall.

"What is it?" Sabre asked.

"Have you seen my mom?"

"No. Have you?"

"Not yet. Aunt Yvonne will take me once everyone agrees it's safe, but I don't think that'll be very soon." Unity was silent for a few seconds. "Do you think she's okay in *there*?"

Vicki was in a mental hospital, but Sabre didn't know how much Unity understood. She had left that to Yvonne to explain to her as she thought best. "Right now, I think she's better off in the hospital than she was in the real world. The doctors will help her with her mental issues. Your mom was in a lot of pain. Things got very confusing for her."

"Aunt Yvonne said she might go to prison." Unity looked up at Sabre. "Maybe she shouldn't have told me that, but she promised she wouldn't lie to me when I ask her stuff."

"That's a good thing. You both need to be honest with each other. And she's right; your mother might go to prison. But first, there will be a trial, so it will take a long time. Right now, all you can do is take care of yourself and be good for your aunt. She loves you very much."

"I know. I'm trying."

CHAPTER 71

Saturday, p.m.

JP was in the backyard with Ron and his girlfriend, Addie. They'd been dating for several months, but this was the first family function she'd attended. Ron and Addie had been out to dinner with JP and Sabre, but Ron's girlfriend hadn't met their mother yet. Ron went inside to get the Pepsi from Sabre to put in the cooler.

"Are you ready to introduce Addie to Mom?" Sabre asked.

"It's time."

"Do you think this is the best way?"

"I do," Ron said. "I know Mom will like her but ..."

Sabre's eyes widened. "You think Addie won't like Mom?"

"Nothing like that. It's just that, well, you know how Mom can be. She'll want to ask a hundred questions right off. She won't have a chance to do that in a crowd. It means we can avoid the grilling for a while."

"You have a point there."

Ron picked up two twelve-packs of Pepsi from the counter and started out. Just as he reached the slider, the doorbell rang.

"I bet that's Mom," Sabre said. "Good luck, bro."

Ron hurried out.

Sabre's mother, Beverly, and her friend, Harley, came in carrying two gift-wrapped boxes. Morgan ran up and gave her a big hug. Beverly handed one of the boxes to Morgan. "This is for you, little one."

Morgan's eyes got big. "Thank you."

Beverly looked around. "Where's your brother?"

"He's in his room. I'll get him." Morgan dashed out and returned shortly with Conner right behind her.

Beverly handed him the other box. He seemed apprehensive to take it.

"Don't be embarrassed. I can spoil you kids if I want to. If Sabre or Ron would just give me some grandkids, I could spend my money on them. Until then, you two will just have to suffer through my spending sprees."

Conner smiled. Sabre knew both kids liked her mother, but they didn't always know how to take her, and they weren't used to getting gifts.

"Well, open them," Beverly said.

The kids sat down and opened the boxes. Morgan was faster and pulled out a pretty, pink and purple dress. "It's beautiful, Beverly. No, it's stunning," Morgan said, holding it up to herself and swinging around. "Simply stunning."

Conner opened his and found a blue, western shirt in his Nordstrom box. "It's real nice, Beverly," he said with sincerity. "Thank you very much."

Sabre told the kids to put their things away, then she escorted her mom and Harley outside.

Ron hugged his mother, shook Harley's hand, and introduced them to Addie. Beverly looked her over, and Addie did the same to her. "Nice dress," Addie said, before Beverly could comment. "It looks like a Liz Claiborne."

"It is." Her mother seemed a little surprised.

"She has designed some lovely clothes, and they look really good on you."

"Well, thank you."

They continued to chat, with Addie doing most of the interrogating. But Beverly was obviously impressed with Addie—as evidenced by her smiles and expressions.

"I guess you didn't need to worry," Sabre said to Ron. "That girl can hold her own."

Sabre heard the doorbell ring and went inside to let Bob, Marilee, and CJ in.

"How's CJ doing?" Sabre asked after Morgan and CJ ran off to play.

"Remarkably well, considering what he witnessed," Marilee said. "And his stuttering has calmed down as well. He was pretty bad for a day or so, but then he applied the techniques he had learned in speech therapy, and he's almost back to normal. He was proud of himself for mastering it again. I think it made him realize it's not a permanent condition."

The doorbell rang again. Bob and his family joined the others in the backyard, and Sabre went to answer it. The last to arrive was Aiden, Conner's friend from school. He'd been there a few times before and seemed like a good kid with good grades. Sabre and JP thought he was a positive influence on Conner.

Sabre did a few things in the kitchen before going out back to join the others. She looked at her family. It had grown so much in the last six months, but it was all good. She felt euphoric.

JP went inside to use the restroom. He was on his way back out when the front bell rang. JP opened the door. "Hey, Marlow. Come on in. You're just in time for a burger."

"No, thank you. I was in the neighborhood and thought I would stop by and tell you the latest on Banks."

"Please come in."

Marlow stepped inside. "Banks has been arrested for murder with a gang enhancement on the Walgreens shooting."

"That's good news. How did you get him?"

"The shooter didn't do his job well enough. One of the gangsters lived and identified the shooter. He, in turn, pointed the finger at Banks."

"That sounds a little shaky if all you have is one gang member testifying against another."

"When Banks made the stop to talk to the three victims, that was the signal for the shooter. We also have a text message from Banks to the shooter, telling him the stop was his target. It's a little cryptic, but I think it'll fly. On top of that, we have his own kid who can corroborate the stop at Walgreens."

"I sure hope it sticks," JP said. "Now, let's go have some beers to celebrate."

"I don't want to intrude."

"You're not. Come on."

Marlow followed him to the backyard. "Okay, one beer."

After everyone had left, Conner helped JP clean up the backyard, while Sabre and Morgan went inside.

"Uncle Johnny," Conner said hesitantly.

"Yes?"

"Nothing."

After a few seconds of silence, JP said, "I see you finished your driver's ed class."

"How did you know?" Conner asked. "I was going to surprise you, then talk to you about getting my permit."

"Your Uncle Johnny doesn't miss much, kid."

Conner looked at him with admiration. "You're a lot like my dad."

For the first time in a long while, JP didn't mind the comparison. He knew Conner meant it as a compliment, and JP was starting to see the better side of his big brother—the one he'd admired so much as a kid. He knew he'd never get back to that point, and truthfully, Gene didn't deserve that kind of admiration. But JP liked getting a little closer. He knew he'd never be able to fully trust Gene, but they had made a start.

"Set an appointment to get your permit, and we'll start clocking behind-the-wheel time."

"Thank you, Uncle Johnny."

"Now, let's get this cleaned up so we can go relax."

Inside, Morgan and Sabre were washing dishes. Morgan asked, "Will that girl be okay?"

"What girl?"

"The one whose mother hurt you and tried to kill CJ's mom."

"Yes, I think she will. It's hard when a child's mom goes to prison." Sabre stopped, realizing why Morgan asking. "I'm sorry. I guess you know about parents being in prison."

"Yeah, but we have Uncle Johnny and you. Not only that, my dad will be out soon. Conner and I are pretty lucky."

Sabre wrapped her arms around Morgan and pulled her close. "Your Uncle Johnny and I are the lucky ones."

ALSO BY TERESA BURRELL

THE ADVOCATE SERIES

THE ADVOCATE (Book 1)

THE ADVOCATE'S BETRAYAL (Book 2)

THE ADVOCATE'S CONVICTION (Book 3)

THE ADVOCATE'S DILEMMA (Book 4)

THE ADVOCATE'S EX PARTE (Book5)

THE ADVOCATE'S FELONY (Book 6)

THE ADVOCATE'S GEOCACHE (Book 7)

THE ADVOCATE'S HOMICIDES (Book 8)

THE ADVOCATE'S ILLUSION (Book 9)

THE ADVOCATE'S JUSTICE (Book 10)

THE ADVOCATE'S KILLER (Book 11)

THE TUPER MYSTERY SERIES

THE ADVOCATE'S FELONY

(Book 6 of The Advocate Series)

MASON'S MISSING (Book 1)

FINDING FRANKIE (Book 2)

Dear Reader,

Would you like a FREE copy of a short story about JP when he was young? If so, please go to www.teresaburrell.com and sign up for my mailing list. You will automatically receive a code to retrieve the story.

What did you think of THE ADVOCATE'S KILLER? I would love to hear from you. Please email me and let me know at Teresa@teresaburrell.com.

Thank you,

Teresa

ABOUT THE AUTHOR

Teresa Burrell has dedicated her life to helping children and their families. Her first career was spent teaching elementary school in the San Bernardino City School District. As an attorney, Ms. Burrell has spent countless hours working pro bono in the family court system. For twelve years she practiced law in San Diego Superior Court, Juvenile Division. She continues to advocate children's issues and write novels, many of which are inspired by actual legal cases.

Teresa Burrell is available at www.teresaburrell.com.

facebook.com/theadvocateseries

twitter.com/teresaburrell

amazon.com/author/teresaburrell

bookbub.com/profile/teresa-burrell

Made in the USA
San Bernardino, CA
31 May 2020